Black Mirror

The Paranormal Investigator Series: Book 6

By

Christopher Carrolli

Published by
Melange Books, LLC
White Bear Lake, MN 55110
www.melange-books.com

ISBN: 978-1-68046-335-4

Cover Art by Caroline Andrus

As always, this book is dedicated to my Mother, Gladys (1937-2011); although she would have cringed at this one. It is also for my late-Uncle, B. Richard "Cookie" Carrolli (1937-1996), with whom I shared a love of horror and mystery. I would also like to dedicate this to my pal, Jeffrey Dougan (1962-2016) for his courageous battle with cancer.

Chapter One

~ Angus ~

Cedar Manor 1970

Angus Marlowe had gotten away with murder—quite a few murders to be exact. He'd committed his violent crimes right here in the underground basement of this dark, malignant house. Mother and Father were gone now, both of them passing within a few years of each other. The safety net they'd so perfectly provided had been ripped away. Now, he was alone. The authorities couldn't prove he'd killed any of those girls, but one day they might. One day when he least expected it, the pursuit and the extent of his evils might be unveiled.

However, the black tome described an exit that would ensure his freedom and would send him on his way to the darkened path he so fervently served. It would be his richly reward, his pathway to the dark kingdom, where all of the treasures he'd been promised would be spilled out before him. The Black Mirror would open its gateway to him, just as the tome described, and through it he would venture toward his dark salvation.

He stood in front of it, gazing into its opaque glass and marveling at the rich, silvered frame that surrounded the dark Victorian masterpiece. This large, rectangular mirror was a counterpart to a gold-gilded masterpiece that framed regular glass. His grandparents had acquired both mirrors from England.

His fascination with the Black Mirror began in his childhood. He

1

would gaze into the glass for hours in hopes of breaching its mysteries and satisfying his curiosity. His quest had been unsuccessful.

The breakthrough came when he was a teenager. It was the first time he'd seen the glass change. For a fleeting moment, the glass was no longer there; it vanished from the silvered frame that surrounded it. In its place a thick swirling mist moved within the frame. Then, the mist disappeared. Instantly, the glass froze back into place. He'd blinked his eyes, and then rapped the glass with his knuckles. It was solid, just like always.

Later, in his late twenties, he'd been rummaging through this very basement, examining the history his family had stowed here. He found artifacts, antiques, small statues, paintings, all from different eras of his family's history. Many of the relics and antiques dated all the way back to the Revolutionary War. All of it had been stashed away, allowing the past to die.

The mirrors originated from the Victorian era, two ornately framed masterpieces, one a dark cousin of the other. He never understood why his parents had displayed the gold-gilded mirror in one of the upper parlors and stored the black mirror here, hidden away in this endless labyrinth. As he rummaged, he soon discovered why.

He'd found an old, antique cabinet that hadn't been opened in years. The rusty lock on the cabinet was ancient in his estimation. He attempted to open it, but the lock was impervious, fastened in a solid grasp by its own rust and corrosion. Angrily, he grabbed an axe and swung it high above his head, busting the lock with a single swing. The cabinet doors creaked when he flung them open.

His hands swept through a thick mass of cobwebs, brushing away age-old nets that blanketed the cabinet's contents in mystery. Once he cleared away the cobwebs, he stared at his discovery. It was a large black book by the looks of it. Something lay atop it. He reached inside and retrieved the object.

It was a handheld mirror with black, opaque glass, just like the larger one. He'd held it up to his face, glaring into its darkness. It showed no reflection of him, only the shimmering of the electrical sconces lining the walls behind him. He gently removed the large black book from the cabinet, blew the dust from its cover, and opened it. The book appeared old, almost two-hundred years at a guess. Carefully, he turned the yellow tinged pages. Their edges were browned by the assault of time.

Beneath the light of one of the electrical sconces, he saw the book contained large handwritten portions in fine penmanship. He recognized the handwritten words as Latin. He'd been familiar with Latin, having studied it at one of the private schools he'd attended, and later continued with a private tutor. Within a year, he deciphered most of the large, black tome, word for word.

Soon, he realized what he uncovered from the cabinet were two missing, key components in the Black Mirror's mystery. In its own obscure, yet fascinating way, the tome detailed how the two mirrors were gateways, portals to a destination or realm otherwise unknown. He suddenly realized something important. He thought back to that quick moment when he was a teenager. The black glass had mysteriously vanished, and a strange mist moved thickly and slowly within the frame. The gateway had briefly opened for him, though he hadn't known it at the time.

Now, it would open for him again. He had waited for years, and this time, he had the key. Angus gripped the handheld mirror in his hand, now fully understanding its purpose. Like all doorways and gateways, there had to be a key. The black handheld mirror would open the gateway and allow him to enter into its welcoming darkness.

His pounding heart made his blood race faster and faster at the thought of what was about to occur. His booming, thunderous voice bellowed out in Latin, echoing from the basement walls. He begged for acceptance, allowance, and the chance to serve within the gateway's shadowy confines. He called out for the acknowledgement of his presence, a faithful servant in desperate need of passage.

"Black Mirror, open to me!"

The upward rise of his arms and the whiplash movement of his head signified his wicked exaltation. His knees hit the hardened floor as he dropped and bowed before the Black Mirror. In its stillness, the dark glass almost seemed to watch him, as if hidden somewhere behind its hardness evil pairs of eyes stared. He resumed his sinister incantations, loudly and rapidly spewing Latin phrases. Unholy words formed an ominous spell, an ancient ritual meant to call forth a perpetual darkness into the light.

He continued to maneuver the handheld mirror in front of the silver-framed masterpiece, casting one dark reflection upon the other. Abruptly, he stopped. His words ceased. Something was happening. Something about the mirror was changing.

The Black Mirror altered itself, just as it had in that brief instance long ago. The glass appeared almost gelatinous and wobbled within the frame. Then, its texture seemed to liquefy and ripple in waves. His mouth hung open in awe; his anticipation mixed with beguilement.

Now, the glass disappeared, and he saw right through the mirror. Where the glass once stood, upward spirals of mist spun into strange dancing shapes and odd formations. The mist thickened into a fog, turning the blackness into an apocalyptic gray. The color beyond the frame looked like the end of all things. Fear suddenly struck him, but he had done it. He'd opened the gateway. Now, nothing was left to stop him.

He slowly rose to his feet, his eyes transfixed upon the gateway, cautious that it would instantly change back into the Black Mirror. Something flashed inside of it. A distant pulse of light flickered within the thick misty fog. Was it lightning? He traced it with his eyes as it penetrated more and more of the gray murkiness. Whatever it was drew nearer. Suddenly, he threw his forearms up in front of him in a blocking motion as flares of electrical light flashed outward, causing small flames to dance and sizzle around the frame.

A quiet ensued. Slowly, he lowered his arms. Fearful eyes gazed beyond the gateway for what came next. He stepped forward, but before he moved any closer, a ball of lightning burst through the gateway, knocking him to the floor and flooding the basement with light. It was as if the dark majestic house had been ripped apart by a powerful storm or a magnificent daylight.

Then, the lightning vanished. Yet, had it actually been lightning? Did it strike here in the house or in the realm just beyond the gateway? Either way, he had experienced it, full force. He felt the heat of it, though he'd not been burned in any way. When he fell, the handheld mirror flew from his hand, skipped across the floor, and came to rest beneath an old chest, but he couldn't focus his thoughts on it now.

Angus lay on the ground, shaking, afraid to glance back at the gateway. He heard the rumble of thunder somewhere beyond the frame, somewhere in the strange realm he'd just unlocked. Again, he rose from the floor, but the need to continue prevailed. After all, it was his discovery, his dark world that dwelled beyond the Black Mirror. He must finish what he'd begun.

He stepped slowly toward the gateway, his eyes searching through the misty fog. The lightning continued to flash, yet something else was coming closer. The fog rolled and then parted, as whatever or whomever it was moved within the gateway. A figure walked toward him from the other side of the mirror.

His heart pounded. His knees shook. He heard no footsteps, yet the image of a figure came nearer and nearer. The unidentified figure embodied the art of all mystery, a subject come alive within an eerie painting.

At last the figure stood only feet from him, but still within the confines of the frame, trapped in the clutches of a netherworld he'd opened with the strangest of keys. The figure's height equaled his, but the murky fog hid the face. Something about the figure was familiar. He continued to watch the motionless being that stood staring outward. Then the misty fog rolled away, unveiling the specter it had hidden so well from his mortal eyes.

His heart stopped. The figure in the gateway was him, down to the last detail. His mind reeled as he stared back at himself. He recognized slight differences, discrepancies so minute that only he would be able to identify them. The face appeared smoother and maybe slightly younger. The hair looked fuller, and the neat attire projected a less disheveled appearance, but it was unmistakably him. He smiled back at himself, as mere footsteps separated him and his doppelganger.

His double extended his hand, beckoning Angus to join him within the depths of the gateway. Together, they would revel in the mysteries of the Black Mirror. Angus looked into the figure's eyes. The eyes were brighter, clearer, and it was with those eyes that the figure spoke. The eyes recognized him, seeming to applaud him for discovering the darkest of secrets.

The figure's hand remained outstretched, an open link to another world that existed secretly within this one. Their eyes remained locked on each other, and without moving its lips, the figure spoke inside Angus' mind.

"Walk through the gateway, Angus," it said. *"And we shall become one."*

Angus watched as the figure turned and began walking away.

"No, no, wait!" he shouted. "Wait for me... Wait!"

As Angus ran toward the gateway, another ball of light exploded through the silver-framed portal. Again, he was knocked to the ground, this time, with greater and stronger force. He rolled across the floor, and through his squinted eyes, he saw the entire basement was lit from the electrical force. It pulsated, flashed, and flickered, illuminating the limestone walls like a great projector. He wondered if this force of electrical current had ripped through the entire house.

However, he wasn't going to fear it. He wasn't going to let it deter him. He jumped to his feet, ran toward it, and then stopped just before the gateway. The electrical current still flashed through the frame where the black glass had been only moments ago, but when he reached his hand through to the other side, he touched coldness, like the frost of October. He could still see his own backside walking away, farther and farther into the shadowy vortex that awaited him.

He heard the voice again. The deep, hollow tone filled his mind.

"Come, Angus, before it's too late."

The murky fog enveloped the figure completely. He saw it no more. It was time. It was his chance to escape, a chance that could not be missed. Angus left all things behind and ran through the gateway before it could close on him. All thoughts of the handheld mirror, the key, were easily forgotten. He turned around, looked behind him, and watched as the open portal he'd just passed turned back into glass. It hardened, closing all things in and out. He was through to the other side of the Black Mirror.

He turned back around and walked slowly, soon realizing that the darkness was not one of pitch blackness. A strange blueness tinged the new world around him, one that cast deeper shadows, like the hour before dawn. He moved through the cold, eventually running in hopes of finding the figure. Then, it happened.

The pain was heavy, hard in his chest. He stopped and struggled for air, inhaling nothing except the coldness that surrounded him. He heaved and cried out. No one answered, except eerie faraway voices that echoed his own pain. His body was shutting down. The blueness began to blur and fade to black. His eyesight was fading. His heart was stopping, for real this time. He fell to the cold, rough ground. Angus felt himself die... and then come alive again.

* * * *

George and Joan Sheffield were driving home from a celebratory dinner that same evening. They lived along the one-mile rural stretch known as Cedar Drive. For years, they'd lived only five-hundred yards away from the steel tycoon, Caspar Marlowe, and his family. They'd met both Caspar, and his wife, Agnes, on several occasions. The Marlowes were a charming, down to earth couple, yet they were reclusive and private. George and Joan had never met the Marlowe's only son, Angus, but they'd heard the stories.

Years ago, a rumor circulated about Angus nearly raping a young woman, but nothing ever came of it. Many stories of his bad behavior existed, and more recently an article in a society column by a well-known columnist had given a rundown of the rumors. Although Angus was never mentioned by name, tales of his blatant disregard for his aging parents, wild parties, sex scandals, and worst of all, his ritualistic cult activities persisted. The columnist suggested this middle-aged reprobate should have been disinherited early; maybe that would have set him straight.

George and Joan never paid any attention to the gossip, but they couldn't help but think of Angus now, after what they'd just witnessed. Once they arrived home and parked the car in their driveway, a flash of what looked like lightning lit the world around them.

"What the hell was that?" George said.

"It can't be a thunderstorm," Joan observed. "Not at the end of November."

George looked up at the sky, and then around him. "It's not. I don't hear any thunder."

Joan commented on the strangeness of it, as they walked down the sidewalk to their front porch. Then, it happened again. This flash appeared larger and brighter, turning the night into a light-blue day for a split second.

"Did you see that, George? It came from Cedar Manor."

The great flash had erupted from around the back of Cedar Manor's castle-like structure, as if it had built up from the bottom of the house, and then burst outward. He stood staring at the now dark and seemingly desolate estate. The place didn't look like it was on fire. Then, Joan's voice distracted him.

"You don't think it could've been gunfire, do you?"

"No," he said, scoffing. "Gunfire couldn't have made that kind of a flash. Besides, I didn't hear any gunshots, did you?"

They stood on their porch, watching the majestic house, and wondering. Agnes had been dead for over a year now; Caspar had been gone for five years. Out of respect for the both of them, George and Joan had kept any and all questions to themselves. Now, Angus lived in the house alone. It was his house now. That single thought made the Sheffields nervous because of what had been happening here in Green Valley over the past couple of years—murder—and rumors convicted Angus Marlowe's of all of it.

Girls had gone missing. Just three years ago on Christmas Eve, a young woman's body had been discovered in the woods not far from Cedar Manor and their own house. Police had suspected cult activity, and Angus Marlowe was said to have been immersed in it.

The police had arrived at Cedar Manor to question Angus, given his rumored activities and the location of the body. They had been unable to pin any of the crimes on him. The family lawyer, Mr. Harold Bennett, briskly intervened. He insisted no evidence connected his client to the recent string of murders. From a legal standpoint, he'd been right. The rest of Green Valley hadn't been so sure.

George and Joan resigned themselves that they would have no interaction with any part of Cedar Manor again, now that Caspar and Agnes were gone. They'd tried to avoid it altogether, but tonight, it suddenly drew their attention, taunting them, and prompting their suspicions of a sinister situation indoors.

8

"Should we call the police?" Joan looked to George.

He thought for a silent moment. "Maybe we should, just to make sure everything's okay over there."

Quickly, the Sheffields unlocked their front door, entered, and phoned the police.

* * * *

James Carlisle also saw the bursts of what looked like lightning erupt from Cedar Manor. He'd been taking out the trash at around the same time that the Sheffields arrived home. Two brilliant blue flares, about thirty seconds apart from each other lit the area. Each time, he checked the sky and saw nothing. He'd even listened for thunder, just to be sure.

He was positive those bright flares had come from the vicinity of Cedar Manor. He wasn't far from the great house. He saw nothing to explain the mysterious eruptions of light.

Like the Sheffields, he'd also known the late tycoon and his wife. He'd even met Angus a few times. All instincts had told him years ago that Angus was a disturbed young man. He'd seen it. It had been evident in the wild, deranged look in his eyes. Now, talk was growing that Angus was suspected of being involved with the disappearances and possibly the murders of those young women. Some called it speculation. Some called it talk, but James didn't doubt the rumors. The authorities remained silent, refusing to answer questions regarding Angus Marlowe.

James had known Harold Bennett, the family lawyer, for years. He was also friends with Detective Ralph Palmer, who continued to investigate the murder of Sheila Barton, the young woman whose body was discovered in the woods not far from Cedar Manor. Harold wouldn't divulge more than the fact that the police had no evidence against his client. He'd hoped for Harold's sake that it was the truth. James knew Ralph Palmer was unhappy knowing he'd looked a murderer right in the face but wasn't able to prove it.

James had often wondered what Caspar and Agnes had lived with during the last years of their lives. God only knows how much cash Caspar had shelled out to protect his miscreant son; all to ensure his own name wouldn't be dragged through the mud, and to spare Agnes the embarrassment and humiliation. Angus had inherited Cedar Manor and the entire Marlowe estate, and there was nothing anyone could do about it. Harold Bennett was the executor of the estate, which meant Angus would forever be under Bennett's watchful eye, as far as the estate was concerned. Yet James had a sneaky suspicion that under that watchful eye, Angus Marlowe would be well protected.

Angus was alone now, introverted, perverted, and probably conducting sick, satanic rituals in that house which had seemingly turned dark after Agnes died. He knew what he'd seen just now, and whatever those two flashes of light had been, they had something to do with Cedar Manor and the only person inside it. He wouldn't call the police. There was no point. The police couldn't control Angus Marlowe, but someone else could. He went back inside his house and phoned Harold Bennett.

* * * *

It was nearly nine-o'clock when Harold Bennett's phone rang. He and his wife were settling down to relax in front of the television. Who would be calling at this hour? He was surprised to hear Jim Carlisle's voice on the other end.

"I think you'd better get over to Cedar Manor, right now, Harold. Something's going on over there." Jim told him about the strange flashes of light that came from nowhere else but the house. "It looked like lightning, but it's not storming outside. Take a look for yourself."

The Marlowe family lawyer closed his eyes, knowing Jim was right. What the hell could Angus be doing now? He listened to more of Jim's repetitive details and then stopped him.

"Alright," he said. "I'll be there in ten minutes."

"I just wanted to alert you before the cops showed up there," Jim explained. "You know how I feel about Angus, but being that you're the overseer and all—"

"Thanks, Jim. I appreciate it. I really do."

Harold hung up the phone and sighed. Linda, his wife, stared at him.

"I've got to run over to Cedar Manor."

"Now?" The incredulity in her tone signaled a silent protest.

"Apparently, something's going on," he said. "It's my job to check on Angus, and make sure he hasn't burned the place down or worse."

Linda sighed. "I told you long ago to rid yourself of the Marlowes and that place. I wish you would have listened."

"Well, sweetheart, I'm now the executor. Should anything ever happen to Angus, I would inherit most of the Marlowe fortune, and probably even the house."

"That creepy castle? No thanks. Besides, don't hold your breath."

"It might take a while." Harold sounded more like a lawyer now. "You never know."

Harold thought about these facts often. If Angus was out of the way, he would become the main heir to the Marlowe fortune. All of it was true, but his respect for Caspar and Agnes and their final wishes remained paramount for him. He'd known and served them for over twenty years. He secretly felt their pain and embarrassment when it came to Angus. He did whatever he could to preserve their good name and reputations. That was his job. In return, they had bestowed upon him their trust and gratitude in the event of their son's untimely demise.

As far as Angus was concerned, it would be only a matter of time before he ended up dead or in jail. However, in the hypothetical event of any murder charges, there would be hefty restitutions to pay, one after another, all of which would deplete the Marlowe fortune. Harold wasn't about to let that happen either.

He'd stopped the police from obtaining a warrant to search Cedar Manor three years ago, insisting they had no probable cause against his client, only unfounded rumors. The body found in the nearby woods was purely coincidental. Three years had now passed, and still no evidence against Angus existed—no fingerprints, no blood trails, and no eyewitnesses. He often wondered if Angus had committed those horrific crimes, but either way, Harold did not want to know.

"I'll be back before you know it." He bent down and kissed Linda on the forehead.

Jim had mentioned flashes like lightning coming from the house. Harold silently scoffed. For a moment, he pondered the very real possibility that Angus had burned Cedar Manor to the ground. Maybe he'd gone up with it. Good riddance.

Harold drove the long, one-mile stretch of Cedar Drive within minutes. At the end of it, the dark majestic house came into view. It loomed silently beneath a light snowfall. Its towering height accentuated the lavender sky of November's end. Harold pulled up to the gate and prepared himself. There were flashing lights, red and blue, and spinning around his car as he parked. Someone must have called the police. Two officers stood outside the gate, and one of them shined his flashlight in Harold's face.

Slowly, Harold stepped out of the car. He approached the officers with his hand outstretched and quickly introduced himself.

"Hello, officers, I'm Harold Bennett, executor of the Marlowe estate and legal representative of the Marlowe family." One of the officers shook his hand while the other nodded.

"Has there been a problem tonight, officers?"

"We received a call not long ago about some strange flashes of light coming from the house." The officer who'd shaken his hand spoke briskly and to the point. "We're obligated to check things out and make sure everything's okay."

"I understand, officer. If you'll follow me, we can check this out together." Harold began to lead the way, fumbling for his keys for the gate and the house. "There's probably some kind of misunderstanding. Everything looks undisturbed, so I'm sure that we can clear this up quickly."

"By the way, Mr. Bennett, what brings you out here at this time of night?"

The officer's quick question caught Harold off guard.

He explained that it was his job to randomly check on the house. He could feel his answer caused the officers to glance at each other behind his back. It made him uneasy.

Walking ahead of them down the long walkway to the house, he turned halfway to face them. "You know, gas lines run beneath this house. Perhaps it may have been fumes from the underground."

"Anything's possible." The first officer agreed. "We just want to make sure everything's alright in there."

"Either way, I'm sure there's a reasonable explanation for what your witness saw." Harold turned the key in the lock of the front door and opened it with a clunking sound. "Right this way, officers."

He led the way. The house was unlit except for the glass candelabra chandelier above their heads. The white light of its candles cut through the dark, creating a soft and comfortable dimness. The house was eerily silent.

Harold turned and faced the two officers. He noticed their eyes roving over the great house in awe. The immense lower balcony stretched around the house's rectangular structure. The upper balcony sprawled just above it. The towering heights of Cedar Manor loomed high over them, a dizzying splendor becoming visible in the beam of their flashlights.

"Angus?" Harold called. No one answered. He continued calling out to Angus, but only the deep silence responded.

Harold escorted the officers into the elaborate drawing room and found no one there. They checked all of the rooms on the first floor and found them empty—no sign of Angus anywhere. A search of the second and third floors proved unsuccessful. Angus' bedroom was unoccupied. Nothing was disturbed. It appeared as though he'd not even been home.

"I'm not sure what to tell you, officers," Harold said, returning to the first floor. "My client is not home, and nothing here has been disturbed. I'll remain and wait for him to return, but I doubt he has any idea of what your witnesses reported. He's clearly not here."

He watched the two officers stare at each other for a moment. The looks on their faces appeared as though they were contemplating something. Harold's heart pounded, wondering if they were going to ask to see the basement. He would tell them to get a warrant. Searching any more would require one, especially after he asserted that a look in the basement was unnecessary. Only artifacts, furniture, and heirlooms were stored there, yet an inner instinct told Harold that was where Angus could be.

"We'd just like to take a look around the back of the house, if that's okay?"

Harold's heart ceased its pounding. "Absolutely, officers," he said. "Right this way."

He led them back out the front door, into the yard, and around to the back of the house. The cold November breeze blasted them as a light snow mixed with the slightest hint of ice.

"As you can see, officers, there's nothing out of the ordinary, no flashes of light, everything is undisturbed."

They shined their flashlights around the back of the house. Harold thought they looked somewhat dismayed at not finding anything wrong or sinister. The officer that did all of the talking was writing something down on a small notepad.

"Please give us a call whenever you speak to your client," he said, tearing the small sheet of paper from the pad and handing it to Harold.

"I'll do that, gentlemen," he replied.

He thanked them for their concern and watched as they got back into the police car. He closed the front door, and then spying through the small window in the hallway, he noticed them linger for a few moments. They were watching the garage, which was not far from the gate. Finally, they drove away. He let out a sigh of relief. It was time to check the basement.

He stepped carefully down the spiraling stone staircase, one foot in front of the other, mindful not to walk too close to the edge or risk losing his balance. At the bottom, limestone walls of a catacomb structure reached ceaselessly above. He'd seen the basement before when there had been some legal issue over one of the myriad antiques stored down here. Once again, he marveled at how the basement appeared more like a labyrinth, an unending maze where one could become lost.

He walked through the various arched entranceways, calling for Angus and hearing only the echo of his own voice. Somewhere within the far reaches of the basement, a sound repeated over and over... drip...drop...drip...drop.

"Angus?" Harold called out again, louder this time, and the reverberation responded. His own voice mimicked him.

He turned the corner, stepped through another arch, and then stopped. He stood still, his eyes wide in surprise. What stood before him was a relic he'd never seen before. It was a mirror, much like the gold-gilded masterpiece he'd catalogued in the Marlowe family history of artifacts, only this one was different. This one had a silvered frame, not gold like the other, but silver. This mirror had one other significant difference; the glass was black, a strange, shiny onyx. As he gazed into it, it cast only a dark, shadowy reflection of him, almost like a funhouse mirror, but not quite. He could see himself, but the image was immersed

14

and overwhelmed by the mirror's darkness.

He looked around, spotting nothing, until something along the limestone walls caught his attention. Something black was spread against the walls, almost like the smoke damage from a fire. He touched it. The limestone was slightly scorched. What had happened here? Had there been a fire? Had Angus ignited some ceremonial pyre in one of his alleged satanic rituals? His earlier concern about Angus burning the damn place down hadn't been so far off from the look of it.

Harold called out to Angus again, though this time his voice was harsher, angrier. No one responded. He could still hear the monotonous drip-drop somewhere in the distance. No one was down here. He felt like a fool. Where the hell had Angus gone anyway?

He walked back over to the black mirror, staring into it, his eyes squinting. Cautiously, he reached out with his finger and touched it. It was cold and hard, like any glass. He moved his finger away and watched as his fingerprint faded. Why hadn't Caspar or Agnes ever mentioned this mirror? Why had they hidden it from him?

It looked like a counterpart to the other mirror upstairs, though this one framed black glass—strange. Was it some kind of occult artifact which the Marlowes had inherited? Harold knew the Marlowe family had acquired the gold-gilded mirror from the ancestral home in England sometime during the Victorian era. They had to have had two of them because this one had a similar frame, ornate and uniquely designed, but of silver, not gold.

He stepped away from the mirror. He didn't like the feel of being down here. It was eerie, leaving him unsure if the chill running down his spine was from the basement's damp cold. Harold took one last look at the black mirror before stepping back through the archway and ascending the stone staircase once again. The sound of his shuffling feet against the stone steps echoed around him.

After leaving the basement, the warmth of the house engulfed him once again. Then, another thought struck him. The police had not searched the basement, and they hadn't even bothered with the garage. If they had spotted Angus' car still in the garage, Harold was convinced they would have returned to the house. Was it there now? He hadn't had time to check because the police met him at the gate when he arrived.

Caspar Marlowe had owned various cars throughout his life, but during his last years he'd owned two Rolls Royce's, and a Mercedes he'd purchased for Angus. Harold quickly ran out to the garage and looked in through the windows. There were three cars parked inside, all of which, now belonged to Angus—two Rolls Royce's, and the Mercedes. Three fine automobiles wasting away in a garage because the creepy bastard rarely drove. Many had spotted him walking late at night not far from the house, which could account for his current whereabouts.

Harold walked back into the house and waited another ten minutes for Angus to return. He never did. Tomorrow, he would have an excellent reason to question him as to his whereabouts tonight. He would have to warn him of the police coming here. Harold checked his watch, locked the door from inside, and returned home to his wife.

* * * *

The next morning at the breakfast table, Harold told Linda everything, knowing that his words would be held in the strictest of confidence. He placed a phone call to Cedar Manor as he sat at the table, letting it ring a full seven times before disconnecting.

"I don't think he's there," he said. "Something has happened. I'm almost sure of it. The house was vacant, undisturbed, except for that scorching I found along the limestone wall. I know Angus doesn't drive often, but he wasn't there, and all three cars were in the garage."

"Maybe he went out for the night." The frustration in Linda's voice was clear and consistent. "Maybe he's doing you know what to who knows who. He's a big boy, you know. What I don't understand is the fact that they want to question him over what, lightning? He wasn't even home at the time." She laughed.

"It sounds to me like they're trying hard to pin that murder on him. Either way, I don't want you caught up in it. If they ever find evidence on him, you better let him fry."

Harold rolled his eyes and sighed. "Yes, dear," he said.

Throughout the rest of the day, Harold phoned Cedar Manor a total of six times. Each time, he got no response. His eyebrows arched in wonder as he sat behind his desk. He looked out the window of his home office, pondering where in the world Angus Marlowe could be. Angus

16

left the house on occasion, but rarely for long durations. Mostly, he was a reclusive loner, stowing himself away in that big, dark house. It wasn't like him to be gone this long, and Angus had always been reliable when it came to answering the phone.

He watched as wet, icy snow began to fall. It grew dark early this time of year, and the bluish backdrop of early winter descended just before dinner. Linda would be pissed if he went out there again tonight. He had a feeling he would find the house empty yet again. Obviously, the police hadn't heard from Angus, so he couldn't have been in any legal trouble.

Harold would stay home and listen for any unexpected phone calls. Tomorrow, in the light of day, he would venture back out to Cedar Manor. Angus couldn't have just disappeared from the face of the earth.

* * * *

After another phone call had gone unanswered, Harold drove to Cedar Manor the next morning and used his key to get inside. Another sweep of the sprawling house turned up no one. He went back down to the basement. The same unidentified drip-drop, stuck in a long, tedious eternity of disrepair, met his ears. Harold turned the corner and walked through the same archway as yesterday. There stood the Black Mirror, just as before.

He stepped over to it and touched it again. Its same cold hardness revealed nothing for a second time. He felt the strangest feeling, the sudden vibe that Angus would never return. He stared at the mirror, unable to remove his eyes and wondering what gave him that idea. No, he didn't believe in that crazy shit. He turned away, and then turned back again.

Suddenly, he knew what he would do. If Angus hadn't returned within one week, he would arrange to have the mirror removed from this house. He would hide it somewhere or maybe donate it to some collector. If this mirror was an occult artifact and Angus was truly missing, he thought it best to get rid of it. He would make sure it was never connected or associated with Caspar and Agnes. He owed them that much.

Angus Marlowe never returned. The following week, Harold made arrangements to have the mirror packed in a large crate and moved to the discreet connection he'd made with a collector and dealer of mysterious artifacts. The man in question was not far outside of Green Valley, twenty miles at most. Harold had explained that the Black Mirror was among many Victorian artifacts left behind by a late client who'd inherited it from a distant relative. He'd made no mention of the Marlowes and was sparse in details. Harold donated the mirror, and then paid the collector handsomely for keeping his name anonymous.

He was notified when the shipment arrived. He felt strangely and unexplainably relieved. Angus would be in no position to argue if he ever returned. Even if he did, Harold would explain the mirror's absence, as well as the continuing suspicion by the cops. Yet somehow, a strange unease still haunted Harold. Somehow he knew it wouldn't happen.

Eight years later, in 1978, Harold made the motion to have Angus Marlowe declared as legally deceased. It was signed by a judge, and Harold became the heir to Cedar Manor and a generous chunk of the Marlowe fortune. Linda had refused to live there, and he didn't blame her. After seeing the basement wall and the Black Mirror, Harold had grown even more suspicious that he'd defended a killer—God help him.

In 1996, Harold sold Cedar Manor to some young, wealthy realtor who wanted the house for herself. Janet Leeds was her name. He'd sold it to her for an extremely fair price, and she soon moved in with her husband, and her little girl.

Harold Bennett lived out the rest of his days. He lost Linda in 2000. Then, he followed her in 2005, at the age of eighty-five. He'd never heard another word regarding Cedar Manor. He'd also been right about one thing—he never saw Angus Marlowe or the Black Mirror again.

Chapter Two

~ Unearthing the Past ~

2008

Detective Tom Goddard sat behind his desk gazing at the cover of a book that he and the Green Valley PD had long awaited. He'd received an advance copy. A young woman with long, blonde, windswept hair graced the cover. He read the title, *Cedar Manor,* and her name, *Leah Leeds* beneath her image.

He'd already read the sections that dealt with her visions in Cedar Manor. Now, something urged him to meet with this young woman and ask her about the man she described in her bedroom vision. Her description fit that of Angus Marlowe—long, straggly hair, beard, and mustache. Years earlier, the Green Valley PD had been unable to obtain evidence against Marlowe for the 1967 disappearances of several young women. As a result, the murder of Sheila Barton had gone unsolved. Of course, psychic visions would never hold up in court, but the rest of the department agreed with him that a meeting with Leah Leeds was essential.

He opened the book to a page he'd bookmarked, reading the section that described his primary interest—the basement. Something kept nagging at him about the author's description of the limestone walls—stones that looked they had been removed, and in some cases, cemented back together. He rubbed his chin while reading. Funny how an innocent child could remember things in a certain way, and then recall those images years later. If he could meet with Leah Leeds and talk to her, maybe she would reveal something that might enable the PD to obtain a search warrant for Cedar Manor. After all, the house was now owned by the city. In an age of DNA evidence, it would be possible to find just about anything.

Leah Leeds was now an investigator with the Paranormal Research and Investigative Society at Green Valley University (GVU)—a wise choice. He also knew she was doing a book signing today at the GVU library. Perhaps he would pay her a visit, if he wasn't too late, and ask her to drop by the station and answer a few questions. He continued to read the well-written pages documented by the young woman, still in her late-teens. He read for another thirty minutes, looked at his watch, and walked out of his office. He headed to GVU with her book in hand. Maybe he would get an autograph.

* * * *

Leah Leeds sat behind a table in the GVU library; a giant poster of her book cover stood erect behind her. She'd signed numerous copies today, some for her professors, but most were students fascinated by the paranormal, as well as locals interested in hearing about what occurred behind the doors of Cedar Manor. The society had commissioned her to write the book, not only to tell of her experiences, but to document a part of local paranormal history. She'd been with the society for about a year now, and she would never forget the day she walked into room 208 and introduced herself.

"I'm Leah Leeds." She'd announced her name to Dylan Rasche; the chief investigator, Brett Taylor, and Sidney Pratt, as though they would know her automatically. They were all guys, guys who looked stumped.

"I'm the girl from Cedar Manor."

Dylan stared straight into her eyes. Behind her, the heavy guy leaped from his chair.

"Yes," the heavy guy said. "Welcome to our little soiree. I'm Sidney Pratt. Wow, Dylan, looks like ya got two live ones now."

She turned to Sidney who was chuckling. Gazing behind him, she saw the ghost of an older man. She knew it was his grandfather. Then, her third eye revealed a fishing dock beneath full and splendid sunshine.

20

"Your grandfather is here, behind you," she said. "The one who took you fishing."

She watched as Sidney's laughter immediately ceased, and his jaw dropped in awe.

"We've heard of you," Brett said. "Don't mind, Sid. He's our joker."

It was that joker who'd helped her compose the book she was now signing. For hours she'd told him stories, and he told her what he'd discovered through his studies of psychic children. The three guys had become her best friends after a short time.

She gasped as something woke her from the reverie. She looked up from the table and focused on a man standing in front of her.

"I'm sorry," he said. "I hope I didn't spook you."

He laughed at his own joke. She hissed in apologetic embarrassment and shook his hand.

"Leah, my name is Detective Tom Goddard of the Green Valley PD. I've found your book to be a fascinating read. In fact, that's why I've come to talk to you."

"Thank you, Detective. How can I help you?"

"Well, I'm interested in a few of the visions you wrote about, especially those pertaining to the man you described. I'm also curious about the vision in the basement that scared you, the one of the woman's body. I was hoping you might come down to the station and answer a few questions for us."

Just then, she saw Dylan approaching the table from behind Goddard.

"Detective Goddard, this is Dylan Rasche, our society's chief investigator." They exchanged greetings and shook hands. "I would love to help you, Detective. Would it be alright if my fellow investigators accompanied me? We always function as a team, if that's okay?"

Goddard nodded and looked at Dylan. "Absolutely," he said. "Say, later today around four?"

They agreed on the time, and Leah signed Goddard's copy of her book. He thanked her, gave her directions to his office inside the PD, and left. She and Dylan stared at each other until they were sure he was gone.

"I hope he doesn't want me to go back into Cedar Manor," Leah said. "I never want to enter that house again."

Dylan looked at her.

"Who knows, maybe someday you will."

At this moment in time, the thought was unbearable for her.

* * * *

Perfect timing, Goddard thought, as Leah Leeds and her fellow investigators arrived at the police station. They, along with Goddard and a few other detectives, were now seated around a long, rectangular table. Goddard obtained Leah's permission to record the session with both audio and video. He tested the recorder by stating the interviewee, the date, and the time.

"Leah, the first thing I want to ask you about is what I call your 'bedroom vision.' I'm referring to the vision you had of two men strangling a woman during what you call 'an act of perversion.'" She nodded her understanding. "You gave physical descriptions of both men in your book. If I were to show you a picture of a man, do you think you might be able to identify that man as one of the men in your vision?"

"If he's one of them," she said. "I know I could."

"Excellent." Goddard opened up a thick, red file folder and removed a picture. He turned it toward Leah, sitting across from him at the table. "Is this one of the men you saw in that particular vision?"

She drew her lips together tightly, breathed deeply, and nodded.

"Yep, that's him. He was the strangler."

Her response was exactly what Goddard had been waiting and hoping for—verification that Angus Marlowe was a murderer. It came as no surprise to him. He found the right picture of Marlowe, one that depicted him with straggly hair, a beard, and mustache resulting in the creepiest of appearances. Now, the objective was to get Leah Leeds to find or direct them to physical proof.

"Leah, that is Angus Marlowe," Goddard continued. "I see that you dug up a little about the Marlowes for your book. Did you know anything about them or Angus, before writing it?"

"I'd heard the stories later in life, but many of them were varied. My father kept me sheltered from much of the stories, until I became too old not to hear them. Sidney and I did most of the research on the Marlowes, though there was a ton of it not vital to my memoir."

"That's right," Sidney interjected. "Leah and I felt that her story should've been the focus of the book, not the Marlowe family."

Leah finished that thought. "I felt that my job was to introduce who Agnes Marlowe was, and prove the fact that she existed, and that I hadn't imagined her. The whole story of the Marlowes was not part of my memoir. This is the first time I've ever seen a picture of Angus Marlowe."

"Understood," Goddard said.

Just then, Goddard's second-in-command, Lance Brock, spoke. "Leah, we also want to ask you about your descriptions of the basement walls. You wrote that some walls looked like the stones were removed and put back in some places, and, in other locations, they looked cemented over. Is that correct?"

Leah confirmed what she'd written. "I never really understood it. I just remember being amazed at how walls could've been constructed in such a way."

"The house is a masterpiece," Goddard commented. He then segued into another aspect about the basement. "Also, in your description of the vision you had in the basement, the one that frightened you, you wrote that you saw bruises strung around the woman's neck, correct?"

"Yes," she said. "It's one of those visions I will never forget. It looked to me, as a child, like a purple necklace."

"The reason we mention these things to you is because we believe the woman in your vision could have been the victim who was discovered in 1967 or any of the young women that were never found. We can't be sure which. That brings me to the reason for these questions. Because of your visions and recollections of the basement, we believe Marlowe and his accomplice had not only committed murder there, but had hidden the bodies behind the stones in the walls."

Goddard watched her face. It drained of color, while her eyes drooped and closed slightly. He guessed her reaction was caused by the thought of having lived in that house and played in that basement while bodies rotted behind limestone walls. He waited for a moment before getting to the question he really wanted to ask.

"Leah, we're hoping you might take us down into that basement, and use your third eye to help us uncover the remains of those forgotten women, if they're even there. I know that's asking a lot, but it could be of tremendous help."

Detective Brock sought to soften the blow of the request. "We would understand if you refused. Keep in mind, Leah, we now have enough reasonable suspicion to get a court order to go there anyway, but having you along might be even more helpful."

Goddard watched her turn her head toward her colleagues. The look on the poor girl's face was one of pain and fear. He wouldn't blame her if she refused. He was asking a lot of her.

She sighed. "I'm so sorry, Detective, but I swore I'd never enter that house again." Tears welled in her eyes. "Not after what I went through, not after what I'd seen inside that house."

"I understand, Leah," he said. "I'm no psychiatrist, but have you ever considered the possibility that going back into that house once again and confronting those memories may give you some release once and for all? You know, it might be a chance to put it behind you forever."

Goddard watched her wipe away the tears that streaked her eyes.

"I wish I could help you by being there, Detective, but—"

"No need to apologize, Leah. You've already been a tremendous help to us."

"I was going to say there is another way I can help you. I remember the stones in question. I still remember where they were. I had to envision that for the book."

She closed her eyes and lifted her head slightly. Her fellow investigators glanced at each other, aware of what was happening. Goddard marveled at how this young woman demonstrated her abilities right in front of him. A trance-like serenity appeared to come over her. She began describing the stone staircase, the foot of which led to open, arched doorways. She spoke of how the basement's layout twisted and turned in lefts and rights, and which walls contained the stones in question. Detective Brock took notes while she spoke.

"Leah, if our theory is right," Goddard said. "You would be responsible for solving this mystery and getting justice for those women." He thanked her and the team for showing up, and the four investigators left the PD.

"That's a uniquely troubled young woman," Detective Brock said. "I hope she overcomes whatever happened in that house."

"Oh, she will," Goddard said. "I have no doubt about that. Meanwhile, I'm getting Judge Matthews on the phone. I want a court order to get into that house and down into the basement ASAP."

* * * *

Goddard descended the spiraling stone staircase with teams of detectives, forensics, and excavation experts behind him. The electricity in the house had been turned on for the excursion, but electrical torches were brought for the basement. Now, as light flooded the dismal underground, a vast labyrinth of limestone walls surrounded them, draped in cobwebs as thick as cotton candy. He ordered his investigative team to follow the directions Leah had provided, and to seek out any stones that appeared unusual or out of place.

Within minutes, they'd arrived at the spot where Leah had described stones that looked cemented over, unlike the other stones in the wall.

"This is it," Goddard announced. The excavation team took over, chipping away at the stones with pickaxes.

Clink...clank...clink...clank...

In less than an hour, the first of two stones had been loosened. It took four men to remove it. They dropped the boulder-like stone to the floor with a resounding boom.

Detective Brock walked over and peered inside the hole with a flashlight.

"What do we have, Brock?" Goddard said.

Brock turned away from the hole. He motioned with his hand to the forensic team.

"Skeletal remains."

Just then, the second stone was removed. Brock looked inside and quickly turned his head away. "There's more over here."

Anger, hot and relentless, surged through Goddard. He could almost feel steam coming from his skin. A fire for justice burned in his eyes. He walked over to the second hole. An unshakable urge made him want to see for himself what that bastard Angus Marlowe had done. He looked inside.

25

His stomach turned at the sight. Dry, brittle, black hair clung to a browning skull. He saw the bones of an outstretched arm, but he couldn't take his eyes away from that skull. There was black where the forehead would be. Goddard thought of a gunshot wound, but the black moved. He watched as a family of spiders crawled into one of the empty eye sockets. Goddard gagged and turned away. The sweat slicked his forehead, and for a moment, heat flooded this deep, dank, underground.

"We've got another one," he shouted to the forensics team. Then, he turned to the excavation team.

"Damn it!" His attempts to control his emotions failed. "Tear the whole goddamn wall down." His voice bellowed and echoed, repeating his every syllable.

The excavation team tore the wall down, stone by stone. No other bodies were found behind the wall, but there was another location Leah had mentioned. They traveled farther into the basement, until they reached a walled section where Leah had described stones that looked as though they'd been removed and replaced. One of them jutted out above the other stones. Goddard and Brock looked at each other. The excavators went to work removing the stones.

The remains of two more bodies were found, skeletal and decayed. Lives had been taken and given shoddy graves. Souls had become trapped in this basement hell forever. A continuous search left several crumbled walls in the basement of Cedar Manor. Another set of remains brought the total recovered to five, the last of which was beyond decomposition.

After making certain there was nothing left to find, Goddard turned to the excavation and forensics teams. "That's it, boys," he said. "Our theory was an accurate one."

The forensics team filed up the stone stairs first, two by two, toting body bags to be taken to the morgue. The excavation team followed. Then Goddard, Brock, and two fledgling detectives continued their search of the basement.

Goddard called out to Brock when he reached another wall and noticed something. "Hey Lance, come and look at this."

Brock walked over to the wall Goddard was facing. Goddard ran his finger across the wall from left to right without touching it.

"What the hell is that?"

Black marks stained the stones in this wall. He touched the charred limestone, removed his finger, and examined it.

"It looks like it's been scorched," he said.

Brock touched it next. "You're right. This wall was burned in some way."

"Yeah, but how?"

"With fire," Brock replied.

"I know that." Goddard was used to Brock's sarcasm. "But how would that happen?" He answered his own question before Brock had the chance. "Rituals, his damn rituals."

"Of course, what other explanation would there be?"

"Goddamn that Harold Bennett." Goddard exclaimed. "He stopped our department from getting a warrant to search down here back in 1967. I blame him for all of this."

They continued their search, examining antiques and artifacts that had obviously nothing to do with Angus, but did with the family itself. One of those antiques was a cabinet.

Goddard crouched down and opened it. Inside was a dusty, old, black book surrounded by strands of cobwebs. Goddard could see the browned end pages. He gently removed it from the cabinet to examine it. The cover was worn by time and dust. What once was pure black was now dusty and grayish. He blew the dust from the cover and opened it.

Flipping through the pages, Goddard noticed words and sentences in what looked like Latin. He saw inserts of sketches drawn by hand, none of which made any sense to him. Goddard closed the book, not needing to see any more.

"This must have been his book of rituals, his black bible, if you will. We'll tag this as evidence."

He handed the book to one of the younger detectives, who tagged it as confiscated evidence. Then Brock noticed something stowed away behind the cabinet on a small shelf.

"Look at this, Tom."

Brock retrieved a brass candelabrum from the shelf. Housed inside of its holders were black candles, much like those used in satanic rituals. The candles stepped in unison, three up to the top, and three down from the top. Black wax stained the brass along with what looked like smoke stains.

"How's this for proof positive?"

The candelabrum was also tagged as evidence, and finally, the search wound down. Goddard gave the order to begin to move out, but something caught the corner of his eye. An object of some sort jutted from the space beneath an old chest.

"Lance, what is that?" He pointed to the object.

Detective Brock walked over to the old chest, bent down, and with his latex-gloved hand, gently coaxed the object from its long held hiding place. He picked it up with the tips of his fingers. It was a handheld mirror, but the strangest thing about it was the black glass cast no reflection except for glimmering shadows from the existing light.

"What the hell?" Brock said.

Goddard examined the mirror in Brock's hands, careful not to touch it for fear of smudging any possible fingerprints.

"I think our friend, Angus Marlowe, was deeper into this shit than we thought," he observed.

"Looks like, what do they call this, a scythe? What in God's name is something like that used for?" Brock was stupefied.

"Whatever it is, it has nothing to do with God; that's for sure."

The handheld mirror was labeled as yet another piece of evidence. They continued to search around for another twenty minutes, but the short extension of time turned up nothing. Goddard was tired and weary. He sighed.

"I say we call an end to it. We have everything we need. We've now proven Angus Marlowe was responsible for the 1967 disappearances, and was in fact, a serial killer. I think we've done our job for today."

"I agree," Brock said. "I just want to get the hell out of here."

"Ditto that."

The junior detectives began carrying the electrical torches up the stone staircase. Goddard took one last look around. He looked at the pile of stones torn out from the wall, the scorching on the other, and the handheld mirror that Brock had.

"It looks like this story is over, once and for all," Brock said.

But Tom Goddard had a feeling that the story was years from over.

Chapter Three

~ Taryn ~

March 2009

Taryn Page had been called many things in her life—goofy, flaky, kooky, and weird, among them. She supposed it was all true, at least in the opinions of certain people. However, they wouldn't understand the truth, even if they'd known it. From an early age, Taryn had possessed a psychic ability. Sometimes she saw things, but not always, and certainly not like that girl who had written a book about a year ago. Taryn was intuitive—she knew things. She knew things, and then they happened.

Her ability was largely responsible for her fascination with the paranormal, which led most people to think of her as weird. She admitted being a little flighty. She was no academic genius, but none of her drawbacks diminished the fact that Taryn Page was what many would call a psychic.

Not only did she refuse to shun her ability in her life, but she immersed herself in it. She read up on psychic phenomena as much as she could. She chanted, and did yoga, all to focus her chakra. She even rearranged her furniture to create the right environment and establish the proper chi within the household. She also loved collecting strange and unusual artifacts.

What surprised Taryn most of all was that she'd passed on her ability to her daughter, Madison, now a five-year-old girl, sitting strapped next to her in the car's passenger's side. It wasn't just that she'd passed on her ability to her child, but the realization that Madison's talent dwarfed her mother's even though she was still a child.

Taryn could see it more and more as Madison grew older. It was the main reason she'd picked up a copy of *Cedar Manor* by Leah Leeds and read it cover to cover. She prayed her daughter would never experience anything like that in her lifetime. Yes, Taryn prayed. God was a big part of her life also. She assumed that was another reason she was called flaky.

The prayers had become more frequent lately, as Taryn discovered Madison's ability was much more than she'd originally assumed. Recently, when Taryn told her five-year-old daughter they could not go for ice cream that day, Madison displayed her temper, which had always been quick in the first place. Now, with that temper came something that scared the life out of Taryn. During her fit, Madison had moved a glass the entire length of the table, until it tipped and then crashed upon the floor. She threw the front door open and upended a dinner plate in the air, so that it spun and landed back on the table, smashing into pieces. Her little girl had done all of this in anger—all without touching a thing, and never leaving her seat at the table.

Taryn knew there was a word for it, but at that moment she'd been unable to recall it. It came to her after searching the internet. The word was "telekinesis." She'd read the definition according to Webster's: *The purported ability to move or deform inanimate objects by mental power.* Her stomach plunged upon reading those words. A word kept popping into her head, one she refused to attach to her precious little girl, but she kept hearing the word over and over again in her mind—witch.

She told herself time and again that her daughter was no witch. Yet Taryn knew damn well her own ability had never manifested into the things her little girl demonstrated time and again. Not only was Madison a telekinetic, but she was also clairvoyant. From what Taryn had read, even Leah Leeds had never demonstrated telekinetic ability.

According to gossip and local chatter, Leah Leeds was said to be one of the most powerfully gifted psychics in the world. Leah had written of being approximately five-years-old when she'd first demonstrated her ability to her father. Madison was five now, and Taryn and her husband, Charley, first noticed her capabilities shortly after her fifth birthday.

She'd told them when their phones were going to ring. She would predict a visitor minutes before a knock sounded on the front door. She'd even picked a few lottery numbers, though Taryn and Charley had been too stupid to play them. Then, their little girl began to move things, especially when she became angry or impatient. Once, Taryn and Charley were to attend a retirement party for someone at Charley's workplace. Madison didn't want them to go because she didn't want to spend the evening with the babysitter. In a fit of anger, she began turning over chairs.

"Stop it," Charley had said, kneeling in front of her, "right now."

She stopped. Madison had always listened to her Daddy, and then she would plead with him to get her way, yet she would fight with Taryn and lash out with her temper. Outside of being a little spoiled and somewhat impatient, her Maddy was a good, sweet girl. She was an only child. Taryn's obstetrician had told her there would be no more, and to be grateful for Madison. So, she blamed herself and Charley for the girl's spoiled temperament.

Now, Taryn glanced at herself in the rearview mirror while driving. She noticed her deep green eyes, her kinky ash-blonde hair, and her milky-white skin. She turned and looked at her daughter in the front seat and saw similar features in the complexion, the hair, although straighter, and the way her eyebrows made a perfect rounded arch. Madison had inherited her father's eyes, an icy, crystalline blue that was often hypnotizing. She smiled at her little girl, who smiled back at her, momentarily distracted from the sights that whizzed past the window.

"Mommy, how much longer till we get there?" Madison's tone was one of curiosity rather than impatience.

"It's not much farther, sweetie. We'll be there in just a few more minutes."

Taryn had made the twenty-mile trip after hearing about a small place that sold strange and unusual artifacts. The man who owned the place was a collector, something they both had in common. She called him, told him who she was, and asked to visit his shop. He suggested she stop by at three-o'clock, the best time for him to show her around. She hadn't planned on bringing Madison, who attended morning kindergarten, but all of the babysitters were at school.

Taryn had no other family than Charley and Madison. Her parents were killed in a car accident when she was a teenager, and like her daughter, she was also an only child. Charley's family lived across the country in Seattle. So it was just the three of them, one small, unusual, but happy family. Besides, she had no qualms about bringing Maddy with her. It was Charley who would not have been so wild about the idea.

Charley shared her interest in the paranormal. His concern may have grown greater on realizing his daughter was gifted in a strange way. He was a freelance writer who wrote articles and tidbits for various regional newspapers. He often wrote of real-life paranormal occurrences and sold quite a few pieces. Still, he was not quick to indulge his daughter's ability.

Taryn rounded a corner and drove up a winding, spiraling road. "It's just up at the end of this road. I told ya it wouldn't be much longer."

She and her daughter laughed in the front seats.

"Mommy, are you going to buy anything?"

That was a good question. Taryn had so many strange artifacts and antiques at the house that Charley had suggested renting a storage unit to stow some of it. She had even thought of opening her own shop back home in Green Valley.

"I don't know, sweetie. Daddy might get mad if I did. After all, I have so much stuff at home." Taryn made a face and Maddy laughed, knowing it was the truth. "But who knows, I don't really know what I'm looking for, but I feel like I need to be here. You know what I mean?"

Taryn asked the question in a certain way. Maddy nodded her head, obviously knowing what she meant. Taryn spoke openly and often about their shared abilities to her daughter. She wanted her daughter to understand her clairvoyance and not traipse through life wondering, speculating, and being constantly surprised, as she had once been. Taryn wanted her to be unafraid of it, and to control it. Although it was fear that prevented her from indulging Maddy's telekinetic talent.

Just then, Taryn pulled into a recently paved parking lot and looked at the neon blue sign that blinked the shop's name, *Enigma's & More.* The letters descended vertically on the large, rectangular sign that clung to the side of the building.

"This is it," Taryn said.

She parked the car and made sure Madison had properly undone the seatbelt that secured her. After locking the car, she held her daughter's hand as they walked. A bell clanged over the door as she opened it and entered the shop. An older man with white hair was wiping a long, librarian's counter in front of him. He looked at her as she stepped through the door. Then, he looked at Madison and smiled.

"Well, hello there," he said.

"Hello, my name is Taryn Page. We spoke on the phone."

"Yes, my dear, I remember. Please come in. And who have we here?"

She introduced Madison, who looked up at the man, studying his face. "I couldn't find a babysitter, so I brought her along. I hope that's okay?"

"Certainly." He bent down to Madison's eye level. He spoke in the voice that grownups use to placate children. "This big girl doesn't look like she's afraid of too much. Am I right?"

Taryn laughed. Madison kept a straight face.

"I'm afraid you're right," she said. "She's fearless."

The old man straightened himself. "Well, there's nothing here to be afraid of, just strange and unusual things that may or may not have a known history. I'm Ernie Mattson. Welcome to Ernie's Enigma's & More."

"Oh? I didn't see your name on the sign."

"They couldn't fit it all on the sign."

Taryn and Ernie erupted in laughter, while an unimpressed Madison stoically watched the man's face.

"Well, my dear, how about a tour?"

"I'd be delighted."

As they followed Ernie through the front part of the shop, he began by telling how he'd first come into business, back in 1969.

"My wife had disapproved," he said. "After all, it wasn't a big money maker, but she eventually came around, especially when we'd sell something to a collector who paid top price. Then, she was ecstatic."

Taryn told him about her hopes of opening her own shop, about all of the relics, antiques, and artifacts she'd collected over the years.

"It takes a great deal of patience, my dear, that, and a wide range of networking."

Ernie led them into a parlor-like room decorated in all green. The walls, the floor, even the ceiling was covered in a shade of green velour that ranked somewhere between pea and forest. In the center of the room stood a display encased in glass. Showcase lights beamed brightly down upon the display, illuminating what looked like two rocks.

Ernie took a key from his pocket, unlocked the display, and removed one of the rocks. "The first of these two rocks is said to contain an electrical pulse. No one knows of its origin or history. Many think it's manmade. Some say it's extraterrestrial, claiming that it's not from Earth." He turned the rock over and showed it to Taryn. "See that?"

Taryn was amazed at what she saw. On the back were two electrical plugs, one below and one above. It looked as though one could plug it right into the wall.

"Wow," she said. "Have you ever plugged it into a wall socket?"

"I have. It sparked, smoked, and blew itself out of the socket. I never did it again. Go ahead, and rub it between your hands." Taryn was leery. "Go on, it won't hurt you."

She took the small rock between her palms and rubbed it back and forth. She felt a quick shock, a zap as if she'd touched the wrong wire. She quickly set the rock back on the display case. Ernie laughed at Taryn's surprise. Madison watched them, not completely understanding.

"Where did you ever find such as thing?"

"A fellow came in here in the early seventies, told me he found it near the Roswell, New Mexico crash site. I was never really sure if he was telling the truth about that, but he wasn't the kind of guy who would've been smart enough to manufacture such a thing. You know what I mean?"

Taryn nodded as Ernie replaced the rock and retrieved the second one from the display case. The second rock was slightly smaller. He placed it in Taryn's open hands, and then closed them.

"Wait and tell me if you feel anything."

After a few seconds, Taryn felt it. The rock was vibrating, throbbing in her hand.

"I feel it," she said, nodding. "What is it?"

"That rock has a magnetic pulse, though that's not entirely unusual. Rocks beneath the earth's crust have magnetic pulses. It's how earthquakes are predicted. What's unusual about this rock is that archeologists have adamantly attested that it is not from Earth, and its level of magnitude is extremely high, higher than what would be found on this planet. Watch this."

Ernie bent down beneath the display case and produced a rectangular magnet, one he obviously kept for this demonstration. He held it up over the rock and continued to speak. Then suddenly, the magnet flew out of his hand and attached itself to the rock. Taryn gaped in open-mouthed awe.

"That's amazing," she said.

Madison continued to watch. Ernie told Taryn to remove the magnet from the rock, and when she did, it was difficult. The magnet was stubbornly attracted to the rock. She could feel the force, the strong magnetic pull as she forced it away.

Ernie took the rock and locked it back up in the case.

"Right this way," he said.

Taryn and Madison followed him to the back of the room, where another display case stood, this one, against the wall. Inside, Taryn saw a rounded, light-green sphere. Ernie unlocked the case and removed it.

"This is one of a few that has been discovered in the Orient, Egypt, and other places. An enthusiastic game hunter brought this to me, said he discovered it in Sri Lanka. These things are called grooved spheres." He ran his fingers across the sphere in a horizontal, parallel motion. "You see these grooves? They're supposed to represent the equator."

Taryn pointed to the sphere. "So, that thing is supposed to represent Earth?"

"Precisely," he said. "Although where they originally came from, when, and who's responsible for such a piece of work is unknown. The strange thing about this sphere is the metal." He dinged the sphere with a pen he took from his shirt pocket. "If it's as old as estimated, this particular type of metal did not exist yet on Earth."

Taryn looked at him, catching on. "So, the question is, where did it come from?"

"Smart girl," Ernie said, making her laugh.

They walked into the next parlor-like room, where multiple colors draped the walls with different shades of red, orange, blue, and purple. In the center of the room sat another display, this one showcasing a large crystal perched on a fitted dais. Ernie led them to it, and then stood behind it, demonstrating like a professor.

Madison eyed the strange rounded stone.

Ernie moved his hands around it as he spoke. "This is said to have come from the lost city of Atlantis, though how anyone could ever prove that is questionable. It definitely came from a mystical somewhere."

He gestured to Taryn with his hand. "Go ahead, move your hands around it."

He laughed when she quickly withdrew her fingers in hesitation. "Don't worry, this one won't shock you. We'll do it together." Ernie and Taryn moved their hands in waving circular motions around the crystal, keeping their eyes on it.

Madison stepped forward slightly. Within seconds, a bright orange glow pulsated within the crystal. There was no shock, no heat, just the invisible presence of a pulse. Taryn quickly glanced at Ernie, and then turned her attention back to the crystal. It had changed to a vivid, vibrant red, and then to a deep, exotic purple.

"It's changing colors." Her voice rose in astonishment.

"No one can explain why," Ernie replied.

Then the crystal changed to various hues, all noticeable shades belonging to the prism of light, but then the stone changed to other vivid and exotic colors: turquoise, gold, and what looked like chartreuse.

"Okay, now let's move our hands away from it," Ernie instructed.

They both moved their hands away from it simultaneously. The colors stopped. Taryn gasped. Madison's eyes grew wide, staring at the stone in silence.

"I've got another artifact said to have come from Atlantis. Let me show you, though I'm afraid it's much less fascinating." From another case, Ernie produced two small, metallic disks, gray in color. He ran his fingers around the edges.

"See these?" He pointed to what looked like writing. "They're hieroglyphics. An ancient language of a time long past is inexplicably carved into these highly sophisticated disks. Interesting, isn't it?"

"Could they be forgeries?"

"Anything's always possible, my dear," Ernie said, laughing.

They moved on to another parlor, this one decorated in the deepest, cobalt-blue. Ernie led them to the room's glass display. Inside of it were three ball-shaped objects the same color as the room. He removed them and placed one in her hand.

"These blue balls mysteriously fell from the sky and landed in a small town about sixty-miles east of here. No one knows what they are or from where they came. They've fallen and landed in the same general area at different times throughout the last century. Many claim the first time was in 1947, then a second time in 1953, and again in 1967. The one you're holding was discovered in 1993. I've heard stories that this continues to happen."

Taryn turned the ball-shaped object in her hand. It was solid, somewhat heavy.

"Are they made of cobalt?"

"Some say yes. Others disagree. To this day, there remains no explanation for them. I even heard the town changed its name to 'Blue Balls' after the strange phenomena."

Ernie and Taryn erupted into more laughter. Taryn then looked behind her at her daughter, whose interest seemed still attached to the color changing crystal in the other room. Ernie continued to talk as they left the parlor and passed a small hallway, where something caught the corner of Taryn's eye. There at the end of the hallway, stood a large, rectangular, black mirror.

She brushed past Ernie and walked toward it, unable to take her eyes away from its opaque glass and unique silvered frame. She felt mesmerized. She hadn't even noticed as Madison closely followed her, and then wrapped her arm around her right leg, immersed in the same ardent curiosity.

Taryn's growing astonishment came out in a mystified tone. "What is this?"

Ernie stepped forward and stood alongside her. Now, the tone of his voice sounded different. It was no longer that of the exuberant and instructional shopkeeper. He now spoke in an even and careful manner.

"That is something I acquired from an anonymous donor back in 1970. It's called 'the Black Mirror.' To be honest, it's been there for forty-five years and has always given me the creeps. The donor gave me a vague story about how a late client of his had inherited it from a distant, unknown relative. At the time, I thought nothing of it. I think now that I should have been a little more cautious. I have the distinct feeling that whatever history lies behind that thing has been hidden."

Taryn stared at the black glass. Drawn to it, she moved closer as Madison trudged beside her with eyes equally unwavering from the dark mystery. She looked into it, studying the dim shadows it reflected. Then, she touched it, feeling its cold hardness respond beneath her fingertips. She sensed Ernie studying the fascinated expression on her face. She could feel his concern. She turned and faced him as Madison let go of her leg.

"Would you be interested in selling this? This would be a rare asset in my collection."

Ernie's expression was one of concern. She sensed his caution, his wariness.

"Young lady, are you sure you want to own something like this? It has always drawn people to it, much like it has with you right now. That's why I keep it in this hallway. Like I said, it's always given me the creeps."

"All the more reason to sell it."

Ernie looked at her, and then noticed Madison, who continued to stare into the glass. He walked over to the mirror and looked into it himself. His unease about the mirror hit Taryn like a fleeting gust of cold wind, and then it was gone. He turned back to face her.

She made her offer. "I can pay you fifteen-hundred dollars for the mirror, and I can have it moved myself. I mean, really, it's just an artifact, right? It's an old black mirror that gives you the creeps. I'd be happy to take it off of your hands."

Ernie inhaled as he thought for a moment. Then, he sighed.

"What the hell, fifteen-hundred dollars for a mirror that cost me nothing and gives me the creeps anyway." Then, he turned, looked into the mirror, and shivered. "You got yourself a deal."

He extended his hand, and they shook on it. Madison continued staring into the mirror.

"Great," Taryn said. "I'll be in touch about picking it up, and thank you for everything."

"Thank you, my dear."

Taryn walked over to Madison, who stood frozen in front of the mirror. "Madison, let's go, and be sure to thank this nice man."

Madison uttered a soft-spoken thank you as they walked out the door, the hanging bells clanging behind them. As they walked away, Taryn sensed Ernie watching her.

* * * *

Ernie stared into the Black Mirror and wondered if he'd done the right thing, selling this damn eyesore to the young woman. Maybe she was right. Maybe it was just an artifact. Ernie had mentioned this damn thing gave him the willies, but he hadn't said why. After all, he didn't want her to think he was crazy or, better yet, a drunk.

It had happened one night in 1975, after a Christmas party he and his wife, Stella, had attended. She had taken the keys and driven the car home, insisting he was drunk. Afterward, he'd been staring into the mirror, just like the young woman had moments ago. He could've sworn he saw this same black glass ripple in waves, and then it stopped. He'd blinked his eyes, and the glass appeared normal. He'd never told a soul about the incident.

Now, this young woman wanted that mirror. She seemed a little flighty, even witchy maybe. That would account for her attraction to this thing. He was in no position to turn down an offer like that for something he considered a strange burden and a constant reminder of his much younger stupidity. So, it would be gone soon. He looked into the glass one last time, freezing in his mind its unexplainable opaqueness that cast wavering shadows.

Then, something happened. For a moment, Ernie saw the glass change. The mirror appeared to have an almost three dimensional effect, as if one could walk right through it. Ernie removed his glasses. His heart pounded a rhythm that hurt his chest. The glass was no longer there. Where the glass had been only seconds ago, he glimpsed an open doorway. Then the surface became glass again, hard and cold just like always.

Ernie's hands shook as he stepped away. Sweat streaked his face. He turned his back and hurried away, never to face it again.

Chapter Four

~ Taryn (Continued) ~

March-June 2009

The men Taryn had hired finally delivered the mirror to her home and set it in the desired location. She had turned what had once been the finely furnished family den into her very own gallery—a unique lair prominently displaying her artifacts in showcase style.

The room was decorated in dark brown hues with maroon paneling, and inside an exhibition of odd displays revealed the strangest of curiosities. She had African death masks, Egyptian runes, a glass case containing an exotic looking violet, and large urns that held heather and belladonna. Odd gold statues twisted into serpent forms, dragons rivaled, and a stone gargoyle sat alone in a far corner. One of Taryn's favorites was the white statue of a vestal virgin. Multiple eyes covered the delicate icon from her head to her feet. The statue was symbolic, and she couldn't help but think of her little girl when she'd first discovered the piece at a traveling bazaar.

Charley hated all of it. She hadn't told him about the Black Mirror. She couldn't. If he learned she'd paid fifteen-hundred dollars for it, plus another five-hundred to have it delivered, it would be the end of it all. Yet she was proud of the new addition to her collection. It took its own place in the corner opposite the gargoyle.

In front of Ernie, she'd tried to downplay just how mesmerized she'd been by the mirror. Her fascination had grown with each passing moment. Now, those moments had turned into days. For days, she stood in front of it, gazing into its odd, opaque reflection. It had some kind of possessive power, some kind of hold over her she seemed unable to shake. She wanted to discover more about it and learn its mystery, its origin. She touched the glass and tried to grasp what her intuition told her, but her instincts failed whenever she stood before the mirror, immersed in its darkness.

Charley was growing suspicious. She'd been spending more and more time in the gallery lately. She wasn't too worried about Charley. As a writer, he was constantly wrapped up in his work. If he were to ever discover the mirror, she would devise some excuse for its presence. Then, another unexpected concern came to her attention—Madison.

Yesterday, Taryn had been gazing into the mirror, trying to figure out how it cast such eerie reflections. Suddenly, she saw another strange, smaller likeness in the mirror. She quickly turned to find her daughter watching her. Madison walked up to her, took her hand, and studied the mirror with her mother. It was then that Taryn realized her daughter's interest in the Black Mirror matched her own. They watched it together, equally spellbound.

Something unexplainable prevented her from discouraging Madison's interest in the mirror. Why should she? There was nothing to fear. Still, her own volition was to be alone. Today, she had wanted to examine the mirror in the morning while Maddy was in school, but Charley was home from work until this afternoon. After he'd gone, she picked up her daughter from school, and left her to watch TV in the living room upstairs.

"I won't be long, sweetie," she said, walking down the stairs.

She held the den door open and took one last look at Madison. The girl's eyes were focused on the screen, watching cartoons. Taryn turned and closed the door behind her. She walked over to the mirror and stood in front of it again. Her odd fascination was now turning into a bizarre obsession.

Taryn looked into the glass, touched it, and whispered to it. "What are you?"

A strange sensation swept over her. She felt like she was being pulled. A sudden magnetic force, not much different than the rock she'd held in her hand, lightly tugged at her body. Her eyes froze in front of the mirror, two wide green orbs unable to escape the grasp of the blackness. Something was happening to the glass. It seemed to be melting, and then rippling in small waves. She let out a gasp as the rippling stopped and the glass vanished.

Her heart stopped beating. She knew what the mirror was. It was a gateway. She saw some kind of mist rising beyond the mysterious entrance she'd just opened. Something moved within that mist. Her heart suddenly leaped to her throat and began beating again.

A tall man with piercing blue eyes and long hair was coming toward her. She couldn't move. Her body was paralyzed, much like her eyes.

Then it happened.

* * * *

Mommy had told her "no displays," and Madison knew exactly what that meant—no moving things. She told her this before they'd made the trip to that old man's shop. Mommy had been afraid she might break something. So, Madison had stayed quiet, careful not get mad.

Madison knew she could break things. She first realized it when she got mad at her doll because her hair wouldn't comb right, so without using her hands, she broke her. She watched as cracks formed in the plastic doll and spread to its face like bulging veins until the face shattered. She hid the broken doll in her closet under some blankets. After that, when Daddy gave her a time out in her room, she turned over her small, play desk chair without touching it. She never meant to get mad, but it happened.

Then, there was the glass of milk. She hadn't wanted to finish her milk. She wanted ice cream. Not only had she moved the glass across the table, but she sent it crashing to the floor, where it shattered into pieces. Mommy had been mad. Madison enjoyed breaking the dish, but she got in trouble for it. Then, there were chairs. That was when Daddy stopped her. She hadn't wanted to stay with the babysitter that night. She didn't like her. All the sitter did was talk on the phone and invite her friends over. Madison wanted to break her like her doll.

Something else Mommy and Daddy didn't know about was that one day the babysitter brought her boyfriend over and asked Madison to go and play elsewhere.

Madison went to play in the garage. She wasn't supposed to play in the garage, but who would know? She'd been bouncing the rubber ball Daddy had bought her. It bounced too hard and got lost behind a pile of Mommy's old junk. Madison got mad and smashed the garage window. She hadn't realized she'd done it until she heard the crash of glass. Then, she ran out of the garage.

Daddy later thought some neighborhood kids had accidently smashed the window while playing. Madison had been lucky. The babysitter hadn't known or cared.

Today, Madison knew Mommy went downstairs to her den to study the Black Mirror. They got the mirror when they went to that old man's shop, where Madison was careful not to get mad. Mommy had also said not to breathe a word to Daddy about buying it, or he would get mad.

The shop bored her. She didn't understand many of the things there, especially the disks and the rocks. What was the big deal? Madison loved the crystal that changed colors. Why couldn't Mommy have bought that instead?

She remembered when she and Mommy saw the Black Mirror. Neither of them could take their eyes away from it, but Mommy liked it. Madison knew there was something wrong with it. It was a bad mirror— that's why it was black. Madison watched it too because in her mind, she had seen it opening. If it opened, and you walked inside, where would you end? Madison had stared, waiting for it to open.

She should have told Mommy about seeing it open because she wished Mommy hadn't brought it home. All Mommy did was stare into the mirror. Maybe she already knew it would open.

The day they'd gone to the shop, Mommy had told her not to break anything. Madison realized she should have broken the mirror, because after Mommy had closed the den door, leaving her to watch cartoons, Madison had seen everything.

She pretended to be watching the TV, but actually, she was tired of Sponge Bob. Mommy had closed the door, so Madison waited. Then, she tired of waiting. She sprung up from the couch and tiptoed silently down the stairs. She opened the door and stood in the doorway. That's when she saw Mommy.

Mommy clutched both sides of the mirror, staring into it like she'd never seen it before. She made some kind of noise like she was crying. Something about the mirror appeared different. It didn't look like glass. Instead, it looked like water. Then, Madison watched it open. She knew it would open because she'd seen it in her mind.

Madison jumped when she saw a man with long hair standing where the mirror's glass had been. He grabbed Mommy by the neck and was choking her.

Madison screamed. Suddenly, the man glared at her. She felt the evil cast of his eyes move through her. Then, he pulled Mommy through the mirror. Madison screamed louder. She ran to the mirror, but the mirror was glass again. The opening had closed. Mommy was gone.

Anger pulsated through her body, heating her blood. She seethed, breathing heavily. Madison focused all of her energy, thinking of all the bad things she'd done lately. She thought back to when she broke the doll and the dish. She directed whatever it was she had inside of her and unleashed it upon the mirror. Nothing happened. The glass didn't break. She tried again. Nothing. The glass was too heavy to break. She felt its resistance repelling her unseen energy.

Madison fell to the floor and screamed, over and over again.

* * * *

He was coming closer and closer. Taryn couldn't pry her hands from the sides of the mirror. She couldn't escape. Those eyes, those menacing blue eyes burned with anger and approached rapidly. Taryn wanted to scream, but she couldn't. All that escaped her were loud, heaving whimpers of fear. The man reached out through the gateway and grabbed her around the neck.

His grip was like an iron fist. The squeeze stopped her air. She feared he would crush the bones and muscles in her neck. Her vision blurred, while multi-colored spots formed before her fading eyesight. She struggled, but he pulled her through, and then tossed her to the ground—a cold, hard ground, unlike the earth her feet had normally trod.

Suddenly, cold, like death, enveloped her. She writhed on the strange ground beneath her, breathing October-like brisk air. She sensed her imminent death as her life passed before her in stages—her childhood, her teen years, marrying Charley, having a precious baby girl placed in her hands. It all faded to blackness, but then she opened her eyes. She felt herself rise from the ground and come alive again.

She looked around her at a world unlike anything she'd ever seen before. It was tinged deep blue like early dawn. Around her was nothing but a strange and unexplored landscape. The cold was gone. She felt nothing. She turned and looked at what lay on the ground at her feet. It was her body. Again, she felt nothing, no emotion, no sorrow, no pain, only existence.

She looked away from what she couldn't change and saw him, the man who had pulled her through. He'd killed her, but some hidden intuition of hatred lay dormant and buried somewhere inside of her. It was an emotion untraceable to who she was at this moment. He came toward her, his blue eyes no longer menacing. He touched her hair, her face.

"Do you know what you are?" His voice was deep and with a scratchy rasp that seemed to fit him.

She tried to think. Her thoughts seemed the same as always. She felt no change in the way she thought, the memories she retained, or in the way she responded.

"Am I a spirit?"

"Not quite," he said. "What you are... is a doppelganger."

She turned her head and looked again at her body on the nearly frozen unearthly floor.

"But I'm dead."

"Your body is dead, but your double, your better other side, lives on. The magic of the mirror has made you what you are. Come, see for yourself."

He took her by the hand, and she let him. She no longer feared him. What she felt inside of her now was a thriving curiosity. He walked her through the deep blue of this realm, hand in hand like a ghostly specter and his newlywed bride. She surveyed her surroundings in wonder, recognizing mountainous rocks and rolling mist. There was no sun, no moon, only blue. A mysterious bird cawed and flew over their heads as they walked through the hidden twilight. She'd seen one like that before in books, an extinct bird, yet alive in this world.

They arrived at a vast clearing. There, the mist dissipated around them on both sides. What she saw in front of her didn't look real, but more like an illusion or a mirage of some sort. It was another mirror or at least the image of one. Its frame was exactly like that of the Black Mirror, though gold, and the glass was clear and perfect. She and the man who killed her stood side by side in the flawless reflection.

"Look at yourself," he ordered.

She stepped forward and looked into the glass. She was different somehow, almost better. Her hair was shinier, her face tighter, her skin smoother. She touched the side of her face with her left hand. It felt soft, delicate, like a flower.

"This mirror is the opposite end of the gateway," the man said. "Both mirrors are doorways. You will use this doorway when you leave."

"Leave?"

"Yes, there is something I need you to do for me. I cannot leave, at least, not yet."

She suddenly thought of her daughter. Would Madison see the change in her, if she saw her? She wanted to see her daughter, yet she felt no urgency. Madison would be fine, maybe even better without her. A sudden intuition told her to keep her daughter's psychic abilities hidden from this man.

"I've already seen your daughter," he said.

Her eyes focused on him. He knew her thoughts.

"She was watching as I pulled you through."

Taryn had not known, but it made sense. Madison had been sneaking up on her in her den for quite some time. She remembered leaving Madison in the living room, watching TV. She'd gone into the den and closed the door behind her. Her hands, she remembered being unable to detach her hands from the sides of the mirror. Then, he had pulled her through.

"What is it that you want from me?"

He raised his index finger.

"In time, all will be revealed. First, there are things you must learn about what you are. I will show you all you need to know. Then, I will send you out into the real world."

* * * *

47

Time. No measure or marker of time existed here. To her, it seemed only a moment ago when the man pulled her through the mirror. Out in the real world, weeks, maybe months could've passed. Taryn had no way to tell.

She learned many things from him. In her doppelganger form, she could appear as a fully-fledged visible human; or, she could dissolve into near invisibility.

"The ghostly form," he called it. In this state, she might be seen, but only by the keenest of human eyes. She would appear as a ghost. She initiated the ghostly form under his direction and watched herself fade and dissipate, vanishing into nothing but a scarcely visible outline of a person. She lifted her hand and looked through it, something she would have marveled at in life, but now, it was if she'd somehow always known.

He led her to one of the many mountainous rock formations of their realm. "Do you see the small mountain before you, the hard, solid rock?" She nodded. "You can move through it, effortlessly."

She stared at him with a hint of skepticism. He moved his arm toward the small mountain and motioned her to enter it. She looked away from him and at the rocky heap. She glided toward it as if walking on air. Her presence penetrated the hard rocky mass.

The small mountain swallowed her, and she moved through rock, passing through atoms and molecules effortlessly. Now, she stood on the other side of the small mountain, examining her surroundings when a sudden movement distracted her. He stepped through the mountain as if he'd passed through a mere curtain. She watched him emerge from it bit by bit, limb by limb.

They stood together on the other side of the small mountain. Again, he took her hand. His even-toned voice had a commanding timbre.

"I am Angus," he said. "Here is what I need you to do."

He told her about leaving through the doorway he had shown her earlier. She would walk through the image of the gold-gilded mirror and emerge on the other side. There, she would find herself in a great and majestic, but abandoned house—his house.

"That is the location of the gold-gilded mirror. It is the end of the gateway. Once you're inside the house, you will descend the stairs and then pass through its great walls, until you are out in the open air. You may long to stay in the old world, but you must not. Here is what you will do."

He dictated his instructions precisely. She was to go to the police station in the ghostly form, move through its walls, and find her way to the evidence room. There, she was to retrieve a black, handheld mirror, opaque, like its larger cousin. She was to bring it back to him.

"It is the key," he said.

She stared at him, unafraid, yet not quite ready to yield to his wishes. "If I don't?" The hint of malice in his blue eyes returned.

"You ended my life," Taryn protested. "What's to stop me from remaining in the real world and living out the rest of my days like this? Why should I help you?"

He stepped closer to her, his eyes filled with anger. Taryn didn't flinch. What was the worst he could do now?

"Remember, I saw your daughter. What was her name again?" He rolled his eyes upward. "Madison. What would she think if she saw what you are now?"

Taryn didn't believe his threat. He needed the key for a reason. It's why he couldn't leave yet. She didn't rebuff him. A powerful intuition told her to leave as he asked. While she felt emotionless, part of her yearned to be in the real world again.

She turned to him. "Take me to the exit, the one you showed me."

The malice melted away in his eyes. "You have chosen well."

Together they walked back through the open clearing and to the strange mirage of the gold-gilded mirror. A ghost of an object, she thought, as she neared it.

He spoke to reassure her. "You will feel nothing, just as you did when you passed through the rock. You are a doppelganger. There is nothing to feel."

She glided toward the fleeting image of the mirror, stopped, and looked back at him. He motioned with his hand for her to enter it. She turned back to the mirror and gazed at herself once more. Yes, she appeared as a more perfect version of herself, but something was different, something she couldn't identify.

He yelled from behind her, his words echoing through a hollow world. "Your imperfections are nothing compared to what has been enhanced. Don't be foolish. Go! I will be waiting for you."

She continued to glide freely toward the mirage. It drew her in, just as the Black Mirror had done. She penetrated the shimmering image of glass. He'd been right—she felt nothing, except for a dull magnetic pull, as if she walked underwater.

Her movement was slow through the lengthy passage, but the presence of light grew brighter. She must be near the exit point. She shot her hand out with as much force as she could muster and watched as it disappeared through the portal to the other side. She had made it.

She moved slowly and deliberately through clear glass, until she stood alone in a shadowy room. Sunshine outside cut through gable windows, creating a soft dimness that allowed her to see. She noticed how the mirror caught the glare of the sun that projected through the gable window.

After the change, her emotions had died but her senses remained. Now the acute smells of dust, mice, and cedar assaulted her. The house was immense, majestic, just as he described, but she felt lost. She wandered around until she found the giant spiral staircase. She stood at the top, looking down. This had been his house, this magnificent masterpiece now draped in thick cobwebs, desolate and abandoned.

She descended the staircase in her ghostly form, gliding freely, and then stopping as she sensed something. She looked above, around, and below her. Taryn's psychic intuition had not died away; it simply merged into the doppelganger during the transformation. Something wasn't right about this house. Many unseen things lived within these aging walls. Taryn's intuition was spontaneous like a voice. She knew what dwelled here—evil. It was of no consequence to her now. She arrived at the bottom of the staircase, planting her ghostly feet on the floor and moving fast through the massive hallway.

The windows in this house had not been boarded over. They'd been left as they were, abandoned to the reality of being smashed in certain places by random punks on the prowl. The light poured through the windows enough for her to see the large wooden front door ahead of her. He'd told her to pass through the walls. Why do that when she could exit through the front door? She absorbed herself into the solid wood of the door, becoming one with it, and arriving outside of the great house.

Its height towered above her. Three-stories stacked high with gable windows freely admitting streaks of sunshine. It was chocolate in hue, and a strange spire pointed upward, almost in defiance. She knew where she was—Cedar Manor, the house Leah Leeds had written about. He'd told her his name was Angus. Now, it all became clear. He was Angus Marlowe, the killer. Yet he was like her, which meant that he was Angus' doppelganger. She wasted no time. Slipping through the front gate and out to the road, Taryn looked around, making sure no one was watching. Then, she materialized.

Bone became bone, flesh became flesh. Feet began to step in sync and walk down the road. She continued to look around as she walked in human form. If someone had seen her, they would've witnessed her slowly take shape and form before their eyes, a shock that would've drawn much unwanted attention. Now, the warmth of the sunshine on her body was real, not a vague sensation. She heard the chirping of birds more clearly than when in the ghostly form. So, this was her life now, both a ghost and a human, an exact replica of who she once was.

She walked a mile away from Cedar Manor until she arrived at Ridgley Park. She sat on a park bench. Angus had been right about one thing. How would her daughter respond to what she was now? Madison was clairvoyant, and she would know. Even Charley would know something was different. How could he not? She was the same, yet she was different.

It wasn't any easier to muster emotion in her human form. She thought Maddy and Charley would be better off without her. However, she had no intention of living out a bizarre existence in some alternate realm with Angus Marlowe. She would go to the police station, she would steal the handheld mirror, but she would not return it to Angus. She had other plans.

She was not near the police station, and getting there in human form would not be easy. She no longer had her cell phone, so she couldn't call a cab, and she surely wasn't going to call Charley. Neither did she have any money.

Taryn wasn't even sure how much time had passed since she'd entered the gateway. She knew her life, as she'd known it, ended during the cold spell of early March. Now sunshine warmed her bones, as if she'd never felt it before, but it was time to go. She rose from the park bench and faded back into ghostly form.

* * * *

Taryn stood across the street from the police station; a small, square building she'd driven past many times in her life. Barely visible in her current state, she remained extra careful and waited for the opposing traffic light to turn red before crossing the street. She glanced at the waiting cars as she glided across the road, wondering if they saw the slightest hint of a ghostly figure. She couldn't tell. Traveling in the ghostly form was like the human dream of flying, covering a lot of ground in a small span of time. Now, she stood in front of the police station, ready for her mission, but not for Angus's sake. She was not about to help a murderer who had claimed her as his latest victim.

Standing outside of the building and contemplating her task, she suddenly thought of something. According to what she understood, Angus Marlowe had disappeared in late 1970. That must have been when he'd gone through the Black Mirror. The man she had just left looked no more than forty-five or fifty years of age, which meant, as a doppelganger, Angus hadn't changed. She wondered if it would be the same for her. Would she continue indefinitely, never to age? Would the being that she was now cease to exist at some point? Only he would have those answers, but she wasn't willing to become his slave just to learn what she could discover on her own.

She examined the building closely, its brown brick exterior she would walk through was thick, but nothing she couldn't handle. She merged herself with the side of the building, penetrating the brick until it was all she saw before her, nothing but brick and cement, which seemed endless. A quick second of panic struck her, but she imagined herself through to the other side, to the building's interior.

Inside the police station, she found herself in a room full of desktop computers, where uniformed cadets sat and surfed in frustration. One man in plain clothes sat back in his desk chair, his hands folded atop of his head as he stared at the screen. No one turned in her direction. No one had noticed any disturbance in their surroundings. A part of her marveled at this fact, but she kept her perspective. This was not the evidence room.

She floated through the station, curious as to when someone would scream "ghost." Through a glass window, she saw a man behind a desk, filling out paperwork. Obviously, he was some type of higher-up, a detective most likely.

Moving through the building freely, she remained cautious. Phones rang in the background, people called out to each other, and the voices of dispatchers crackled from police monitors. Finally, she arrived at a closed door. A plaque on the door contained the words *Evidence Room*. Her gaze moved across the hallway to the opposite wall. A video camera hung from the ceiling, moving left to right as it scanned up and down the hallway. Then, it peered in her direction. It didn't matter because the camera would capture nothing of her ghostly image.

Again, she merged her ghostly form with the door, allowing it to absorb her as she became part of it and all of its physical components. She emerged in darkness as the Evidence Room was unlit. Large, stacked metal shelves stood side by side throughout the room. Boxes, folders, manila envelopes, all were stored haphazardly high to the ceiling.

How was she supposed to find anything in here? It wasn't like any particular piece of evidence was laid out in the open. Time was not a problem nor was the possibility of her being discovered. She materialized in the room and flicked the light switch on the wall. The flickering bulbs above provided minimal light. The door was locked, so she would have ample time to fade back into the ghostly form if anyone tried to enter.

She looked at tags on plastic bags and labels on boxes. Nothing struck her eye. Then she noticed the shelves were assigned to house pieces of evidence alphabetically. She moved across one of the shelves, and then over to the other side, to the section designated as "*C*." She read through the various labels, and again saw nothing of relevance. Then, a manila envelope triggered her intuition. She hesitated for a moment, and then slowly, she pulled it from the shelf. The envelope was labeled with the two magic words she'd been searching for—*Cedar Manor*.

She undid the flimsy brass fasteners on the back of the envelope and removed its contents. The only thing inside the envelope was a mirror, handheld and opaque. Its glass was identical to the larger Black Mirror. She held it in her hand for a moment and gazed into its glass. Strangely enough, it cast a shadowy reflection of the ghostly image she'd abandoned only moments ago. Something akin to surprise woke within her consciousness.

She returned her attention to the shelf. Next to the envelope was a large, black tome, as well as a black candelabrum. She assumed they were part of the Cedar Manor evidence as well. Angus hadn't mentioned a book or a candelabrum, so she left them where they were.

Suddenly, the sound of someone jiggling the lock on the door of the Evidence Room surprised her. Quickly, she faded fast into her ghostly form. She moved behind the door just as it opened. A female officer stepped inside and looked around the room, obviously wondering why the lights were on, yet she saw nothing. The officer walked over to a pile of stacked folders and began rummaging. Taryn wasted no time. She drifted through the open doorway and into the hallway. The unexpected moment came as a lucky break.

She waited until the video camera's focus turned down the hallway. Then, she materialized and strolled past the Ladies Room. As she was about to leave the station, she stopped and turned. A calendar on the wall above one of the desktop computers caught her attention. She looked at the month—*June*. So, it had been three months since Angus had pulled her through the Black Mirror. Three months she'd spent in that strange realm, and it had only felt like one day. Taryn didn't stop to dwell on it. She had something to do.

She walked to the front exit and left the station, making it outside with the handheld mirror safely in her pocket.

Angus Marlowe would never get his hands on this. She would never unleash something like him on the rest of the world. His soul was trapped, and it was trapped for a reason. She was not going back to Cedar Manor. She knew exactly where she would leave this "key".

Taryn fled through town, taking to alleyways and shortcuts she remembered well. Unable to travel with the mirror in her ghostly form, she remained vigilant so as not to be seen. She soon arrived at a place she was anxious to reach—home. She felt as though she'd only been gone for a day, but it seemed like a lifetime when it came to her home. Charley's car was not parked out front. He must've been at work, though she wasn't sure what time of day it was. Maddy could be at school, but maybe not. She used the key hidden by the backdoor to enter.

Once inside, she went to her living room. No one stirred. The house appeared empty. It was a good thing. How would she explain where she'd been? How would she explain what she was? How could she tell them that she was dead, but alive in this form? She couldn't reveal herself to them, at least not yet.

She was certain no one was home. She walked around her house, revisiting her kitchen, her dining room, and even the stairs that led to her den. Yet she didn't feel the same. She felt like a near perfect shell of who she once was.

A feeling like somberness passed through her the same way she'd passed through walls. She stood atop the stairs, staring at the door to the room that was hers—all hers. Another fleeting feeling like fear stirred inside, but it was hard to identify. What was there to fear anymore?

Angus could not harm Maddy, not if he stayed trapped within the gateway. She descended the soft, carpeted stairs, one by one. She would feel the plush beneath her feet only in this form.

At the bottom of the stairs, she opened the door to her den once again and went inside. It was her room, and nothing had changed. The Black Mirror remained in the far corner, the gargoyle in the opposite. Slowly, she walked over to the mirror, the catalyst that had caused all of this. She eyed its sleek darkness, no longer transfixed by its sinister enticement. It was black glass to her now, nothing more. In front of the doppelganger, the glass no longer morphed or changed.

She suddenly realized why it had in the first place. It had been Angus, trying to open the gateway from the other side. He couldn't do it without the handheld mirror—the key. It was the same reason he couldn't leave through the mirage of the gold-gilded mirror and get back into Cedar Manor. That was why he needed a willing, ignorant participant like herself. He needed the key. His intention was to make a slave or an accomplice out of her, but that wasn't going to happen now.

At first, she'd thought to leave the handheld mirror behind in the den amid her vast collection. It would've been right at home. Then, she thought better of it. She had no doubt Maddy was still coming into this room, staring at the Black Mirror as she had. She had probably even tried to break it, unsuccessfully by the looks of it. What if Maddy got older and eventually made a connection between the two mirrors? What if she released Angus or, worse, took her place by his side? That would not do. She couldn't leave the mirror in this room.

She would leave it in Charley's home office. Maybe he would take it as a sign. Maybe he would know it came from her. Charley wrote about paranormal things. Maybe he would research the handheld mirror and the Black Mirror, and solve this mystery. The mirror was better off in his hands than in Madison's.

In Charley's home office, she set the mirror down on his desk. The passing feeling of oncoming tears came and went. She would visit this house again and often, but now she needed to leave. She needed to experience who or what, she was. She looked through her house one more time. She would return when the time was right.

Chapter Five

~ Trapped Within the Gateway ~

Taryn never returned with the key, and Angus remained trapped here in the gateway. He'd assumed she'd been under his spell, ready to learn under his direction, but he was wrong. She represented his first chance to get his hands on the key. It didn't matter. There would be another.

Time was all the same here. The past, present, and future all merged into one existence. He wasn't sure how many years had passed since he'd entered the gateway through the Black Mirror, but he had no concern for time where it didn't exist.

He discovered many things in this bizarre realm. It was supposed to be his salvation, his reward, but it was a vast wasteland. Here, the blueness of early dawn seemed eternal. Extinct birds called and flew overhead. Rock formations and mountains unlike any other rose beneath wisps of mist and thickening fog. Occasionally, he heard a desperate cry from some lost soul somewhere within his earshot, but far away. Then, many mirages all depicted one thing or another. They formed his windows to the real world.

He'd always known the gold-gilded mirror was another portal, but he'd never understood how. The tome had only briefly mentioned it. Eventually, he realized it was the exit, as the Black Mirror was the entrance. He had found the exit. It was more than a mirage, or an image. It was a portal, one that would lead through the gold-gilded mirror and into Cedar Manor. He had tried to leave via it and could not. Taryn made it through the gold mirror successfully, but now, she had failed him.

Long ago, he'd memorized much of the tome, and he thought back to it now, recalling words about the key that had been cryptic. The English equivalent of the Latin words was something like *"without the key, death would befall the gateway's traveler."* He'd translated words that insisted on the key remaining with the person who entered, but he'd never thought much of it. He hadn't understood it at the time.

The night he'd entered the gateway through the Black Mirror, he'd been too overwhelmed to think back on it. He'd had the key. He had the handheld mirror in his hands, but the lightning knocked him to the floor, and the mirror had flown far from his grasp. He'd never been sure where it had landed, or what happened to it, but eventually the mirages showed him. The night of his escape, he'd been in the thrall of fear and excitement. Beyond the mirror lay his reward and redemption. Then, his doppelganger beckoned him like a princely brother. The urgency of wasting important time had swept through him. He'd dashed headlong into the gateway before it closed on him forever.

However, he had left behind the key, and death had befallen him. The secret of the gateway was that once a person entered, his or her doppelganger would be born within the blue realm. That was the malevolent mystery it perpetrated upon the world, the mockery of mankind, and the contradiction of divine creation. Without the handheld mirror, the traveler through the gateway would die, and the doppelganger would emerge. If the traveler held the key, then the doppelganger and its host would coexist.

Now, Angus understood why he couldn't leave through the gold-gilded portal. He hadn't entered the gateway with the key. Taryn had died without the key, but she could leave by the gateway because she hadn't entered it willingly. He'd pulled her through the Black Mirror, making her an unwilling victim and thus able to escape through the gold-gilded mirror. With the key in hand, she could reenter, but Taryn had never returned.

The mirages and images he saw appeared to depict the passage of time, though such transitions were unnoticeable to him. They showed a little blonde girl. She saw things. She saw his murders as the past replayed before her eyes. She witnessed his rituals and what resulted from them, demons he had unleashed within Cedar Manor. He was almost sure that with the powerful third eye she possessed, she had looked out into time and space and seen this blue realm. Their eyes had met for a fraction of a second, and then the image vanished.

Another mirage had appeared before him, one that elicited a deep emotional response from the cold, unaffected shell he'd become. He thought he'd been long devoid of such reactions, but the alarming image caused him to reconsider. His home, Cedar Manor, was burning. He saw flames bursting from the gable windows and reaching up to the roof, the floors sinking from the destruction, and billows of smoke surrounding the great structure. A familiar face appeared in the image of the house. It was a young female, long blonde hair, deep blue eyes. It was her, the child he had seen, though she was grown. The flames were her fault.

Then, he thought about the gold-gilded mirror. He ran to the open clearing where he'd brought Taryn. He searched for the image of the portal. There it was, on fire, burning just like the house. Flames surrounded the golden frame, and glass shattered from the intense heat. It was happening before his eyes. Not only was the house gone, but so was the exit.

"NO!" he screamed.

The bellowing of his voice echoed throughout the desolate realm, much like it had in the basement of Cedar Manor. Lost souls cried out in response, yet he received no comfort, no assistance. He watched helplessly as the portal became smaller and smaller, until it was no more. Black smoke overcame the image. The exit vanished. His pain was the first thing he'd felt in what could have been decades.

More images appeared—another little blonde girl, but he knew her—Madison, Taryn's daughter. This girl, like the other, had the powers of a witch. She watched the Black Mirror, waiting for it to open. She watched it even more now with her mother gone.

He saw Taryn walking the streets in the guise of human flesh. She meant to fool the world, but she still hadn't returned to her family.

Angus saw and could almost feel Madison's pain. She longed for her mother. She wanted desperately to open the Black Mirror and enter. Perhaps he could open the gateway again. Perhaps he would help Madison.

Taryn had refused him, but maybe Madison would not. He would enhance her talent, her ability, shape it, and mold it. She would be his key to escape.

When he managed to free himself of this realm, he would find the young woman with the third eye, the one who had destroyed his home and trapped him here without an exit. He would find her and kill her.

Chapter Six

~ Present Day ~

Susan Logan sat behind her office desk at University Hospital. She'd had a moment to unwind, and now she took a brief respite to think of how things had quieted down the last few months here in Green Valley. The recent UFO business had placed them all in not only a local spotlight but a national one as well. The team had been interviewed by several paranormal TV shows. The press conference she'd held had been played over and over, and she and Dylan had even been offered book deals, though nothing extraordinary. Yes, things had quieted down. The phone calls from reporters had dwindled, no more aficionados roamed the campus grounds, and the MIB had never been heard from again. Susan thanked God for the latter.

She thought of all this as she awaited a visitor. She'd had the most interesting phone call this morning. The caller's introduction had put her on guard.

"Dr. Logan, my name is Charley Page," he said. "I work as a freelance writer for the Valley Tribune, and I'm also a writer for Paranormal Magazine. The reason I'm calling—"

"Yes, Mr. Page, I remember you well," she confirmed. "You recently persisted on getting a story from Dylan Rasche after he reappeared. I believe Dylan has told you he's not interested in doing a story. He isn't ready to talk about things just yet."

"I'm sorry, Dr. Logan. You're right. I did. That's not why I'm calling you. I'm not calling on a professional basis, but a personal one."

Susan scrunched her eyebrows in curiosity. "Oh?"

"I understand you work with children who possess psychic abilities. If that's true, Dr. Logan, I need your help."

Susan sat forward, closer to her desk. "Tell me more, Mr. Page."

"Please, call me Charley. It's about my daughter, Madison." He inhaled and then sighed through the phone, his breath crashing like static in her ear. "When she was about five or so, her mother and I discovered she had a very powerful psychic ability, clairvoyance I believe, but then she began to move things." Susan sat forward, stunned by what he'd said.

"You see, Dr. Logan, my wife disappeared a little over six years ago. Madison knows what happened to her mother, but I'm afraid that's where the story becomes fantastic. Madison is eleven now, and I really think she could use your help. Would it be alright if I explained all this in person?"

"Absolutely, Charley," she replied. "I'm at my office at University Hospital." She told him what floor and where to go. "I think it's best if I meet with you alone, first, before meeting Madison. Please forgive my jumping the gun when you called. It was a very rough time for us, and we're all still recuperating from such an unexpected case."

"Not a problem, Dr. Logan. I understand. Ironically, I'm afraid I'm going to have to ask for the same type of discretion. I'll explain when I see you."

Susan explained that any case she took on was treated in the same manner as any psychiatric patient. She maintained the doctor-patient confidentiality rule as sacrosanct.

"I'll see you at three-o'clock then?" He agreed.

Now, she sat contemplating what Charley would reveal "...but then she began to move things," he'd said. A telekinetic. Interesting. So, her mother had disappeared, and the child knew what happened to her. Susan wondered if Madison suffered from child abandonment issues, or if the reality was something darker. She checked her watch—three-o'clock. A knock sounded on her office door.

She walked to the door and opened it. A man, approximately in his early forties, medium height, black hair, and blue eyes, greeted her. She'd seen his picture before, probably in the paper.

She extended her hand. "Charley Page, I presume?"

"Dr. Logan?" He shook her hand. He carried a small bag.

"Please call me Susan," she said, ushering him in with a wave of her hand.

"Thank you for seeing me on such short notice. I'm afraid I have nowhere else to turn."

She sat down behind her desk, and he took the chair directly across from her. She spoke in the soft coaxing tone she'd used so well with her patients and others.

"Charley, I want you to relax, and tell me everything you can from the beginning."

He took a deep breath, looked up at the ceiling, and then faced her eye to eye. "The beginning?" he said. "It all started about six years ago when Madison was five. To understand, my wife, Taryn, also had some form of psychic ability. As you know, I write and research a great deal about the paranormal. I discovered Taryn was what they call 'intuitive.' She knew things, and she knew them automatically." He looked away and shrugged. "Many people thought of Taryn as flaky, flighty, if you will, and I guess she was to some extent. She may have immersed herself in her ability, but she understood it."

Susan smiled at his description of his wife. She could see the love and the loss in his eyes.

"And then Madison came along," he continued. "She was a beautiful child, still is. When she was around the age of five, we noticed a few things."

He told her about Madison's knowing things beforehand, how her predictions had come to pass, and how at some point, she began to move things.

"When she became impatient, or angry, she would break things without touching them." He told her about the glass, the plate, and the incident with the chair. "There were many other instances, as well, little things. Taryn and I realized our little girl was telekinetic. We also spoiled her. Maddy was our only child. Taryn couldn't have another.

"My wife collected odd and unusual artifacts. She redesigned our den into her very own gallery. I always thought it was creepy, not to mention junk, but I let her have her gallery."

He detailed all of the things Taryn had collected. Susan sensed he avoided the most painful part of the story. He took another deep breath and blew it out in frustration.

"Then, my wife suddenly disappeared."

Susan sat forward in her chair.

"My neighbor called me at work one day," he recalled, his eyes staring at the floor. "She'd heard Maddy screaming inside the house. She was uncontrollable. My neighbor couldn't get a word out of her, other than the fact that she wanted her Daddy. I rushed home, and Maddy ran into my arms and squeezed me tighter than she ever had before. I knew something had happened. When I calmed her down and asked what was wrong, she took me into Taryn's gallery. She kept pointing to an artifact I'd never seen before. It was a large, rectangular, black mirror."

Susan felt her heart sink at those last words—black mirror. It couldn't be. She instantly thought of Leah Leeds, of Cedar Manor, of the night they fought demons in that house. She said nothing. Instead, she let Charley continue.

"This is where it gets crazy. She told me Mommy had gone into the Black Mirror. A man had grabbed her when the mirror opened, and he'd pulled Taryn through. I thought Maddy had imagined things, even though she was never the type of child for make-believe and imagination. I didn't call the police; I thought it was crazy. I called a friend of mine, who is a doctor. He gave Maddy a light sedative to calm her.

"I thought for sure Taryn would be back. I kept staring at that mirror and waiting inside the den. I called everyone she knew, and they hadn't seen her. Taryn had no family other than us. Her parents were killed when she was young. I waited inside the den for hours. I waited inside our house for years, but Taryn never returned. To this day, she remains missing."

He forced his thumb and index finger into his eyes to stop the forming tears, a self-imposed dam that would stop the oncoming flood. Susan had a suspicion about what he wanted to say next but couldn't.

"Did you ever report Taryn missing?"

He began to cry. "How could I? They would've called my little girl insane." He heaved between words. "They would have suspected me, tried to pin it on me, although I had an air tight alibi. I was at work. The thought of what would've happened if the authorities angered Maddy was even worse. Taryn and I had only guessed at the full extent of her abilities.

"Eventually, I made up a lie and said Taryn left me and Madison. Nothing could be farther from the truth. We had a great marriage, a comfortable home, and a quiet life, but I never saw Taryn again. All of her belongings were left behind—her phone, her purse with all of her money and credit cards, and her car keys. Her car was parked in the garage."

Susan remained calm when asking the next question. Those two jarring words, "black mirror" were still stuck in her head.

"So, tell me more about this black mirror."

"Madison told me she'd gone with her mother to a shop that sold the type of junk Taryn collected. That day, Taryn had purchased the Black Mirror without my knowledge, or consent. I have reason to believe this shop was somewhere near Pittsburgh. Madison later told me Taryn was fascinated by the mirror, and that she kept staring into it."

Susan's heart pounded. She thought of Janet Leeds.

"What's more, Maddy said she had visions of the mirror opening. I've never known my daughter to be wrong in what she sees. Not even when she was a little girl. Her story has never strayed, never been inconsistent since the day it happened. She says the mirror opened up, and a man pulled her mother through."

"Did she ever describe what the man looked like?"

He related the vague description Madison had given him, a man with long, brown hair and a beard. Madison hadn't seen him all that well, and the description had come from a five-year old. Susan didn't want to overreact, but Angus Marlowe was said to have had a beard and long brown hair. He and the Black Mirror had mysteriously disappeared in 1970. Her heart still pounded, but she tried to concentrate on everything Charley was telling her. The society's next case might be sitting right across from her.

"Then the story gets even stranger," Charley said. "It was about three months after Taryn disappeared when I found this on my home office desk." He opened up the bag he'd brought with him and pulled out a handheld mirror with dark opaque glass.

Susan couldn't believe her eyes. It was the same mirror, the handheld mirror that had disappeared from the police station in 2009. The mirror that Charley held was one of the many antiques that had belonged to Cedar Manor. Susan was at a loss for words. She played it carefully.

"May I see that for a moment?"

He handed her the mirror. She held it in her hands and looked into its black glass. It cast only a vague and shadowy reflection of her, aided by the light above. Yes, she was sure of it. This had to be the missing handheld mirror stolen from the police station. It had belonged to the Marlowes. It fit the description Sidney had stumbled upon a few years ago before they'd gone into Cedar Manor.

"I've seen this thing before," Charley said. "I know it never belonged to Taryn. A colleague of mine wrote a description of this for the paper. I also saw the picture. I have reason to believe this is the mirror the police found in Cedar Manor in 2008. I stepped out of my home office one day to pick up Maddy from school and take her to lunch. When I got back, it was on my desk. It wasn't there when I left. I don't mean to sound intrusive, Susan, but another one of my colleagues, Cory Chase, died when you all ventured into Cedar Manor a few years ago. So, do you see why I'm making connections?"

Susan handed the mirror back to him. Telling him everything she knew about this mirror, and what happened to her and the team a few years ago in Cedar Manor was not the way to go, at least not yet. She needed the team for that one. They would all have to explain, especially Leah.

"Well, I assure you, Charley, we've known nothing of this mirror's whereabouts. You are the one who has now provided the missing pieces of this puzzle."

"There's another reason that I've made a connection to Cedar Manor." He opened up the bag again, and this time, retrieved a book. "I found this among Taryn's things. I didn't know that she'd read it, but with Madison's ability, I think I understand why."

Taking the book in hand, she saw the cover and felt it was not just a sign, but an omen. The title and author read *Cedar Manor Leah Leeds.*

Susan smiled and tried to steer the subject away from Cedar Manor. "I can introduce you to the author. She'll even sign it for you. You're right, though, Charley. Taryn was reading this because in it, Leah writes extensively about being a child with a powerful psychic ability. Leah was five at the time, and you say that you discovered Madison's ability at the same age, right?" He nodded. "If I were in Taryn's position, I would have picked up the same book."

She handed it back to him.

"You know, sometimes, I feel Taryn right next to me," he said. "I can't see her, but somehow I know she's there, whether it's a breeze that blows past me inside the house, or a wet peck I suddenly feel on my cheek. I know she's there. I can feel her around me. Susan, you're a parapsychologist, do you think that means that she's dead, and what I'm feeling is the presence of a ghost?"

Susan lifted her eyebrows in thought. "That's a hard one even for me to answer. As a parapsychologist, I would say it's a definite possibility, but I would need more evidence of a ghost or spirit. On the other hand, as a psychiatrist, I might tell you that you want to feel Taryn around you, so you do. For me, it's like having a split personality."

Her attempt to make him laugh was a success. A smile cracked across his face as he laughed.

"I know this, Charley. Wherever your wife is, she needs you to be Madison's father. Madison needs you to be her father. If your wife is gone, you still have a daughter to think about, especially if she witnessed her mother's abduction. She has been traumatized. She needs your strength."

"That brings me to the main reason I'm here," he said. "Madison's ability has flourished since she was a five-year-old girl."

"Naturally," Susan agreed.

"However, I'm not so sure it's for the better. You won't believe some of the things I've seen since then. Once, she lifted all her toys up in the air until they danced in a frightening parade. Then, in her anger, she crashed them to the floor. She has anger issues since Taryn's been gone. She shoved one of her friends up against the wall without touching him. The boy went home, and told who knows what story. Of course, I continue to cover for her, like everyone else is imagining things."

"I'm afraid you could be smothering her ability, and that's what's causing her to act out with it the way she does."

"So, what do I do?" The frustration in his voice echoed defeat and long suffering. "I can't let her upend whatever she chooses, and ignore how she can turn her ability on people when she's angry. She continues to try and smash the Black Mirror. It won't break. I've forbidden her to go into that room."

"It sounds to me like Madison's real problem is her anger, not her ability. She needs to learn how to control it. I'm glad that you came to me, Charley. I think I can help you, probably more than you know." He looked at her quizzically, but she didn't elaborate.

"I want to ask your permission on something, and if you decline, I'll certainly understand, but it will help tremendously. I want you to allow me to bring the team in on this one, which would mean I would have to share with them everything you just told me about Madison, Taryn, and the mirror—all of it. You know Sidney Pratt also works with psychic children. I believe I can help you even more with the team involved."

"Certainly," he said. "Anything you all can do to help would be greatly appreciated."

"One more thing, Charley," she continued. "May I hold onto the handheld mirror?"

He agreed. She reassured him once again that she and the team would do everything they could to help him and Madison.

"I may want to meet her first, without the team," she said. "Then, I'll fill them in, and we'll figure out a time when we can all sit down together."

"I don't know how to ever thank you, Susan."

"Just one more thing," she said. "For now, let's keep quiet on the Cedar Manor aspect."

He shook her hand. They exchanged business cards, and she led him to the door.

"We'll be in touch," she said.

He thanked her again, and she closed the door behind him. She stood with her back to the door, her eyes cast up at the ceiling. She did her best to control her amazement. How on earth did a young woman like Taryn find the Black Mirror? They had to find out where she'd bought it.

...Mommy had gone into the Black Mirror...a man had grabbed her when the mirror opened up, and then he'd pulled her through.

Those words sent chills down her spine. How could Angus Marlowe be alive? Was he a ghost? Was it even him? She had to get a look at that mirror.

She continues to try and smash the Black Mirror. It won't break.

As the words replayed in her mind, she realized it was imperative that she assemble the team. She sat down behind her desk and picked up the phone. There was one person on the team she needed to call first—Leah Leeds.

Chapter Seven

~ Come Together ~

Leah Leeds stepped through the doorway of her cottage-style home, her arms full. She dropped her purse to the ground, and then set her briefcase, along with a pile of file folders, on the coffee table. It was her first semester as a Psychology professor at Green Valley University. Her day had been filled with classes, and she was still getting used to the grind. As she took off her jacket, her phone began ringing. She retrieved it from the jacket's inner pocket. It was Susan. She answered, and they exchanged greetings.

"I'm sorry," Susan said. "I didn't know you'd just walked in the door. You can call me back, if you like."

"No, not a problem," Leah said, sitting down on the couch. She ran her fingers through her long blonde hair, combing back the bangs from her forehead. "What's up?"

"Are you sitting down?"

Leah looked at the couch on which she sat, wondering in jest if Susan had suddenly turned psychic. "Yes, I just sat down. Why?"

"I've just had an interesting visitor. Leah, I'm going to say this flat out. I think I've found the Black Mirror."

The laughing smile suddenly melted from Leah's face. A dead silence hung between them. Leah had never expected to hear those words, ever. Memories of the past exploded inside her mind. She could find no words to respond.

"Leah, are you there?"

"Yes," she said, almost numb. "You mean; you think you've found *the* Black Mirror?"

"I know I have," Susan responded. "Leah, I'm holding the handheld mirror that disappeared from the police station in my hand as we speak."

Susan told her about Charley Page, Taryn, and how Taryn acquired the mirror shortly before disappearing. She told Leah about Taryn owning a copy of her memoir and why, providing details about Madison and her ability.

"So, the girl's a clairvoyant, like me," Leah said. "She's also a telekinetic?"

"That's right. It sounds like her anger is controlling her ability."

"So, how did this Taryn come to own the Black Mirror?"

"Apparently, she'd bought it from a shop near Pittsburgh, and that's where we need to begin. I'm calling the team together, but I wanted you to hear what this meeting was about before we convene. I didn't want to spring this on you at the meeting. I'll explain everything in greater detail then. I was thinking tomorrow at one-o'clock?"

Tomorrow was Saturday. Leah had no classes. "I'll be there."

Leah recognized that her own voice had turned distant. A million thoughts preoccupied her. The day had suddenly turned dark at the mention of the Black Mirror.

"Leah, there's more I have to explain, but I'll do so in person. I don't want this to reawaken memories for you. I don't want you being too close to this. If you want to sit this one out, you're more than welcome."

"I can't sit this one out. If this girl is in danger, I'm one of the few people who can help her."

"I was hoping you'd say that. I'll see you tomorrow. Don't let this get to you. Remember, no matter how close this is to you, you're an investigator, and you're one of the best."

"I'll try," Leah said, as they disconnected.

Leah sat on the couch, rapt in thought. Just a few months ago during the UFO mayhem, she'd sat on this same couch before graduation. That day Angus Marlowe and the Black Mirror had entered her mind out of nowhere. She'd wondered how a man and that strange mirror could have disappeared without a trace for so many years. Now, if Susan was right, the Black Mirror had resurfaced. Where had it been? What had happened to it? What about Angus Marlowe?

The past came alive. She remembered being a child in Cedar Manor, her mother gazing into the gold-gilded mirror and becoming mesmerized into submission, and the image of her hanging from the balcony. Then, there was the night she'd returned to that house, dragging the investigators with her. She recalled the snowstorm that nearly stranded them, the demons that spoke, the lightning that struck from the mirror, and the hand that had fatally touched Cory Chase. She remembered the smell of his scorched body as it lay on the floor. The house had burned to the ground. She and the investigators barely escaped in time.

She shook her head vigorously as if to shake away the memories, but it only snapped her out of the dark reverie. She sighed, knowing that a new case would've come along soon, but she'd never expected it to be this. The Black Mirror. She sensed another chapter in her haunted history beginning.

* * * *

Sidney Pratt sat at his kitchen table indulging in his guiltiest pleasures—a Snicker's bar and the daily crossword puzzle. He'd given a speech on clairaudience today at a symposium in Pittsburgh and arrived home early. Now, he thought he'd relax before starting dinner. He had just solved twenty-four across when his phone rang. He recognized Susan's number.

"Sidney's House of Pancakes," he answered.

"Funny, Sidney," Susan said. "What I'm about to tell you is no laughing matter."

"Would this be for pick-up or delivery?"

"Sidney, I've found the Black Mirror."

He choked on his Snicker's bar, coughing and spitting pieces of chocolate across the table. Had he heard her right? Her words were undeniable.

"You're kidding, right?"

"I'm not the jokester, Sidney, you are." Susan paused. "I know the location of the Black Mirror, and the handheld mirror is sitting right here on my desk in front of me. I had an interesting visit from someone today. That's why I've called a meeting for tomorrow, at one-o'clock. Sidney,

I'm giving you permission to collect the black tome from our archives and bring it to the meeting tomorrow."

Sidney thought about the black tome. Detective Goddard had donated it to the society before they'd all gone into Cedar Manor. Sidney had researched and read it extensively. He'd promised to continue examining it, interpreting what little of Latin into English that he could, but it hadn't been easy. He hadn't been a student of Latin. Paul Leeds had been helping him, but after what happened in Cedar Manor, Leah had wanted her father as far away as possible from anything to do with that house ever again. Sidney had continued to work on it alone, but the Cedar Manor episode was behind them, behind Leah. After the house had burned, Sidney no longer felt that interpreting the contents of the tome was of any immediate urgency.

"I take it you've been interpreting what you could of it over the past few years?" Susan's question ignited a small spark of guilt within him.

"Well, I managed to make out a few things, but Susan, I needed help. Paul was definitely out, and I had no time to find a translator, especially after everything we've gone through since then. I mean, it no longer seemed important, and Brett needed us, and then Dylan."

"It's nothing to worry about now, Sidney. We'll find a translator. Just be sure to bring the tome to the meeting tomorrow. I have a feeling once deciphered, it's going to explain some things we hadn't looked into before, but now is the time."

Sidney asked her for details about her visitor.

"Charley Page, the reporter and paranormal writer, contacted me," she answered. "I've already updated Leah on the whole story. I felt she had to know right away. I want to wait until the meeting to discuss further details. I want to tell this story once."

Sidney understood. He would be in room 208 tomorrow afternoon at the allotted time. He ended the call and sat thinking, flabbergasted by what he'd just heard. The Black Mirror, so where had it been all these years? An old and mysterious occult artifact goes missing in 1970, and then suddenly resurfaces more than forty-five years later. Where could it have been? Then, another thought popped into his head. What about Angus Marlowe? Suddenly, a chill rippled down his spine.

* * * *

Dylan Rasche had no memory of the twenty-four-hour period in which he'd gone missing. Leah was certain he'd been abducted by the phantom in the sky, but he had no recollections. Nothing formed in his mind when he tried to remember and doing so resulted in complete frustration. Susan had hypnotized him a few months ago, but it hadn't worked. He had remembered seeing the object, its green light, its warm heat, but then blackness swallowed the recollection. He didn't want to experience yet another let down after a failed hypnosis session. The disappointment had been too great.

Since then he'd moved on with his life. He had no alternative. His sister, Denise, had driven all the way to Green Valley from Philadelphia after seeing the story on the local and national news. She stayed with him for a few days, and he told her everything from the beginning—what he'd seen, opening the safe, and reading their father's journals, the witnesses, the MIB, and discovering the storage facility beneath Eagle Rock Mountain. She grabbed him and held onto him when he'd told her about his missing time. She'd even talked to Susan before going back home.

It was over now. He'd experienced no ill effects from his disappearance, no radiation exposure, which was yet another mystery, no nightmares, and of course, no memories. He'd often wondered if it was a good thing that he didn't remember. Either way, life returned to normal for him, and it was time to live it.

Just then, his phone rang. He checked the name on the screen. How odd. He'd just been thinking of Susan.

"Dylan, as chief-investigator, I thought you should know I've called a meeting with the team tomorrow at one-o'clock."

He heard urgency in her voice. "Why? What's up?"

Her answer stunned him. His heart jumped at two words—black mirror.

"How the hell did this happen?"

She told him about Charley Page's visit.

"Charley Page? You mean that hack who kept bugging me for my story?"

"The same, but Dylan, he's experienced a traumatic event and has lived with it for quite some time now. He spoke to me in doctor-patient confidentiality, but he gave me permission to explain everything to you all. I told him we, as a team, could help him more efficiently than me working alone. I'll fill in the details for everyone tomorrow. Charley Page and his daughter Madison are our next case. I need you to be nice."

"No problem," he said. "Have you told Leah about this?"

"I have, and she's ready, as you all must be. I have a feeling this is going to be a dark case because it's connected to Cedar Manor."

"I'll see you then," he said. They exchanged goodbyes and ended the call.

Dylan sat thinking, but now, all thoughts about his own dilemma evaporated like the memories he couldn't recall. Leah must be worried, knowing that a past she'd buried was resurfacing. He thought of the girl they were about to encounter. What kind of trauma had she experienced? He wasn't aware yet of all the details, but was history repeating itself? Leah Leeds would not let that happen.

* * * *

The wolf ran through the woods and over the hills adjacent to Brett Taylor's farmhouse. The cool October day had a slightly gray overcast, and the solitude of the wolf's run had been peaceful. The freedom of roaming the hills unnoticed enthralled and invigorated the dual soul that dwelled inside. Now, the wolf arrived at the starting point in the woods where the run had begun.

It sniffed at the pile of clothes on the ground, recognizing a scent that it knew well. All memories flooded to the forefront. The soul inside awoke, and the transformation began. Fur receded back into pores that shrunk. Wedge-shaped ears folded back and morphed into those of a human. Canine skin became flesh that formed an elongating shape. The shape writhed on the ground. Then, it became a naked man.

Brett Taylor pushed himself up from the ground with his hands, and snatched the pile of clothes from the ground. He dressed quickly. In the woods, no one saw him.

He walked into the house via the kitchen door, groggy and sedated by the rush of endorphins. He felt a vibration against his thigh. His phone was ringing. He pulled it from his pocket and looked at the screen. Susan was calling him.

"What's up, Suzy Q?" He spoke with a slow, sleepy drawl in his voice.

"You've been out on a run again, haven't you?"

"Yeah, how did you know?"

"I hear it in your voice, not to mention, I've been calling you for over thirty minutes. Didn't you get my messages?"

Brett looked at his phone again and saw that he had two messages awaiting him. "No, sorry about that. I just got in."

"Well, Brett, be sure to stay current in the journal I told you to keep."

"I do." In the living room, he slouched back on the couch with his eyes closed, and the phone to his ear. "So, what's the news?"

"Our next case," she said. "Brett, I've called everyone and told them what I'm about to tell you. I've found the Black Mirror."

He opened his eyes wide, rolling them back and forth as he thought for a moment. Then, he sat up from the couch, fully awake.

"You don't mean—"

"Yes, Brett, *the* Black Mirror. I've also come into possession of the handheld mirror that was stolen from the police station."

"No shit?" His words came out as a loud exclamation.

Susan related the basics of the story, explaining that she would go into all of the details at the meeting she'd scheduled for tomorrow. "I need everyone there, Brett. This case not only continues what we thought had ended a few years ago, but it also involves the disappearance of a young woman, not to mention her psychic daughter, who's been traumatized since she was a little girl. We have to help them. We're the only ones who can."

"Of course I'll be there," he said. "How has Leah taken the news?"

"She's stunned, as we all are. This revives more memories for her than we could possibly imagine, but she's determined to help this girl."

They talked until Susan announced she was going home; her shift was ending.

"I'll see you tomorrow," she clarified. "For now, Mr. Taylor, there's a journal awaiting your attention."

He laughed.

"You got it, Suzy Q."

"You should feel special. You're the only one allowed to call me that." They exchanged goodbyes.

Brett felt more dazed by the news than his run as the wolf. There had always been something unspoken between them after the Cedar Manor excursion. They all wondered if the Black Mirror would ever be found, and if the whole mystery would begin all over again. Now it had, and he was sure the rest of them were as equally speechless. He sat remembering that night in Cedar Manor, the snowstorm, the death of Cory Chase, but what had recurred in his mind often since then was the speaking demon that had almost exposed his secret.

"Shifter!" It spoke in a demonic, twisted warble that heaved and gasped in what sounded like agony.

Tahoe had already known his secret. He'd remained silent as they looked at each other from across the room. The moment had quickly passed, but the night continued on in mayhem followed by tragedy.

That was all behind them now, and Cedar Manor was no more. He recalled something Sidney said when they'd been pondering on what happened to the Black Mirror.

"Who knows, maybe someday we'll all find out," he'd said.

It appeared Sidney had been right.

* * * *

One-o'clock couldn't arrive soon enough for any of them. Room 208 was unchanged. It was the way they'd always kept it and exactly the way they wanted it. As always, they sat at their normal places around the long conference table, Susan at the head of the table and Dylan on the opposite end. Leah sat to Susan's right, and Sidney and Brett were to her left. Their eyes met each other's, one by one, pondering the imminent details with skepticism, wonder, and unspoken fear. For the first time in months, they had come together.

Susan called the meeting into order. "As I explained to you all on the phone, Charley Page came to visit me yesterday. At first, I thought he was calling me in yet another attempt to get a story from Dylan, but he assured me he wasn't. He told me about his little girl who is not only a clairvoyant, but a telekinetic. She'd witnessed the disappearance of her mother, his wife, and was traumatized by it. He seemed at a loss on how to deal with her ability. I told him to come by my office at the hospital. I assumed that was the extent of it—another case of a child psychic. When he showed up in my office, I soon realized it was so much more."

Susan folded her hands in front of her. She looked out at them all, especially Leah, wondering if they were ready for everything she was about to reveal, or even remotely prepared for this newly opened chapter of Cedar Manor.

"Taryn Page had taken her daughter with her to a shop near Pittsburgh," she continued. "It was there that she'd purchased the Black Mirror. We need to find out exactly where this shop is, and how its owner acquired the mirror in the first place. We'll begin there."

She turned her attention to Leah.

"Leah, I wanted to prepare you for the next part of this story. According to Madison, her mother was fascinated by the mirror, mesmerized by it. She told her father that her mother was constantly looking into the mirror, as if she couldn't take her eyes away from it."

She saw Leah close her eyes and nod her head. The words were all too familiar to one who already knew. Susan told them about Taryn's fascination with strange and unusual artifacts, and how she'd maintained a collection displayed in the family den. Susan suddenly realized that Taryn's hobby was ironically, a dark commonality to Janet Leeds collection of traditional antiques. Strangely, the two women had much in common.

"Madison told her father she'd followed Taryn into the den one day. She'd been gazing into the mirror. Madison claimed the mirror had 'opened up,' and a man had pulled her mother through the mirror."

Gasps of surprise erupted around the table. Leah's eyes closed tighter. Sidney and Brett sat forward even closer, and Dylan watched Susan's face, his eyes wide.

"Now, you must understand," Susan said, "Charley and Taryn had claimed that when Madison became angry, she showed her displeasure by smashing plates, breaking glasses, and other destructive forms of behavior, all without laying a finger on the objects. Madison is an only child, so I suspect much of her temper is because she's spoiled.

However, after witnessing her mother's disappearance, Madison has continually tried to use her telekinesis in an effort to smash the Black Mirror. She's failed so far."

"She's trying to get inside," Sidney said, the black tome in front of him. Heads turned toward him. "It's a gateway. I remember that Paul and I deciphered the fact that the gold-gilded mirror was a gateway. We'd realized it not only from the written words, but from the drawings we found inside of this." He placed his hand on the tome. "I would bet the Black Mirror is the opposite end. That would explain the connection between the two mirrors."

"So, which end is which?" Brett said.

"Good question," Sidney replied.

"Then that would mean that what Madison witnessed was real," Susan concluded.

A familiar silence surrounded them once again.

"That would be my estimation, yes," Sydney said.

"Well, team, there is much more to this story, and I'm about to reveal it. Madison gave her father a description of the man who pulled her mother through the mirror." Susan paused. "She described the man as having long, brown, straggly hair, and a beard and mustache."

No one gasped this time. Instead, the team stared at her. Shock filled the room, accompanied by the silent pulse of a collective heartbeat.

"Angus Marlowe." Leah's low voice, a result of her surprise, sliced through the silence with those two words.

"How is that possible, Leah?" Dylan demanded. "We've been through this before."

"Nothing's impossible to us, Dylan," she retorted. "It's possible just the same way that you were sucked up into that UFO."

"Team, let's not get ahead of ourselves," Susan said, "or should I say behind ourselves?"

"So, if it is him, do you think he's a ghost, maybe a poltergeist?" Brett said.

"It's impossible to know at this point, Brett," Susan responded. "However, that is a valid guess." She reached behind her, where she kept her purse, and produced the bag Charley had brought with him to their meeting. "Charley brought this to me, claiming he'd found it on his home office desk three months after Taryn's disappearance. I was as stunned as you all are about to be."

She took the black handheld mirror from the bag and held it up in front of them. Now, the gasps were louder than before. Susan saw Sidney's jaw drop. She saw the worry in Leah's eyes and the astonishment on all of their faces.

"Charley says he doesn't know how it got there, but there it was when he got home. He also never knew about the Black Mirror until the day of Taryn's disappearance. She'd kept it a secret from him."

Susan passed the handheld mirror around the table. Leah looked into it with what looked like anger.

"So, he never went to the police about any of this?" Dylan said. "This mirror was stolen from the police station. As a reporter, surely he knew that."

"Charley went into all the reasons as to why he never called the police. We all know that going to them with such a fantastic story would've put Madison in the spotlight as a mentally disturbed child. Plus, with such an unlikely story, much suspicion would've fallen his way. No, I agree with his decision not to report this to the police. I just wish he would've contacted us sooner."

"So, you think he's above suspicion?" Brett said.

"I thought of that, and yes, I do. How else would he get his hands on the Black Mirror? His story about Taryn buying it can be easily verified. The devastation this man has been suffering is real. I could see it. He's worried mostly about his daughter, and with good reason by the sound of it."

Susan turned to Leah once again. "Leah, there's one more thing you should know. Charley brought something else with him. It was your memoir. Taryn had picked up a copy of your book and read it when she and Charley were trying to understand Madison's abilities. She was interested from the aspect that you were five-years-old when your ability was first noticed. Madison had been the same age when they'd discovered hers."

Leah closed her eyes again and shook her head.

"Now, here's how I want to proceed," Susan continued. "I want to meet with Madison alone, as a parapsychologist, and as a psychiatrist. I think I should get to know her first, and then introduce you all. I'll try to get as much information as I can from Madison about the day her mother bought the mirror. Then, I want you all to try and find this shop. A big piece of this mystery is how the Black Mirror got there in the first place. Then, we can all sit down with Charley and explain the connection to Cedar Manor."

They glanced at each other again, the reality of their next case becoming real. Leah looked at Dylan, and then at Susan.

"Sounds like a plan," she said. "I've known since Cedar Manor burned that this lingering mystery connected it to it would come back to haunt us, and it looks like it has. We vanquished the demons in that house and brought it down along with them. There's one thing left to do—destroy the Black Mirror."

They all agreed, but Susan suspected it would be easier said than done.

Chapter Eight

~ Meeting Madison ~

Sunday, the following day, Susan found it to be the perfect opportunity to meet Madison Page. Now, she heard footsteps approaching the door as she stood on the porch, ringing the doorbell. Charley answered, his face bearing a cautious expression. He invited her in, and she stepped through the doorway into the modest, yet elegant, ranch-style house. He thanked her for coming, but the eleven-year-old girl who sat on the couch distracted Susan. The girl looked up at her with deep blue eyes, much like her father's, eyes that secretly wondered if she was in trouble.

"Maddy, this is Dr. Logan. She's a friend of mine, and she's anxious to talk to you."

"Hello, Madison," Susan said, walking over to her and extending her hand. "I'll tell you what, since I'm a friend of both you and your father, you can call me Susan."

Madison rose from the couch and slowly extended her hand, her eyes wide in skepticism. She shook Susan's hand with a weak, careful grasp.

"May I sit down?" Susan said.

Madison looked at her shyly, and then at the couch. She moved her hand to the place next to her, offering Susan a seat. Susan thanked her, and they sat next to each other on the couch.

Charley proceeded as he and Susan had planned earlier. "Maddy, how about if I go get some work done in my office, and let you and

Susan get to know each other a little better?"

Madison, still bashfully silent, looked at Susan, and then back to her father before nodding her head. Susan smiled at her, and Charley left them alone in the living room. Susan began by asking her about everyday things such as school, friends, teachers, and even her favorite subject. She tried to gauge the girl's reactions before mentioning her psychic abilities.

"Well, Madison," she said. "You may come to think of me as your special friend. Do you know why?"

Madison, now more receptive, smiled shyly as she shook her head. Susan swooped in toward her and then winked.

"It's okay to show your ability in front of me." The girl's smile expanded across her tiny face. "You might say I'm a doctor for people who have abilities such as yours, and no, you're not the only one."

Madison's eyes widened. Susan gathered that it was the first time the girl had realized she was not alone in her capabilities. She was about to test the girl's level of performing telekinesis. She remembered her way with children, and proceeded with caution.

"Madison, how about we have a little fun by showing me what you can do?" Madison nodded her head and smiled. "But, this is just between special friends, okay?" Susan warned. "You must still remember your father's rules." She paused to whisper. "It's okay to show me."

Madison nodded, still smiling. She was ready, and unsuspecting of Susan's game. Susan opened up her purse and pulled out a yellow balloon.

"You like balloons?" Susan said, stretching the balloon back and forth.

Madison nodded vigorously. Susan blew up the balloon to its full capacity, and then tied a knot at the end of it. She held the balloon up in front of her.

"Okay, Madison, I want you to force the balloon from my hand with your ability."

Susan watched the girl's face. Her expression hadn't changed. The playful smile Susan had cajoled out of her showed Maddy's interest in the little game they were playing. Suddenly, the balloon flew out of Susan's hand. It floated across the room, and Susan startled when it popped in mid-air. She realized Madison had done it without any effort at all.

It was the first time she'd heard Madison laugh. Her lighthearted, repetitive giggle revealed exactly what Susan had originally suspected, that the girl needed to control her ability. Susan laughed along with her, and then she took another toy from her purse. It was a blue and white spinning top made of tin, the type of toy won at a street carnival.

Susan showed it to her first, watching Madison's growing excitement ignite a fire in her eyes. She held the top in place on the surface of the coffee table, and then spun it quickly in a clockwise motion.

Her eyes darted between Madison and the top, which now danced in a rapid topsy-turvy spin. Then, Susan watched as the top spun faster and faster in frenzied acceleration. Suddenly, it leapt from the table and whirled across the room, making a clanging sound as it bounced off the wall. Madison's telekinetic ability was much greater than Susan had assumed. It was blatantly obvious why Charley hadn't notified the police. That could've led to complete disaster.

Madison's laugh grew louder as Susan's blood raced, and her heart pounded harder. She playfully gave Madison a dumb smile, as if she'd lost the game. Madison laughed even harder. Then, Susan became distracted by the sound of something moving; something heavy scraped across a hard, wooden surface. She looked around and saw an empty glass vase sliding itself along the mantle above the fireplace. She bolted from the couch.

"Madison, no, don't—"

Before she could finish, the vase fell to the floor and crashed inside the grate. Susan covered the lower part of her face with both hands as Madison continued to laugh. Then, she turned to Madison and placed both hands in front of her.

"That's enough, Madison. You've shown me your ability."

Charley came out of his office. "Is everything alright in here?"

Madison went silent, her laughter suddenly stifled at the sight of her father. Susan looked at Charley and motioned with her eyes to the fireplace.

"Don't worry," she said. "That was my fault. I'll clean it up."

Charley shook his head, as if he was accustomed to the sound of breaking glass. "No need, Susan. I'll get it later."

He walked back down the hallway to his office and closed the door behind him. Susan sat back down on the couch next to Madison. She took the girl's hands in hers.

"Madison, let's talk for awhile, shall we? Your Dad tells me you saw something you will never forget when you were a little girl. Is that right?"

Madison's smile faded. She lowered her head and nodded.

Susan gently touched the side of the girl's face. "I know you love your mother very much, don't you?" She used the present tense when referring to Taryn. Madison looked up at her and nodded again.

"Madison, I want to help you and your Dad find out what happened to your mother. Would you like me to do that?"

Madison continued to nod. Susan wiped away a tear that slowly streaked the girl's cheek. Then, she gently lifted Madison's face to meet hers at eye level.

"Then I'm going to need you to tell me everything you know about what happened to her."

Madison said nothing. She stared at Susan, thinking. Susan wondered what was going through the child's mind. After a pause of seconds, Madison nodded again, this time, with conviction.

"Okay, then," Susan said. "Madison, I want you to tell me all about the Black Mirror, and the time your mother took you with her to buy it. Then, your father has given his permission for you to take me to the den and show me the mirror. Would that be alright with you?"

Susan watched as Madison's sadness turned into determination. The girl focused her eyes on Susan's, blinked, and then nodded. Then, she spoke again.

"Okay," she said. "Do you think you can find my mother?"

It was a hard question for Susan to answer, regardless of how many degrees graced her office wall. She couldn't build this child's hopes up, and yet she couldn't let her down.

"I'm certainly going to try, Madison, but I'm going to need all of your help." Susan told her about the team, about how she was going to introduce her to people who had abilities just like she did. "They're going to help me find out what happened to your mother. I'll introduce you when the time comes. First, tell me what you can remember about the day you went with your mother to the shop." Madison raised her gaze to the ceiling, squinting as she tried to remember.

She spoke in a soft voice; one Susan assumed was used for strangers and completely opposite of the spoiled, angry Madison.

"It was pretty far away," she said. "It took us a while to get there." Then, Madison became excited, as if she remembered something. "The man whose shop it was had a crystal he showed us. It changed colors."

"You liked that crystal?" Again, Madison nodded. "What colors did you see?"

Madison's eyes squinted again, remembering. "Orange, red, purple, blue..."

Susan nodded, showing that she understood. "Madison, do you remember the name of the shop?" Madison shook her head. Susan hadn't thought so, but it was worth a try. "What about the man's name who ran the shop?"

Susan watched as the question caught Madison's attention. Her gaze wondered off, remembering something or someone.

"His name was Ernie," she said. "I remember him telling Mommy he couldn't fit his name on the sign."

"Good girl, Madison," Susan said. "So, Ernie sold your mother the Black Mirror, right?"

"Yes, but I wasn't supposed to tell my Dad."

"Then your mother placed the mirror here at home, in her collection in the den?"

"She kept staring into it, more and more," she said, "like she was trying to find something. She was always in front of it." Janet Leeds entered Susan's mind once again. "I stared at it too, inside the shop, but I stopped. I hated that mirror. I still hate it."

"Do you remember telling your father that it was a 'bad' mirror?"

"Yes." Madison looked straight at her. She spoke with the same conviction Susan had seen her muster only moments ago.

"What made you call it a 'bad' mirror?"

The expression on Madison's face turned to one of anger. It was in stark contrast to the laughing girl who had popped the balloon. Susan had no doubt Madison had experienced something real. She felt certain she was not about to hear the ramblings of a child's imagination.

"What did you see when you looked into it, Madison?"

"It was like watching a movie," she said. "I saw it opening up, like you could walk through it. Mirrors aren't supposed to do that. The glass was black. Mirrors aren't supposed to be black."

A third eye, just like Leah. Madison's words clearly confirmed why Taryn had been reading Leah's memoir. Madison's lips tightened. Susan saw a child unsure whether to scream in anger or cry in grief.

Susan took her hands in hers. "It's okay. You can do this."

Madison told her how she'd followed her mother into the den one day. She walked into the room and stood behind her, watching. She described Taryn's hands gripping the sides of the mirror, and seeing the black glass ripple like water.

"Then it opened up," she said. "I knew it would. I think Mommy did too. She sounded like she was in pain, and she couldn't take her hands away from it."

Madison's eyebrows bridged together; a look of pain scrunched her face. Susan squeezed Maddy's small hands tightly.

"I saw the man. His arm shot out through where the glass had been, and he grabbed Mommy by the neck. He choked her, and I started to scream. He pulled her through the mirror, and when I ran after her, it closed. It became glass again." Susan wiped more tears away from the girl's face.

"I couldn't save her. She was gone, and I couldn't do anything." A painful moan escaped her. "I tried to break the glass. It wouldn't break, and so I screamed until my Dad came home."

Susan hugged her, trying not to show her own tears. Soon, Madison stopped crying.

"I'll never forget his face, ever. I still dream of it."

"Tell me what he looked like, Madison."

She echoed the description she'd given to Charley. The man had long, straggly brown hair, and a beard and mustache. Madison called him creepy looking. Susan had hoped the description would differ slightly from Charley's second-hand account, anything that didn't point to a killer who'd been missing and presumed dead for over forty-five years.

"Madison, I want you to take me to see the Black Mirror. Will you do that?"

"Yes," she said. The nod of her head this time was quick.

She was ready. The child had been waiting for someone to help her find her mother. Susan only hoped she didn't fail her.

Madison led the way down the stairs, straight to the door of the room her father had forbidden her to enter, except for today. Madison opened the door, and Susan stepped inside. Before her she saw the strangest artifacts—death masks, strange statues, paintings, and a gargoyle among other oddities. Susan turned her eyes directly across from the gargoyle, and there it stood—the infamous Black Mirror. For over three years, its whereabouts had been an unsolved mystery for the society, and now it stood before her somehow beckoning.

Susan walked toward it, marveling at its sleek, opaque glass, its ornate, silvered frame. She gazed into it, seeing only a shadowed reflection of herself, an image of a person, cast and distorted in the blackness. She felt a slight strain in her eyes, as she was unable to take them away. For a moment, she felt the fascination, the allure of this strange object. She thought to take the handheld mirror from her purse, and try to figure out what the connection was between the two mirrors, but she couldn't now, not with Madison watching her.

Her fingers reached out and touched it. It was cold and hard. Her fingerprints quickly faded as she removed her fingers. She continued to stare at it, waiting for it to open, but nothing occurred. She stepped away from it, feeling an eerie reluctance the farther she moved. Suddenly, Susan felt herself overstepping a boundary.

"Madison, try to break the glass again."

She watched as Madison walked closer to the mirror, unaffected by its mystery. It cast no spell over her, as if the child saw things for what they were, not as what the adult hoped to prove. Madison closed her eyes and tried to force something out from within her, some kind of energy that was unseen to either of them. She directed whatever it was at the mirror. The mirror stayed strong, solid. It was not a balloon, or a small vase. The fact that an active form of telekinesis powerfully embedded in this child failed to even scratch its surface was something that mystified Susan even more.

"That's enough, Madison," Susan said. "You've demonstrated your ability enough for one day." She walked over to her, placing both of her hands on the girl's shoulders. "I'm extremely proud of how you opened up to me today. Whether you know it or not, you've made great progress today. You've released a great deal of stress, and we're going to continue to try and find out what happened to your mother, I promise."

She hugged Madison as they stood before the Black Mirror. Suddenly, Susan felt a rush of cool air, a draft that wafted from nowhere. The windows and door were closed. She sensed someone else in the room, an unseen presence, but saw no one besides Madison, herself... and the Black Mirror.

Chapter Nine

~ Following Susan ~

Some things remained with Taryn in this new existence, like her sense of smell and her psychic intuition, but some aspects of being human had left her. The need to sleep, and even hunger were no more. After all, she was dead, but existing in this doppelganger form. She lived, though unlike before.

Now, she watched as the world around her thrived while she roamed aimlessly, seen or unseen. Time no longer meant anything to her; she no longer had any conception of it. It was all one to her. She was oblivious of its passage, unaffected by minutes as they ticked away, numb to the moving world around her. She would watch the sun come up, and she watched it go down. It meant nothing. She heard the ticking of clocks, but no longer felt her heartbeat.

Taryn's powerful intuition had remained, as if her psychic being had never died. It continued on, a constant reminder of who she once was. Today, she had felt it, an instant inkling both strong and overwhelming. She needed to see Madison. Her daughter needed her.

In the ghostly form, she went home. She'd been there many times since the day she'd left the handheld mirror on Charley's desk, six years ago, though the passing of time was something she would check on newspapers, calendars, glimpses of her growing daughter, and the stray grays that shot through Charley's black hair. She would walk through the walls of what was once her home and sit with her daughter. She often kissed the cheek of her lifelong love. They would never know that it was her among them, but she was keenly aware that all thoughts of her had not died.

Today, she walked through the walls of her own home yet again. She stood in the living room in her ghostly presence. Who was that woman sitting on the couch with Madison? Why was she provoking her abilities? Taryn watched as her daughter popped a balloon, spun a top and flung it across the room, and even made her once favorite vase crash into the fireplace grate. Why was her daughter being tested in such a way? She watched the woman's every move.

The woman began asking questions about her. Maddy described everything from Taryn acquiring the mirror, to the day that Angus pulled her into the gateway. It was the day that she died, though they didn't know that.

"I couldn't save her. She was gone, and I couldn't do anything." Maddy began to cry. Taryn felt loss, but it was an empty feeling. The twinge of heartbreak was distant, if it had even registered. She watched Madison, wishing she could appear to her, but now was not the time.

Then, Madison took the woman into her den. The woman seemed taken aback by her collection, except for one piece—the Black Mirror. She walked over to it, gazed into it, much like she had. Her expression when she stared into it was all too familiar. The woman touched the mirror while Madison watched. The mirror was what she was after.

The woman then asked Maddy to break the mirror using her ability. Taryn knew that wouldn't happen, and it didn't. When Maddy's failure was accepted, Taryn walked over to the woman and stood close beside her. Oddly, she looked familiar, but Taryn's emptiness overwhelmed minute memories. She promised Maddy one thing—that she was going to continue to try and find out what happened to her mother. Taryn moved about the room, passing in front of the woman, and then the woman looked around as though she sensed something. The woman had already been here when Taryn entered through the walls. Now, as she was leaving, Charley had called her Susan.

Susan…

Taryn decided to follow her, find out where she was going, and discover who she was. As the woman left, she followed her out through the front door. She entered the back seat of Susan's car with no trouble and sat in the rear passenger's side, an unseen ghostly figure watching silently and patiently as Susan drove. While she was driving, Susan phoned someone named Dylan, and Taryn overheard her side of the conversation.

"Dylan, it's Susan," she said. "I've just met Madison." She sighed. "My heart bleeds for this poor girl. I believe every word she's told me. What she saw was real. There's no doubt about it. I've seen the Black Mirror... Yes, it was right there among all these creepy artifacts her mother had collected." Taryn grimaced. "The extent of this child's telekinetic ability is something I've never seen before. Her ability to move and break objects is phenomenal. Except for the mirror, she couldn't break the Black Mirror."

There was a pause as Susan listened.

"Yes, I got her description of the man," she said. "She may as well have been describing Angus Marlowe."

Taryn had been listening, but looking out the window, and then her head shot back to Susan. She mentioned Angus. How did this woman know?

"We can talk about all this tomorrow. I have to go to the hospital to check on a couple of patients. I want you to rustle the team together, and see if we can all meet tomorrow at four-o'clock. Yes, not only is she a telekinetic, but I think she has a third eye, much like Leah's."

Taryn sat up closer from the back seat. Leah? She mentioned someone named Leah. Taryn remembered the book and its author, Leah Leeds. Was this woman connected to Leah Leeds? Leah Leeds was connected to Cedar Manor, and so was Angus. Pieces of a mystery floated in the air, but she couldn't connect them. So, this woman was a doctor. Taryn recognized the hospital and its parking garage.

She followed Susan into the hospital, all the way through the lobby, into the elevator, and down the hall to a door with a plaque on the wall. Susan retrieved a set of keys from her purse and unlocked the door. Before the door opened, Taryn read the words on the plaque. *Susan Logan; MD, PsyD.*

A psychiatrist. Susan closed the door behind her, and Taryn walked through it. She watched as Susan turned her desk lamp on and donned her white coat. Taryn followed her to the nurse's station, where she picked up two patient files. Then, she trailed her back to the elevator. The more she thought of this woman's name, the more familiar it became, but she was still unable to place her. She followed her out of the elevator, gliding stealthily like a ghost behind her, and then she stopped.

A memory overcame her.

It had been a few months ago, that UFO business that had been all through the papers. Charley was trying to get a story from someone named Dylan. She couldn't remember the last name. There had been a press conference. Shock rippled through Green Valley. Susan Logan had ordered the press conference because this Dylan person had disappeared. Susan Logan. She was the head of the paranormal investigator group to which Leah Leeds belonged.

Now, it all became clear as an invisible fog suddenly lifted. The paranormal investigators she'd read about on so many occasions were investigating her daughter and the Black Mirror. Could Leah Leeds have been looking for Angus? Taryn knew what she would do next. She would follow Susan Logan home. She would be at that meeting of the paranormal investigators, tomorrow. They were investigating the Black Mirror, and Taryn realized her own tragedy was about to become the focus of their investigation.

* * * *

Taryn spent the night in Susan's stately home. No longer requiring sleep in her new existence, she simply lingered within the house, waiting to leave it once again. She watched as the day darkened into night, as Susan turned off the lights and ascended the stairs, and as the rising sun turned the dimness into daylight.

Susan arose early and worked throughout the day in her home office, a room situated in the back of the house's lower level. Taryn heard her tell someone on the phone that she was not due at the hospital today. Taryn eavesdropped on a few phone conversations, hoping that the callers would be Dylan, or possibly, Leah Leeds. None of the calls were from the investigators.

She hadn't realized the day had worn on. It became apparent when Susan removed her glasses, stored a few things away in her desk, and closed her computer program. Taryn looked at the clock in the hallway;

it was 3:30. Susan walked back up the stairs to ready herself, while Taryn waited at the bottom of the staircase. Finally, Susan came down, and Taryn watched her don a light jacket and sling her purse over her shoulder. It was time for the meeting.

Taryn once again sat in the back seat of the car, waiting as Susan started the ignition and drove away. She stared out the window at the passing trees that were beginning to change their colors. The magnificent red, orange, yellow, and pink leaves meant nothing to her now. She felt no reaction at what had once been beautiful to her. Soon, they arrived at Green Valley University. Susan parked the car, and Taryn followed her into Levin Hall.

Susan was the second to arrive. Dylan had already been inside room 208, doing something in front of one of the many computers.

"Is everyone coming?" Susan spoke to Dylan.

"They'll be here," he said.

"Good, because this mystery is much deeper and more complex than we could've possibly imagined."

"So, this girl's really a telekinetic?"

"She's an off-the-chart telekinetic. I saw why her parents were concerned."

It was then that two men walked into the room. One was a heavy-set guy with glasses; the other had wavy brown hair and a slight goatee. Susan called the heavy guy, Sidney, and the other, Brett. She thanked them for being on time. They removed their jackets, hung them around the backs of two of the chairs surrounding the long conference table, and sat. The heavy guy placed the black tome in front of him, the one she'd seen in the police station. Dylan took a seat at the end of the table. Then, the door opened.

It was Leah. She looked slightly older than she did in her jacket cover photo, but it was her. Taryn recognized the long, blonde hair and the beautiful, angelic face. She wore a fringe-laced denim jacket and jeans, and exchanged greetings with her cohorts. Leah took her place at the table, and the meeting began.

* * * *

Susan took her seat at the table, opposite Dylan, and began the meeting.

"Team, I've called this meeting because as you all know, I met Madison Page yesterday. I was just telling Dylan this child's telekinetic ability was something I've never seen before in all of my studies or investigations. I'd always heard of telekinesis, as have you all, but I'd never seen it until yesterday. Madison Page possesses something beyond a psychic ability. It's more like a paranormal anomaly. I tested her abilities."

Susan told them about the balloon, the top, and the vase.

"I didn't instruct her to touch the vase. She was showing me how strong and fluent she was in her ability. Her laughter rang out as she demonstrated the impossible with ease. Then, I got her to tell me the story of how her mother acquired the Black Mirror. I saw the pain on this girl's face, the agony, the grief, and then the tears. I'm convinced everything that happened to her was real."

She looked at Leah and Sidney. "We're not dealing with a child's imagination, as I'm sure you both can understand."

"Leah, when Madison described her mother's infatuation with the Black Mirror, it was as if I were reading your memoir all over again. I immediately thought of Janet. She told me her mother became more and more absorbed in the mirror and continued to stare into it, 'like she was trying to find something.' Those were Madison's exact words. She even told me she too had stared into the mirror.

"It had provoked her curiosity in the shop. She said she stopped staring into it because it was a 'bad mirror.' When I asked what she meant, she said she'd seen it 'opening up.'" Susan paused and turned her eyes to Leah again. "She described her foresight as 'like watching a movie.' That's when I realized her third eye must be akin to yours. This is a powerfully gifted, psychic child, much like you were, Leah. Madison said she knew the Black Mirror would open up, and it did."

Susan described how Madison had followed her mother into the den, spying on her as she stood transfixed before the mirror, unable to take her hands away from the sides, and sounding as if she were in pain.

"Then, she said the glass rippled like water before it opened. That's when she saw the man. The man grabbed her mother around the neck and began choking her. Madison ran to help her mother, but the man pulled her through the mirror, and as Madison reached it, the mirror became glass again.

"Madison gave me the same description of the man she'd related to her father. Team, I know it still sounds outlandish, but Madison's description fits Angus Marlowe. Whether he's a ghost, or a spirit, or a poltergeist, we must assume he is somehow trapped within this mysterious gateway."

"*Porta un abyssus*," Sidney said. They all looked at him. "Those were the words we read here in the tome, a few years ago." Sidney pointed to the big, black book. "Paul interpreted them to mean 'gateway to Hell.'"

None of them noticed as an invisible, ghostly face turned and watched Sidney speak.

"One of those mirrors belonging to the Marlowes is an entrance into the gateway. The other is the exit. The gold-gilded mirror was destroyed when Cedar Manor burned to the ground. So, is it the entrance or the exit that no longer exists?"

"Taryn Page and my mother were drawn to the mirrors," Leah said. "My mother was obsessed with the gold-gilded mirror. Taryn focused on the Black Mirror. Could they both be entrances?"

Taryn's eyes darted back and forth, watching each of them speak.

"We could get a better understanding of the mirrors," Sidney said, "if I had some help interpreting this bitch of a book. I'm no Latin expert. I need an interpreter. Leah, your father is a Harvard graduate. He's studied many languages, including Latin. I'm hoping you might consider letting him continue deciphering this book."

Leah shook her head. "No, I don't want to involve him. This is too close to him. I never should've let him come with us to Cedar Manor."

"Leah, his issues were about the house and what went on there," Dylan said. "This is a book, one he never had any connection to, or even knew existed."

"That's true," Susan added. "Leah, as your father's psychiatrist, I can assure you, the past is behind him. He's much better now."

Leah pointed to the book. "What if delving into this book resurrects the past for him?"

"We'll all be there alongside him, especially you," Susan responded.

"If it becomes too much for him, or if I see the slightest hint of stress, I'll find another interpreter. Why don't we let it be his decision?"

Leah sighed and looked up at the ceiling. "I don't know. I guess."

"Well, the issue is not even pertinent at this moment. Our primary concern right now is finding the shop where Taryn bought the Black Mirror and interviewing the proprietor. We need to find out how, and when, he came into possession of the Black Mirror."

"Yeah, but what if he doesn't talk to us?" Brett said.

"He will," Susan replied. "The fact that a woman disappeared shortly after purchasing the mirror, and under mysterious circumstances connected to it, is not going to look good for him."

"Right, but we can't throw him under the bus or we expose the girl." Brett pointed out.

"No, but the implication will be enough for him to talk, if he doesn't." Dylan said.

"We already know the shop is not far from Pittsburgh, thanks to Charley," Susan said. "Madison left me a few clues. She couldn't remember the name of the shop, but she remembered the name of the man who owned it. His name was Ernie." Susan told them about Madison recalling the joke that his name hadn't fit on the sign.

"Then, she imparted something interesting. Madison told me she'd been fascinated by a crystal displayed in the shop. It was a crystal that changed colors on its own."

The investigators were jotting notes as Susan spoke. Taryn's eyes continued to dart back and forth between the speakers. Her expression was one of awe at their motives, their plans, and how connected they were to this mystery. So, they were responsible for Cedar Manor burning to the ground. She'd heard they'd been inside investigating, but their clandestine discussion revealed so much more than she'd known.

"Then, I saw the Black Mirror with my own eyes," she continued. "After our talk, Madison led me into her mother's den." Susan detailed all of the odd artifacts. "Apparently, Taryn had been a genuine lover of the unusual. It stood in the corner amid her bizarre collection. It was sleek, black, opaque, onyx, whatever you want to call it. The frame was silvered. It cast no real reflection, just a distorted reproduction of an image. It was beyond eerie. For a moment, I could almost see why Taryn couldn't remove her gaze from it. It didn't ripple in waves as Madison claimed, and no one jumped out at me, but I could almost feel a bad vibe emanating from it. It was as if it were aware of my presence and enticing me with its strange allure."

"Did you physically compare the handheld mirror to the larger, black one?" Dylan said.

"I couldn't, not with Madison there," she explained. "I didn't think it was a good idea. In any case, I want to meet with Madison one more time alone, before I introduce you all. I'll try to compare the mirrors then. While I'm doing that, I want you all to do some research and find that shop. When you do, I want you to go there. We'll keep each other updated as we go along."

They all agreed. Suddenly, Leah leaned forward and roved her eyes across the room as if she sensed something.

* * * *

Leah saw a disturbance in the closed atmosphere surrounding them. A shape, an outline of something, moved before her eyes. She blinked, attempting to shake off what could have been nothing but her tired eyes. The strange form or outline remained there, stationary and across the table from her, though she'd seen it move. She focused her eyes on the shape no one else was seeing. It became clearer and clearer, developing like a Polaroid picture. It was a face, a woman's face that stared back at her. The hair and eyes became visible in a ghostly way and peered right at her.

She closed her eyes, and when she opened them, her third eye saw a young woman with ash-blonde hair and green eyes. This strange ghost in the room had been watching her. The phantom female leaped from the chair, apparently realizing she'd caught Leah's attention. Leah's naked-eye vision resumed with a flash, and her eyes moved across the room, tracing a shape that vanished through the wall. She shot upward from the chair and moved away from the table, her eyes searching the walls around them.

"Leah, what is it?" She heard the alarm in Susan's voice. "What are you seeing?"

"Someone was in here with us."

Chairs swiveled and bodies moved behind her. She closed her eyes again and opened them. She saw through the walls, but only for an instant. Her naked-eye vision switched intermittently with her third eye view, like a peepshow. There was nothing now, only the five of them, and the room undisturbed.

"She's gone." Leah's tone was a mixture of amazement and defeat.

"Who?" Susan demanded.

"She was a ghost, an apparition, or something. She was sitting right there, across from me. I saw her watching me. I saw her move." Leah extended her arm, pointing to the wall.

She turned and faced them, straining her voice in her persistence. "It was as if she went through the wall. I saw her quickly with my third eye, but the vision kept cutting out. I saw a woman, blonde hair, green eyes, and then I saw the shape of her again. She just disappeared."

They were all standing, roused by the sudden upset. They glanced at each other and looked around them. They trusted what Leah saw.

"She realized I'd seen her. That's when she fled. She'd been in here, watching us and listening to our every word."

"Alright, team," Susan said. "Let's sit back down. Leah, keep watch, in the event that you see her again. I was just about to end the meeting. We all know what our assignments are. The sooner we get to them; the sooner we can solve this mystery. I'm going to make arrangements with Charley, so I can pick up Madison from school tomorrow. I'll take her home. I'll try to compare the handheld mirror to the larger one then. I assume you all will be searching for this shop of strange artifacts. We'll touch bases the day after tomorrow—Wednesday."

Susan adjourned the meeting, and the investigators left room 208.

* * * *

Susan sat alone at the long conference table in room 208, deep in thought, her index finger resting across her upper lip. The team had just left. She was more spooked by what had happened at the meeting than she let on to them. She'd been aware Leah was seeing something, and surely enough, she had. A ghost... right here in the room with them. What perturbed Susan the most was the brief description Leah had given—blonde hair, green eyes. She was sure Charley had described

Taryn the same way, but it all seemed distorted right now in her aging mind. She sighed in frustration.

She called Charley and explained she wanted to pick up Madison from school, bring her home, and speak with her further. He agreed and thanked her. It helped out with his work schedule. She didn't reveal what had happened at the meeting, but she asked him for two things Dylan and the team would need in the event they located the mysterious shop and its owner. Charley complied, and she ended the call. Now, she would devise a plan to examine the Black Mirror tomorrow, without Madison this time.

The image of it kept entering her mind.

* * * *

Taryn had made it out of room 208 and across the campus. She should've known. She should've realized Leah Leeds might be able to see her, and she had. She'd been sitting right across from her, studying that angelic face, trying to fit the person Leah was now into the memoir she'd read with much fascination. Leah's powerful sight had spotted the ghostly image Taryn had assumed was infallible. How would she have explained herself, exposed in the light, but not as a ghost, and not as a human either?

She'd fled through the wall, the fastest she remembered moving in this form. Now, she sat on a bench outside of one of the campus buildings, flesh covering a figure and becoming visible in the daylight. No one had seen her. She was suddenly a woman sitting on the bench.

Then, she thought of something. Susan had said she thought Madison possessed a third eye much like Leah's. So, why hadn't her daughter seen her yet? Would Madison, at some point, see her as Leah had? She tried to separate her wavering thoughts, the good from the bad, logical from illogical, and sense from nonsense. It seemed impossible. Her thoughts were now myriad notions and images merging into cohesion, as if all of them belonged together. Frustration was beyond her. Her existence was now as part of the world, not as one within it.

The slight October chill made her unearthly flesh feel alive. She got up from the bench and walked. Maybe one day her daughter would see her. Maybe one day Taryn would show herself. For now, she would masquerade as a normal human being. Autumn's cool breeze kissed and caressed her flesh. The brisk air recharged her lingering soul. She now walked through the world as a visible person, but remained unnoticed.

Chapter Ten

~ Enigmas & More ~

After having breakfast together in the Levin Hall cafeteria, the four investigators assembled once again in room 208 on the following morning. Each of them took a seat behind one of the many computers that aligned the wall in room 208. Each of them had a mission: conduct an internet search for any and all listings of local shops that sold odd and mysterious artifacts. Four computers booted up simultaneously, displaying four different background screens. Once they were all online, they searched using various terms: odd artifacts, Pittsburgh; mysterious antiques, western Pennsylvania; strange heirlooms; the list went on and on. Soon, they uncovered several possibilities.

"Check this one out," Brett said.

They all gathered around his computer screen. It was a page for a place called "Antique Taboos." It wasn't far, almost twenty-miles and near Pittsburgh. They read the details of the place, looked at the pictures adorning the web page. The Black Mirror would have been a perfect fit for this place. The pictures of the odd artifacts did nothing to explain what they were, leaving the team to rely on the descriptions. They looked through the pictures—no black mirror. Then, Brett clicked on a page that displayed the shop's information. He scrolled to the bottom, where they read the proprietor's name—*Mimi Dodd*.

"Nope, that's not Ernie." Sidney pointed out.

"I found something," Leah said. "It's a little far to be the place we're looking for." They turned their attention to Leah's screen. "It's a listing for a shop called, 'Mysterious Antiques.' It's in Hazelton, which is farther than the range, according to Madison's story, but she was a five-year-old child at the time. It's possible she underestimated, or overestimated the time it took to get there."

There was no proprietor's name this time, only the location of the shop, but the listing did include a phone number. Leah took her phone from her purse and dialed the number.

"What are you doing?" Dylan said.

"Watch," she replied. She pressed the speakerphone button, so they could all hear. On the third ring, a woman answered the phone.

"Mysterious Antiques?"

"Hi, can I speak with Ernie, please?" Leah used her friendliest voice.

"I'm sorry. You must have the wrong number."

"Oh, I'm sorry," Leah said. "You see, I'm a collector, and I assumed that this was the shop owned by Ernie..." She hastened to the others for a fast last name, her eyes wide as her mind raced. "Smith," she said, quickly.

Sidney winced with a sour face at her bad choice.

"No, I'm sorry. There's no Ernie here."

"Well, maybe you can help me," Leah continued. "I've been searching for mirrors, specifically those of the Victorian era. Many of them, at the time, were crafted with black glass. They're extremely rare and unusual, as I'm sure you can imagine. I was wondering if you have anything like that in your shop."

"No, I don't have anything like that here." Now, the woman spoke in a more helpful and businesslike tone and less as the curious recipient of a strange call. "I've never had any mirrors, or anything from the Victorian era. I have things from later eras, but no mirrors."

The woman sounded genuinely sorry that she couldn't help. Neither was she able to recommend any other shops like her own. Leah thanked her for her time and ended the call.

"We can scratch that one off," Leah said.

They continued to search through phone listings, internet postings, and social media sites. Then, Sidney had an idea. Rather than search for shops, he decided to search for collectors and dealers of odd antiques and artifacts. Soon, a name jumped out from the screen—*E. Mattson;*

collector, owner and proprietor of "Enigma's & More."

"Everyone, come and look at this," he said, his voice ready to announce victory. They gathered around his screen. "Someone whose name starts with an 'E' owns a place called, 'Enigmas & More.'"

Dylan noticed the location, Monroe, a city nearly twenty-miles away and near Pittsburgh. "It looks like it would be the right distance."

Now, Sidney took his phone from his jacket and dialed the number listed for 'Enigmas & More.' He placed the call on speakerphone. Dylan attempted to speak, but Sidney lifted up his finger as a man answered.

"Enigmas & More, can I help you?"

"May I speak with Ernie, please?" Sidney said.

"Speaking," the older voice replied.

"Ernie, this is David Smith," Sidney lied. "I'm calling local businesses in your area to talk about our foundation's charity work on behalf of—"

"No thanks, pal," Ernie said. "Not interested."

They all heard a beep, followed by a dial tone. Sidney put his phone away. They stared at him, smug and self-congratulating.

"That was brilliant," Dylan said.

"I know," Sidney said, laughing.

He printed out the listing showing the address to Enigmas and More. It would take them anywhere from thirty to forty-five minutes to get there.

"So, should we all pack into the van and go talk to Ernie?" Sidney looked to the others.

The rest had already risen from their seats and donned their jackets.

"Let's roll," Dylan said.

* * * *

The van's wheels rolled into the city of Monroe in less than forty minutes. Restaurants, shopping malls, plazas, and business locations filled the busy Pittsburgh suburb. Cars crowded the highway, but the GPS told them they were minutes away from the road they sought. Sidney made a right turn when the GPS alert directed him. The road spiraled, twisting and turning until straightening through another part of the vast suburb. They passed bars, diners, auto shops, and bargain stores.

A row of non-descript buildings stretched northward. They read the signs, searching as the GPS guided them through the area.

Then, a neon blue sign flashed in the gray October daylight, attracting their eyes and attention. It hung on the side of a building; its vertically listed letters spelled something unseen from their distance. Sidney turned off from the right lane and drove closer to the building. The sign was now within eyeshot.

"Enigmas & More, this is it kiddies," Sidney said.

"Ernie's Enigmas & More!" Brett suddenly realized.

"He couldn't fit his name on the sign," Leah echoed, remembering.

They looked at the sign. It was large, but not enough to squeeze in a person's name before the word "Enigmas." It flashed blue, beckoning like a sideshow attraction. Sidney pulled the van into the shop's parking lot and immediately found a space. They walked to the front of the shop.

"Is everyone ready?" Dylan said. The three of them nodded.

A string of bells jingled as Dylan opened the door, and they walked inside. It was an old-fashioned house now renovated into this shop full of parlors in the present day. The front room was clean and well-kept, recently vacuumed and absent of a single speck of dust. A long glass counter enclosed a large portion of the room, and behind the glass were small trinkets and statues, all unidentifiable at their quick glances.

A man walked out from a back room. "Hello, there," he said. "Can I help you all?"

He appeared to be in his early to mid-seventies with white hair and glasses, a friendly face and a smile to match.

Dylan took the lead as chief investigator. "We certainly hope so," he said, extending his hand. "I'm Dylan Rasche." He introduced the rest of the team. "We're from the Paranormal Research and Investigative Society from Green Valley University."

"Ernie Mattson," the older man said, as he shook Dylan's hand. "Imagine that, a paranormal team showing up to look at strange artifacts."

"Yes, well, that's what we're hoping you might be able to help us with," Dylan said. "You see, we're looking for something in particular, a mirror, to be precise."

"Oh?" Ernie's tone suddenly dropped from the level of the

welcoming connoisseur. Dylan and the rest of the team watched the man's face for a change of expression.

"Yes. It's a black mirror. The glass itself is black. It's an artifact from the Victorian era. We have reason to believe you might be able to help us."

Dylan noticed the older man's surprise as he shot him a quick glance, and then lowered his eyes, hoping to stifle his hasty reaction. The old man had been caught off guard.

"No, I'm sorry," he said. "I don't think I can help you."

How ironic, Dylan thought, that a man named Ernest just blatantly lied. Dylan knew the old man intended to cut this conversation short. They'd all deduced that however this man had acquired the mirror was either scandalous, or illegal. Before breakfast in Levin Hall this morning, Susan had emailed him a picture of Taryn Page. She had requested one from Charley after the upset at the meeting yesterday. Dylan had saved it to his phone, and he was about to use it, but he waited a moment as Brett spoke.

"So, you've never seen, or come into contact with this black mirror?"

Ernie shook his head, still avoiding their eyes. "No, can't say that I have." His response was short, clipped.

Dylan took his phone from his inner jacket pocket and ran his finger across the screen, retrieving the images stored there. He opened a picture of Taryn Page and sized it to fit the entire screen. Then, he turned the phone around and held it up to Ernie's face.

"So, what you're saying is that you've never seen this young woman before?"

Ernie's eyebrows lifted and met, forming a bridge across his forehead. The visible grip of stress and fear wrinkled his face into a troubled expression. He looked away, unable to lie as Taryn's face stared back at him. Dylan had another piece of evidence. Charley had faxed Susan the bank statement listing the transfer of funds from Taryn's account to Ernest Mattson's. Susan had faxed it to him, and now he took it from the same jacket pocket with his other hand.

"This is the bank statement containing the transfer of fifteen-hundred dollars to your account. She purchased this mirror from you in

2009."

"Remember her now?" Sidney said, stepping forward.

Ernie sighed, his eyes fixed on the floor. "Yes, I remember her."

"So, why did you lie?" Leah demanded.

He looked up at them. "I always hated that thing. I began to despise its presence not long after I received it. I wanted rid of that thing for years. I also needed the money. She offered it, and I wanted that damn thing gone. Do you understand? I didn't think it would be a big deal. I was its owner for over forty-five years. So what if I sold it and made a few bucks?"

"It's not that," Dylan said. "That's not why we're here. This young woman disappeared not long after acquiring this mirror from you."

Ernie took a deep breath and nervously exhaled. "Dear God," he said, obviously unaware of what had happened to Taryn. "I had nothing to do with that."

"We know that," Leah assured him. "However, we need you to tell us everything you know about that mirror. It's important we find out what happened to this woman."

"We need you to tell us exactly how you came into possession of that mirror," Dylan said. "I'm sure you've heard of Caspar Marlowe?" Ernie looked up at him, recognizing the name. "That mirror is an occult artifact. Its last owner was Caspar's son, Angus, the serial killer responsible for the disappearances of at least four women back in the late-sixties." Dylan watched as the color drained from the old man's face.

"Alright, alright," Ernie pleaded with his hands up in the air in defeat. "I'll tell you everything from the beginning."

He led them into another room, a private one with a couch and several matching lounge chairs. The investigators sat on the couch. Ernie took a chair facing them.

"I was contacted by a man back in 1970. It was just before Christmas. He came in here one night and told me he was in possession of a rare, Victorian artifact. He was a lawyer, and he explained that one of his clients had just passed away. Among his late-client's possessions were many unwanted antiques and artifacts that he'd inherited long before his passing. He described the mirror to me, and I thought it would be a unique addition to the shop I was just opening up. He told me that I was to consider it a donation, but there was a catch. I was to keep his name totally anonymous, and he paid me well to do so—five-thousand dollars. All these years later, I sold it back to the young woman."

"Do you remember the lawyer's name?" Sidney prompted.

"Back then, I wrote it down in an old ledger, just in case I ever needed to remember him, but after all this time..." He thought for a moment, his eyes wondering, staring away into the invisible past. "I think his name was Harold, Harold..."

"Harold Bennett?" Sidney finished the thought for him.

"Yes, that's it!" Ernie pointed his finger.

"He was the lawyer for the Marlowe family," Dylan explained.

"I had no idea," Ernie continued. "I was young, in my late-twenties, and just starting out. My wife and I had been recently married. We had nothing at that time, and this man came out of nowhere, made a donation, and then compensated me to keep his name out of it. At the time, it wasn't something I could refuse, nor did I know of any reason to do so. I'd heard of the Marlowe's, but not of their son. I've never lived in Green Valley. I've lived here all of my life. I took the mirror, and I placed it in one of the many rooms."

"You said that you eventually wanted rid of the mirror," Leah said. "What made you come to hate the mirror so much?"

Ernie told her about how people became eerily fascinated by it. It seemed to cause obsessive responses from those who admired it. Then, he told them about the Christmas party.

"I swear, to this day, I saw that thing ripple just like water, and then it was solid again. I'd been drinking, but I wasn't drunk, certainly not that intoxicated. I knew I sure as hell wasn't crazy. No one had any interest in taking it off of my hands. So, I placed it away in a far corner. There it stayed for many years."

"Until Taryn arrived," Brett concluded.

Ernie nodded his head, his eyes closed. "There's more. After I sold that mirror to her, I looked into it one last time. What happened the night of that Christmas party started to happen all over again. It changed. It looked almost three dimensional, and then I realized the glass was no longer there. It looked like it was an opening." He shuddered. "Then, the glass was normal again."

The investigators exchanged glances.

"That young woman insisted," he said. "I hadn't seen fascination like that in many years. Even those who'd admired it years ago weren't that enamored. She offered me a generous amount for that mirror, and I accepted. Even all these years later, nothing was different. I still needed the money. My wife passed away shortly before then."

As they offered belated condolences, Ernie appeared thoughtful for a moment. "That young woman came in here with her little girl." He searched their faces, one by one. "The girl, is she okay?"

"She's suffered the loss of her mother," Dylan said. "However, physically, she's fine."

"The girl remembered your shop because of the color-changing crystal," Sidney said.

"Yes, her favorite," Ernie remembered. "Tell me about the young woman. What exactly happened to her?"

Dylan wondered how much information they should divulge to this man. Leah noticed his hesitance.

"What interests us is the fact that you saw the glass change," Leah said. "Taryn's obsession with the mirror increased the more she looked into it. Her daughter, Madison, says she saw the mirror open up, and her mother had entered through the mirror. Taryn was never seen or heard from again. Apparently, the mirror is some kind of gateway to another realm."

Leah had conveniently omitted the part about Taryn being pulled through the mirror, as well as any suspicions regarding Angus Marlowe, yet Ernie didn't seem surprised by the revelation. He'd filled his life with the unknown and the obscure. His face displayed conviction, a long awaited vindication that he wasn't crazy after all.

He wagged his finger at them. "I knew it. I always knew there was something about that mirror, something evil. You could almost feel it when you were around it, like someone or something was watching you from beyond it. It was the type of thing that drew you into its mystery, its allure, like it was trying to tell you something. I'd seen the glass vanish after she left that day. I was sure of it that time. Then the damn thing was a mirror again, just like nothing had happened."

"When you saw it open for that brief duration," Leah prompted, "did you see anything else? I mean, did you see beyond where the glass had once been?"

Ernie's eyes misted over, remembering the moment. He shook his head. "No, it all happened so quickly. It was like I couldn't piece it all together fast enough." He told them about how Taryn had arranged to have the mirror picked up and delivered to her home. "She took care of everything." He sighed. "Now, I wish I'd never sold that damn thing to her. I was reluctant at first, but I gave in. I feel badly for the little girl."

"Well, as we said, it's not your fault." Dylan's tone was now one of understanding. "You can relax because all of this has to remain a secret for the girl's sake. The best you can do for her is say nothing about our visit, or anything that we've told you. Of course, your role in this will remain unknown except by us. We'll say nothing about your deal with Harold Bennett, and the Marlowes must never be mentioned either."

Ernie nodded and shook his hand in agreement. The conversation shifted as the investigators made their way out. They asked questions about what kind of artifacts he collected and sold, and he described most of the attractions in his shop. The string of bells jingled once again as Dylan opened the door.

Brett turned back to Ernie. "So, the color-changing crystal, is it real or a hoax?"

Ernie shook his head. "Oh, no, it's real. It's just one more thing around here that has no definite origin. I still remember how the little girl's face lit up when she'd seen it."

"Maybe we'll be back some day to check it out," Brett said, smiling.

Ernie smiled back. "I'll be here."

The string of bells clanged as the door closed behind them.

Chapter Eleven

~ Dark Fascination ~

Charley had arranged for Susan to pick up Madison from school, and now she waited for the girl outside of the office at Green Valley Elementary School. Normally, Charley picked up his daughter every day. Susan considered it slightly overprotective, but she sensed it had everything to do with Madison's insurmountable ability, and how it separated her from other children. She could unleash that ability at any moment, especially given her ongoing state of grief. Madison continued her life with no confirmation that her mother was dead. To her, her mother was abducted and continued to be missing. Susan was glad to spend a few hours with Madison, even if she had ulterior motives.

Today, Charley would get to finish his work at the newspaper, and she would speak with Madison privately. Then, she would examine the Black Mirror one more time. The handheld mirror remained discreetly stored in her purse. She wanted to compare the two mirrors in hope of discovering a connection. Images of the Black Mirror kept surfacing in her mind. She'd even seen it in a dream last night. Her subconscious mind was alerting her to the dark fascination that had suddenly flourished in her. Her conscious mind denied it, overruling those thoughts in favor of the view that she was pursuing the truth for Madison, Charley, and Leah. After all, she was a psychiatrist, and she could handle this.

Suddenly, a loud blaring tone signaled the end of the school day and made her jump. She remembered how her own school bell sounded like the loud, rapid ping of an old-fashioned alarm clock. An army of fourth and fifth graders passed her in the hallway, talking and laughing amongst themselves, playfully nudging each other, and making haste for the front exit. A few stragglers trailed after the parade of happy, laughing faces. Those were in no hurry, content to dawdle behind and remain separate from the usual crowd. They appeared more studious and less playful than the others, although some seemed shy, lonely, or bored. Then, a familiar face came down the hallway. Her eyes were focused on the floor as she walked, hugging books closely to the front of her chest. Those vivid blue eyes glanced up and saw her standing there, waiting.

Madison's eyes widened at seeing her. A smile spread across her face. Susan felt relief, joy, pity, and even guilt; Madison was happy to see her. The girl quickly approached her and wrapped her arm around Susan's waist in a half-hug. They exchanged bright hellos and walked together through the hallway. Susan asked her about her school day.

Madison shrugged. "It was okay, I guess. Are you any closer to finding my Mom?"

Susan suddenly worried about the level of trust Madison had placed in her. Yet, finding out what happened to Taryn was why she was studying the Black Mirror, wasn't it? She tried to ignore the creeping guilt. At the same time, warnings of a sudden obsession blared like a neon sign in the back of her mind, but who else could help this young girl outside of her and the team? They knew the real story behind the mirror, at least the twentieth-century part of it.

"Well, that depends on what you can tell me," Susan replied. "Why don't we discuss it in the car?"

Madison nodded, and they strolled out the front door together. Susan saw no sign of the impatient, spoiled child Charley had described. It wasn't there whenever the girl was with her. Could Madison have outgrown it or was Susan's presence providing Madison with an older, female figure in her life, something she'd been lacking for years? Soon, they were strapping themselves inside Susan's car.

As Susan drove, she asked Madison more questions about her foresight and how she "saw" things. Madison described her visions much the same way Leah had, like a movie playing in her mind. Then, whatever she saw happened, or maybe had happened before.

"Mom and Dad would look at each other when I knew things," she said. "They knew I was right. I don't think they liked it."

"It's scary for parents who have children with psychic abilities," Susan said, "especially if they don't possess it themselves like your father. It's because they don't understand enough about it. That's another reason why I'm here, Madison. I can help you and your father to understand your abilities. There are people I'd like you to meet, but for now, we need to put our heads together."

Susan changed the subject and moved toward the next phase of her questioning. She came to a red light, one well known for its monotonous wait time. Susan kept her foot on the brake as she turned to Madison and spoke.

"Madison, if you were to see the man who pulled your mother into the mirror, do you think you'd recognize him?"

Madison thought for a moment. She nodded and turned her head to look at Susan with a fierce glare of conviction in her eyes.

"Yes," she said. "I know I would."

Susan mindlessly stared at the red light. Yesterday, she asked Charley to email her a picture of Taryn, and to fax the bank statement for the purchase of the Black Mirror. He'd made a copy of it years ago and held onto it. They were the two things Dylan and the team would need if they'd found that shop. Then, she'd searched through the society's archives, retrieving the pictures of Angus Marlowe that Sidney had found a few years ago. She sent the one from 1962 to her phone. It was the picture that portrayed his drastic transition from a clean cut but delinquent young man, to the grizzly and visibly disturbed character he'd become.

The light was still red, so Susan quickly took her phone from her purse and pulled up the picture of Angus Marlowe.

"Madison, I don't want you to become angry or afraid when you see this. It's a picture of a man. He may be the one who took your mother, or he may not be. Either way, I want you to stay calm, and know that the closer we get to the truth the better, understood?"

Madison's usual consent with a simple nod made Susan want to shake her into speaking. She handed Madison the phone, the old photo of Angus filling the screen. Madison stared at it, while Susan watched her face for the slightest flinch or movement. The girl's blue eyes grew bigger. Susan saw an angry fire burning inside them. Madison drew a deep breath through her nostrils, her lips tightly sealed. Susan wasn't sure if what she was seeing was pain and hurt that would cause tears, or an anger that would ignite something else. Madison's gaze remained locked on the face before her.

"That's him. That's the man who took my mother."

Susan heard ringing in her ears. It was confirmation, one that would not be easy to explain. How was it possible? Angus Marlowe had been presumed dead for over forty-five years. He would be in his mid to late eighties if he were alive today, yet Madison identified the man as he appeared in 1962. Never in the girl's description had she made mention of an old man.

"Are you absolutely sure, Madison?"

"Yes, I'm sure," she responded. "He looked a little more normal than this, but it was him."

"What do you mean by 'normal?'"

"Well, he wasn't so ugly or shabby looking. He looked..." Madison appeared at a loss for words.

Susan helped her out. "You mean, cleaned up?"

"Yes."

Interesting. The description of his appearance increased the possibility of a ghost, but he had grabbed Taryn with a physical hold around her neck. How?

Madison handed the phone back to Susan, her glance averted. Susan noticed the girl's attention to the red traffic light in front of them. Her small chest heaved up and down, while anger brewed inside of her. An inner fight to subdue it came close to failing.

Suddenly, the light changed. Susan stepped on the gas. Her car barreled through the light, and the sound of screeching brakes could be heard behind her. The light had changed early and unexpectedly, and only she and Madison knew why.

It wasn't long before they were inside Madison's home, sitting at the dining room table, and basking in the warmth from the furnace. Suddenly, something disrupted the comfortable heat that filled the room. Susan felt the same wafting chill that had breezed by her the other day in the den. She thought of the incident in room 208 and gazed around her, now suspecting the cause of the quick draft. Her suspicion made her think of a question for Madison.

"Madison, this may sound like an odd question, but have you ever heard people say they can still feel their loved ones around them even after they're gone?" Madison offered a half-shrug that indicated she understood. "Do you ever feel the presence of your mother around you? I'm not implying that your mother's gone in that way, but do you ever feel like you can sense her near you."

"Yes." Madison spoke clearly and convincingly. There was no simple, uncertain nod. "I feel her around me lots of times. I think my Dad does too. So, I guess that means she's dead."

"You don't actually know that yet, Madison. We must never assume without proof."

Susan looked around the room, subtly accentuating her last words in a way Madison would not detect. She meant those words for a presence that may or may not have been in the room with them. Her eyes moved to the surrounding chairs, to the open space around them, and even into the next room. Susan noticed nothing, yet she remained alert. Now, she was about to set her plan into motion.

She opened her briefcase. "Madison, there's a small assignment I'd like you to complete for me." She took two sharpened pencils and a yellow legal pad from her briefcase and placed them in front of Madison. "I want you to think back to all of the times that you've used your telekinesis."

Susan had spent some time explaining the word to Madison and what the word meant, instilling in her that what she possessed was a genuine psychic ability. "I want you to make a list of all the times you've become angry and lashed out with your ability, and I want you to include all of the instances when you've used it without your parents knowing. Then, write a few words about how you felt afterward. Remember, anything you tell me is between us. What you've done in the past is no longer an issue. I won't be ratting on you." Susan smiled when she said this, eliciting a laugh from the otherwise melancholy child.

Madison agreed, taking a pencil in her hand and moving the legal pad closer toward her. She lowered her eyes, as if remembering the past.

"While you're doing that, I'm going to take another look at the mirror in the den," Susan said, rising from the chair. "There are things I need to write down, so if you'll excuse me for just a few moments, I'll leave you alone to concentrate, okay?"

There was that nod again, though this time the girl was distracted by her memories. Susan walked away from the table, out of the dining room, and proceeded down the stairs to the den. She stood in front of the door, glancing behind her at Madison, who was now deep in thought and pushing the pencil across the page.

Susan turned the knob slowly and flicked on the light switch before entering. Light flooded the room, and in the southwest corner stood the Black Mirror, just as she remembered it. She closed the door behind her.

She walked toward the Black Mirror, stopped, and spun around quickly. That draft wafted again, yet she was alone in the room. She saw nothing. No ghosts lurked in the shadows. She turned back and walked to the far corner of the room and stood before the mirror. Its appearance was uncompromising. Its ornate and antique frame, the sleek blackness that distorted light into shadow, and its silent, innocent beckoning brought back a bad vibe she remembered well. The mirror gave her the same sensation she'd felt when standing outside of Cedar Manor for the first time. It was as if it awaited her presence.

She stared into it for what had to have been minutes, just glaring into the perfect black glass until she became unable to remove or divert her eyes. It was as if they were fastened to the mirror. Her dry and strained eyes winced in pain, and she whirled her head with a quick motion, forcing them away from the sight that held them captive. She fumbled with her purse, her heart hammering hard in her chest.

She pulled out the handheld mirror and held it up in front of the Black Mirror, glass upon glass, her hand shaking as she gripped the handle. She stared into it, waiting, and then her sudden obsession revived within her. She felt abandon, submission, and the need to discover. She wanted to learn of the mirror's mystery, to go beyond the glass. She wanted it to open.

Something was happening. She saw movement within the frame, as if the glass was no longer glass, but something fluid and shimmering. Then, Susan watched it ripple in waves, like rolling black water confined within the frame. Her eyes were fixed. She gripped the handheld mirror harder.

Then, the glass was gone, and beyond it was darkness. She moved closer and gazed inside the gateway. The mirror had opened, and the team was not with her, but that seemed irrelevant at this moment. She tried to move her head to check the door, hoping Madison would not interrupt what was happening, but her effort at movement failed. She stood frozen, transfixed by the sight before her.

Wisps of white caught her eyes. It was a mist, a fog within the darkness, but something else was penetrating the gloom. She saw a flash of light, like lightning piercing twilight for a single moment. Someone was walking toward her from beyond the mirror. Between the faraway flashes of lightning, she caught intermittent glimpses of the figure's familiar movement. A recognizable face came closer and closer. Then, the figure stood fixed within the frame. The face she recognized stared back at her. It was her face.

Shock froze her. Her hair rose from her scalp, and goose pimple hives covered her flesh. She stared back at herself in the mirror, yet there was no mirror, and what her eyes beheld was not a reflection. There was no mimicking of her eyes as they widened, or her brows as they lifted. The figure in the mirror simply stared at her. It was a definite reproduction of her, but something was different, an unidentifiable imperfection not quite visible to the naked eye.

Susan once read that people don't actually see their true reflections in mirrors because mirrors reflect the inverse of the subject before it. Mirrors switch things from right to left and vice-versa. Yet, Susan felt it was something so much more than that.

Was it the hair, the shape of the face, or the blank expression that seemed not quite animate? The figure wore the same clothes—a white shirt covered by a beige knit sweater and matching pants. The eyes appeared the same, almond-shaped and blue, her inheritance from her mother. Every wrinkle, frown line, and crease seemed fainter. The flesh appeared to glow with a vibrant pulse, seemingly dormant and contained within the figure's familiar form. A finger flexed with a beckoning gesture from the figure's outstretched hand.

"Susan," the figure said. Its voice called out with an eerie, echoing

timbre that reverberated no farther than the frame and the recesses of her mind. She remained unable to move, her eyes held captive by the figure's appearance. She tried to speak but couldn't. The figure pointed to the handheld mirror in Susan's hand.

"Bring the key," it said.

She looked at the handheld mirror. The key, she was holding the key that opened the gateway. So, that's what she had done. She'd opened the gateway that led to some alternate realm. Her sudden obsession had caused her to forget the world around her. In this moment of fascination and fear, this quest for knowledge and understanding, all thoughts of Madison, Taryn, and the team seemed far away. The need to explore and discover became overwhelming. She felt dizzy, hypnotized by the beckoning figure that called to her.

The lightning beyond the silvered frame intensified, making her shield her eyes with the back of her hand. She looked into the gateway once more and watched as the figure turned away from her.

It spoke one last time, its face looking out over its left shoulder. *"Time is running out, Susan. You want to solve this mystery, don't you?"*

The key—she held it in her hand. She had to find out. She had to enter. The obsession was an irresistible itch that persisted from inside, one she couldn't scratch. Quickly, she walked through the frame, where the glass had once been. She had no thoughts of anything other than what was in front of her. She followed the figure, but the mist clouded her vision. Ahead, she saw blackness segue into indigo in what looked like a strange reverse motion of the spectrum. Behind her, she heard a voice call her name.

"Susan, come back!"

She turned and looked at the gateway's entrance. She could still see the room she'd just left with its odd artifacts and dark-colored hues. A woman was calling for her, a woman with blondish hair and green eyes. She looked familiar. Susan started back, but stumbled as the way forward became foggy and murky.

Then, the gateway closed in front of her. The glass reappeared and solidified within the frame. The Black Mirror was whole once again. She turned and looked behind her. Another figure was moving quickly toward her, a man with menacing eyes. She recognized him, his beard, his long brown hair wafting as he walked.

Susan's screams echoed out through a lost world.

* * * *

Taryn knew of Susan's plans to visit Maddy today. So, she remained in her ghostly form, lingering and watching in the place she once called home. She listened to all of the questions Susan asked her daughter and paid close attention to Maddy's answers. Susan asked Maddy if she'd ever felt her mother's presence, even though she wasn't there. Madison's answer made Taryn want to show herself at that moment. The slightest hint of yearning nagged at her, and then it passed.

Susan must have realized something following the episode in room 208. Surely, they had assumed she was a ghost, but Leah had seen enough of her to provide a decent description.

At the table, Susan had moved her head in all directions, her eyes searching for an invisible someone. She spoke to Madison, projecting her voice slightly in what Taryn thought may have been a hint to the ghost she failed to find.

"We must never assume without proof."

Was that a covert message to her? Was Susan telling her that she was aware of her presence? Could she have been nudging her to reveal herself to her family? Susan and the team had concluded she was a ghost. They couldn't have been more mistaken.

Then, Taryn followed Susan down the stairs and into the room that still displayed her bizarre collection, as though she'd never left. She glided through the doorway just as Susan took a final peek at Maddy and closed the door behind her.

Taryn followed closely behind her, until Susan whirled around, feeling the presence of someone behind her. This woman was sharp, but she was no Leah Leeds; she couldn't spot her within the very atmosphere that surrounded her.

Susan turned her attention to the Black Mirror, still in the southwest corner, undisturbed. Taryn recognized something while studying Susan's face. Susan was bewitched by the same dark fascination, the same sudden obsession that had possessed her in only a short time after acquiring the mirror.

She watched as Susan's eyes became fixed by the mirror's allure. Soon, Susan managed to turn away and rummage through her purse. That's when Taryn saw her pull out the black, handheld mirror, the key to the gateway.

Something like surprise, alarm, and fear all combined inside of Taryn, as if she were learning human emotions all over again. Susan had opened the gateway with the key. Taryn wanted to warn her, but something was happening. Susan stood spellbound and enraptured by the portal that lay open before her. She was watching something.

Taryn stood behind Susan, looking into the mirror. She saw the mist, the flashes of lightning, and a figure that came closer and closer. Yet the looming presence wasn't Angus. It was a woman. It was Susan, but it wasn't Susan. It was her doppelganger. The figure spoke to her, luring and enticing her to step through the strange portal. Taryn saw Susan's failure to resist, her weakness within the grips of passion and fascination.

Then, Taryn began to materialize. She concentrated, allowing flesh to become flesh. She felt her hair touching her skin, her clothes hanging from her body. She sought to warn Susan, but it was too late. Susan had stepped quickly through the frame where the glass had once been. She was through the portal and inside the gateway. Taryn saw the white mist overwhelm the blackness. She couldn't see Susan anymore, but she saw movement.

She couldn't go back in there; she would never return this time. And if they were both trapped within the gateway, no one would ever know. There was nothing else to do but call out to Susan.

"Susan, come back!"

Susan's face emerged within the murky white mist. She was trying to return, and then the gateway closed. The mirror became glass again, hardening in front of her, swallowing its latest victim alive. Taryn just stared. What could she do? She had to help Susan.

Soft footfalls descended the stairs—Madison. She must have heard her voice when she yelled. She faded back into the ghostly form, watching her flesh dissipate and her presence fade into nothing. She couldn't see Madison, not right now. If she revealed herself, she would have to explain, and there was no time.

She became one with the surroundings once again, just as Madison opened the door.

* * * *

Madison had been deep in concentration, focused on the memories behind her and the writing in front of her. The deepness of thought carried her away to a place where she felt most comfortable, most relaxed. Then, she was shaken from the reverie, rudely awakened from her train of thought by the sound of a woman's voice calling out. She heard it clearly.

"Susan, come back!"

She jumped from the chair and stood, startled. There was a reason for her shock. It wasn't just a woman's voice. It was her mother's voice; she was almost sure of it. Madison walked away from the table and approached the stairs. She stepped down them cautiously, one by one, somewhat scared and not wanting to inflate her hopes. It had sounded like her mother, but how could that be? She hadn't seen her mother since she was five-years-old. Besides, how would she get in the house? Susan was in the den alone.

Madison opened the den door and discovered the room empty. Susan wasn't in the den. She looked around. All of her mother's spooky artifacts were in place, even the Black Mirror. Madison walked over to it. This is what Susan had come to see, but where was she?

Madison stared into its glass, until a vision entered her mind. She saw the mirror open into a dark entry, like the day her mother had disappeared. Then, she saw two Susan's. The two Susan's merged together into one. The vision ceased. It was gone, but so was Susan.

She looked behind her, feeling a draft chill the back of her neck. Madison looked around the room once more. Could Susan have gone into the mirror like her mother? She'd been busy at the table, remembering and writing. She hadn't heard anything other than that voice. Was it possible Susan walked off to another part of the house? Madison wouldn't have noticed, but she would find out before calling her father. She ran out of the room. Where was Susan?

Chapter Twelve

~ Into the World, Once Again ~

A woman had entered the gateway. He'd seen her in one of the many mirages, his windows on the world. She had the key, and the entrance opened for her. He plodded one foot in front of the other through the shadowy realm. The dark glass had captured the image of the woman, and then distorted it. Then, the doppelganger image made an effort to coax her through the entrance. It had happened the same way with him and now with her. His plan to use Madison as an exit was no longer necessary. This woman had discovered the key, but how?

Thoughts of his runaway Taryn had entered his mind. None of that mattered now. He walked through the murky mist toward the entrance and his one chance at release.

He saw the woman's face through the wispy white that surrounded him. Flashes of lightning lit the way forward. The gateway's entrance had closed behind her, trapping her inside, but it was of no consequence to him. The woman held the key as she entered. He would take it from her and release himself from this realm, redeem himself from his stupidity. Long ago, he'd assumed that through the gateway, he would obtain his ultimate freedom. How foolishly mistaken he'd been. Outside, in the world he had left behind, he would continue to exist as he was now. He would see the sunlight once again. He would also seek his revenge.

The woman had dashed through the entrance and followed her doppelganger, as he himself had done an infinite number of years ago.

He came closer and closer to her, until their eyes met. She screamed in a world where no one would hear her except him and the lost souls who cried out in agony.

He grabbed hold of her by her shoulders. He could almost feel her shock, the convulsive trembling at his touch. Her screaming abruptly stopped in speechless terror. She was silent except for the heaving gasps of her hyperventilation. An audible attempt at speech was suddenly stifled as the words died upon her lips. Then, her eyes rolled up; her lids flickered and closed. Her body slouched and crumpled as she fainted.

He caught her in his arms, breaking her fall. He grabbed the handheld mirror from her limp hand just as it began to slide from her grasp. Angus held the smaller mirror in his hands. The key was his once again. He hadn't seen it since it flew from his grasp that night, many years ago, though how many he couldn't be certain.

He still held the woman in his arms, watching her unconscious face, and her chest as it slowly rose up and down. She wouldn't die because she'd entered the gateway with the key—the key he now held firmly in his hand.

The woman's double came forward through the mist and stood next to him, studying her sleeping host. The double was unaffected, expressionless. Her eyes fixed in a blank stare. Still holding the woman in his arms, he looked at her doppelganger.

"I am Susan," the double said. She stared again at her host. "Will you leave her?"

"I must," Angus said. "You must come with me. There is work to be done."

He hoisted the real Susan higher in his arms and carried her. The doppelganger followed. They walked through the misty fog, the darkness, and into the never-ending indigo of the mysterious realm. A strange, large bird cawed and flew over their heads. Angus lowered Susan to the ground, laying her limp body on the hard, unearthly floor. She would awaken, and soon, but he and Susan's double would be long gone by then. Angus felt as if time had suddenly stepped forward to pardon him. It was time to rejoin the world and to even the score.

"Let's go," he said in deep and abrasive voice. He surveyed his surroundings with a glance. "It's time to leave this realm."

They walked side by side in a gliding motion, wafting through the white fog, while lightning flickered above their heads. Soon, they arrived at the entrance. The other side of the Black Mirror offered darkened, shadowy glimpses of what lay on the opposite side. They could see into Taryn's den, but it was much like looking at the negative of an old photo. No human figures were present on the opposite side. Angus lifted his hand, held the key up to the entrance, and waited.

Before him, the entrance rippled in waves. The glass on the other side undulated like water, a familiar effect he'd seen long ago. They stood within the mist, watching as the glass disappeared and the portal opened. He stepped through the frame, the handheld mirror still clutched in his hand. Susan's doppelganger followed behind him, and they both re-entered the world.

He remembered catching a glimpse of Taryn's den when he'd pulled her through the mirror and into the gateway. Now, his glance moved around the room, absorbing it and all of its contents. A gargoyle sat straight across from him, peering at him with its piercing eyes, as if it knew his secrets. A wild flower remained alive within a glass case atop the mantle, while odd trinkets and statues created strange displays throughout the room. He saw no sign of Taryn. Where was she? The answer to that question would have to wait; there was no time to linger. Taryn's daughter was not in the room, but it wouldn't be long before she returned. He could hear footfalls in another part of the house. He took the doppelganger's hand.

"We must leave like ghosts through the wall," he said, "but you will return here. You must take her place with the child and the rest of the world." Angus then told her how Susan was connected to Madison. The girl had shown her the mirror. "First, I will show you everything you need to know."

Clutching her hand, they merged with the southern wall of the room, walking in ghostly form and passing through wood, parting atoms and molecules, and moving like unseen swimmers. They arrived at the back of the house, away from any onlookers. Angus coached her on how to manifest her human-like form.

"See your flesh with your mind. Imagine it covering your bones. Consider how the heart beats, how it pumps blood. Feel that blood as it rushes through your veins."

Together, the two doppelgangers materialized, bringing flesh, blood, and bones together in an almost perfect display of human character. Hair shot from pores, eyes filled with color, and lines and wrinkles crisscrossed as features formed. Now, two ghostly figures became visible in the daylight, mocking the world and its inhabitants from where they stood, unnoticed.

Susan's double looked at her arms, her hands, and felt the smoothness of her face. Angus looked around him, reacquainting himself with the world and seeing it for the first time in what could have been decades. He noticed the dim sun, feeling the slight chill in the air against his unholy flesh. Hickory smoke from a distant fireplace drifted through the air, teasing his sense of smell and telling him autumn prevailed. He'd left this world in 1970. He wondered what year it was now. Still holding the key in one hand, he pointed with the other.

"Now, you must go back, back through the wall as I've shown you. There is much to learn and much to accomplish. Trust your instincts, your feelings, and your memories. Live her life. I will find you when I need you."

Angus watched as Susan's double dissipated, becoming a barely visible specter. She merged with the wall again and disappeared within the structure of the house, evaporating through matter like a ghost. He thought of finding Taryn, but she was of no importance now. He had the key, and he had his release. He would find the young woman, the long, blonde-haired beauty with the third eye. She would pay for the destruction of his home, for his being trapped within the gateway, but he would bide his time.

He strode through the daylight in the cleverest of disguises, a man returned from the corner of Hell and walking discreetly through the streets. The sight of parked automobiles told him significant time had passed. Cars looked nothing as they once did. He saw an inspection sticker in the window of a car. If the year was correct, then over forty-five years had passed.

He gazed into the car window. As far as his appearance was concerned, he appeared more refined, and not a single moment had passed. He looked the same age as he was in 1970, though he was no longer human. He'd inadvertently given up his old existence for this new one. How long would he exist as a doppelganger? He didn't know, but he had returned. Angus Marlowe laughed to himself as he walked back into the world once again.

Chapter Thirteen

~ Susan's Memories ~

Susan's doppelganger faded into a ghostly form and merged with the house's sturdy exterior, penetrating and walking through its thick, wooden wall, just as Angus had shown her. She was in the room with the mirror and all of the other outlandish artifacts.

She'd known automatically she was Susan. She was a doctor. Now, Susan Logan's memories flooded her mind, developing inside of her, making her one with her lost host. Angus mentioned Susan's connection to the girl. Yes, Susan was studying her, examining the child's ability with a microscopic eye. She, Susan, was a parapsychologist. She was also a psychiatrist, though secretly, her love of paranormal studies far outweighed her duty to her patients.

Susan's double sensed her host's excitability, her aggressive undertaking, and even her occasional unethical approach. She felt it all in the racing blood that coursed through the veins of this body. She looked at the Black Mirror, understanding the dark fascination that had so enraptured her host. She had known all about the Black Mirror.

Memories flashed through the doppelganger—she and the team, a night in Cedar Manor, the house burning to the ground. Susan had been the one who eventually located the mirror. The mystery of the Black Mirror was part of a greater enigma that hovered over her and the team for the past few years. Solving that mystery was their agenda, but she couldn't let that happen.

A list; she had told Madison to make a list of all the times she'd used her ability. Soft footfalls descended the stairs yet again. Madison was returning. She thought fast as the den door opened. The girl's puzzled expression gazed back at her.

"Where were you?" Madison said. "I heard something, so I came here to find you, but you were gone."

"Yes, dear, I apologize." Responding as Susan felt and sounded natural. "I was here, and then I used the bathroom quickly. I hope I didn't scare you." She spoke, smiled, and laughed lightly.

Madison looked around, her expression somewhat skeptical. "I heard a voice calling out for you. I thought I heard my mother."

Susan's natural reactions became the double's quick instincts. The words formed in her mind naturally. She tilted her head in apologetic sorrow.

"Oh, Madison, I'm so sorry. I'm afraid I could be to blame for that. I asked you to remember, to think back, and I hadn't realized that some of those memories may have been too much for you. My little assignment could have triggered your imagination, which allowed you to think you heard your mother's voice."

Madison focused on the ground, somehow deflated, but undeterred. "Yeah, but I heard her calling your name. My mother didn't know you."

Susan's double smiled. "You were thinking about your parents, especially your mother, as you wrote, a task I asked you to perform. I'm afraid it was your subconscious jumbling everything around in your head." Madison said nothing, her hand still clutching the door knob. "Madison, I am so sorry if I've caused you any pain by asking you to remember."

Madison shrugged and shook her head. "No, it's okay. You didn't, but I'm sure I heard someone calling you."

"Well, it's over now. So, would you like to show me how far you got with the list?"

Madison nodded, and Susan's double followed her back to the dining room. She knew instantly where Susan had been sitting because the chair was pulled away from the table where her briefcase still lay. She sat and looked at the legal pad Madison handed to her, skimming through the handwritten items. Included were brief notes of breaking dolls, vases, and windows, as well as moving chairs. Suddenly, the doppelganger began to remember why Susan was here, the conversation with Madison's father, picking her up from school, Susan opening the gateway. It all became clear.

"A job well done, Madison," she said, placing the legal pad back in Susan's briefcase. She glanced at her watch. It ticked in time with the world in which she now sat. It read four-o'clock. Charley had told her he would be home then. "That will be all for today. How about we call it a day?"

Madison smiled and nodded. "Thank you for picking me up and coming over."

"It's never a problem, Madison."

Just then, the door opened and Charley entered. She watched his facial expressions as he also thanked her. As far as she knew, neither he, nor Madison, had noticed anything unusual about her or anything that would make them think she wasn't Susan. After all, she was Susan, to a large extent.

"I'll call you soon," Charley said. "I'm anxious to meet the team."

The double assured him the feeling was mutual. She knew their names and saw their faces in her mind: Dylan, Brett, Sidney, and of course, the object of Angus' vengeance, Leah Leeds. She also knew about tomorrow's meeting.

"I'll see them all tomorrow, and then I'll let you know."

As they exchanged goodbyes, a cool draft swept past her. She turned her head and saw a moving outline. A ghostly figure quickly whisked through the room and away from her. What was it? Who was it, the girl's mother? Perhaps Madison had heard her mother's voice. Perhaps she dwelled right here in her own house with her family. Susan's double would tell Angus, but for now she walked out the door like a human being, and stepped back out into the world.

Everything about operating a vehicle was part of her existence. Susan knew her blue Chevy Malibu well, and so did her double. She unlocked the door, slumped into the driver's seat, keyed the ignition, and then drove away. As she drove, she wondered what would happen when all facets of Susan's life became imprinted on her like a stamp. Would Susan wither away and die within the gateway? Angus had said she would survive the transition into that world because she had entered with the key. Would she ever gain release as Angus had? What would happen then?

Her curiosity continued even as Susan's memories, habits, and thoughts became her own, a process that unfolded more as time passed. At some point, it would all be complete. She would live her life as Dr. Susan Logan.

It was different for her than it was for Angus. He had died and been reborn within the gateway. He was free to resume his old life, but in a new and unusual way. She was born as a result of Susan's entering the gateway. She would coexist with the real Susan, a thief of her memories, her past, her present, and her entire life.

Now, she drove through every twist and turn of King's Haven, knowing the winding streets well, as transplanted memories thrived upon what was once a blank slate. She knew exactly which house was Susan's, the immense, two-story palatial home with copper-toned bricks, gable windows, and lampposts flanking the walkway. An image of the house's interior formed in her mind as she found the right key and turned it in the lock of the front door.

It was just as she'd seen it, although she'd never known it. The plush carpeting, the wide, three-piece sectional, and the fireplace set in the towering marble hearth. She would think of the best plan to approach the team. She would also wait for Angus. For now, she enjoyed the comfort of home as she became Susan Logan.

* * * *

Something wasn't right about Susan. Not only did Madison know, but she could see it. She knew what she'd heard. Maybe it wasn't her mother's voice, but she'd definitely heard someone call out Susan's name. When she walked into the den the first time, Susan wasn't there.

Madison turned around, shut the door, and searched in the rooms upstairs. No one had been there. She'd picked up the phone to call her father, but then she'd heard movement in the den downstairs. She hung up the phone and ran back to the den.

When she reopened the door, there was Susan. She'd been walking toward the door to leave the room. Madison had asked where she'd been, and Susan gave the strangest response— that she'd used the bathroom and quickly returned. Madison sensed it was a lie.

Madison had passed the downstairs bathroom when she left the den the first time. The door was slightly open. She hadn't seen her inside. Why would Susan lie? Where had she been? Then, as Madison insisted she'd heard her mother's voice, Susan tried to make her think it was just her imagination, the result of jumbled memories in her mind. For a moment, Madison had assumed it was possible, but she'd grown accustomed to the fact her mother was never coming back. She didn't just hear what she'd been hoping to hear.

Madison sensed from across the table that something was slightly off with Susan, as if she were hiding something. Madison couldn't tell what it was. Maybe she was imagining it, but Susan seemed to walk differently, slower somehow. She didn't talk as much after leaving the den, and soon afterward, she seemed in a hurry to leave. Madison didn't tell her father about the episode. She didn't want to alarm him. However, she mentioned Susan's slightly different demeanor after seeing the mirror, and how much quieter she had been afterwards.

"Yeah, it has that effect on people," he agreed. "Madison, the only reason I've kept that thing in this house is because of you. I know you're hoping your mother will return someday, but I want Susan and her team to find out what they can, and soon. When they're done, I want rid of the mirror. I never want to see that thing again."

Madison said nothing. She was growing up and arriving at the same conclusion. She thought about the vision she had when she'd first gone into the den. The image of the mirror opening flashed in her mind. Two Susan's stood side by side, and then the pair became one. Madison was convinced Susan had gone into the mirror. Something was not right. The truth dangled out of her reach. It existed, but Madison couldn't make any sense of it.

* * * *

She awoke on the cold, hard ground of another world. Her eyes fluttered and caught the blueness of a strange firmament, but it was not the sky she knew so well. Above, it bubbled with billowing swollen masses that were not clouds. A bird she'd never seen before cawed and flew overhead. She reached and touched the ground beneath her. This was no dream. This was real.

She rose quickly from the ground and shrieked. It was the type of yell let loose upon waking from a nightmare, but she didn't wake. Unrelieved terror pounded her heart against her chest and in her ears. She turned this way and that, her head jerking from left to right. Nothing about her current surroundings looked familiar.

She gazed around her, absorbing a setting she'd never seen before. Mist rose from the ground and surrounded her. Solid, craggy rock formations imitated mountains like strange doubles. The sky and atmosphere were awash in a deep indigo that reminded her of a quiet, wintery dawn. Yet it wasn't quiet here.

Strange birds cawed from above. Voices in agony cried out for reprieve, startling her into twists and turns, searching for what she couldn't see.

"Hello?" she called. No one answered, not the voices or the birds. Only the echo of her own voice reverberated around her. "Somebody help!"

Her echo rebounded. "Help...help...help...help..."

She tried to clear her mind and remember. Madison; she'd been with Madison. She'd gone into Taryn's den, and then... She opened the gateway. She'd followed her own image through the Black Mirror and into this. The unfamiliar world around her must be the realm beyond the gateway. Her heart pounded harder. The image she'd chased had disappeared into the fog, but someone else came closer. A man. He'd walked right up to her. She felt as though she would die from fright. It was him—Angus Marlowe.

She remembered his face, the beard, the mustache, and those sinister eyes. He'd grabbed a hold of her, and that was the last thing she recalled. She was alone now. She could feel it. He had trapped her here. The panic exploded inside of her, loosening her muscles, her bowels. She ran her fingers through her hair, raking it away from her forehead. She had to escape. She had to make her way back to the entrance, back to the Black Mirror.

Where was the key? She turned her head frantically in every direction and searched around her. She dropped to the ground, exploring its cold hardness with her hands and finding nothing. The handheld mirror was gone. Angus had taken it. She rose from the ground, gripping the sides of her head. Her breath surged in fear and anger. She did the only thing she could—she ran in search of the portal.

She moved and flailed her arms in front of her, hoping to part the misty fog, but the billowing whiteness engulfed her. Flashes of lightning flickered overhead, giving her only intermittent glimpses of shadows. She thrust her hands outward, feeling around her with pushing and pressing motions, hoping to touch something hard. Her hands touched nothing and fell through the air around her.

"No! Help me!" Her pleas went unheard.

She ran in all directions, failing to find the other side of the Black Mirror. The portal was nowhere, and what could she do without the key? Her mind slipped away as her failure to wake from this incessant nightmare became apparent. Then, she stopped. She was a psychiatrist. She needed to compose herself and think. To panic was to remain trapped here forever. As a parapsychologist, she needed to investigate, but a large part of her knew the likelihood of her dying within this realm was greater than being rescued.

The mists seemed to diminish around her, rolling and remaining low to the ground. She looked around and noticed she'd arrived at some sort of vast wasteland, a clearing of some type. It was an empty void, absent of the craggy rocks, birds, or the rough ground on which she'd woke. It seemed a calm, peaceful vortex, where the mists caressed rather than engulfed, rolling like soft waves at her ankles.

Something shimmered in the atmosphere. Some small remnant of light grew larger in its attempts to appear. It was a vision, though not a psychic one. It had an appearance, like a mirage. She moved closer to it, until the image became clear. It was a moving image, like watching a film. In front of her, scenes of her life were depicted as though on a screen.

She saw herself as a little girl with pigtails, wearing a white and red dress her mother had made for her. Her father pushed her on a swing. The child looked up at a darkening sky as the rain began to pour down in sheets.

"Time to go inside, Susie," her father said. She begged for more time. He shook his head. "I'm afraid not. We'll get wet, and then your mother will have my head if you get sick."

The old swing swayed behind her as she leaped from it and followed her father inside. Another scene showed her in bed, feverish from the chicken pox.

"Bob, we need to get her to the doctor," her mother had said. "Her fever is too high."

Suddenly, the scene changed, and she was older, still in high-school. She'd been helping her mother prepare dinner. She'd been rushing, and as she turned to strain a boiling pot of pasta, she bumped into her mother and dropped the pot. Boiling water had splashed everywhere, scalding her mother's legs and feet. The guilt had tormented her for years afterward. A tear rolled down her cheek as she watched the scenes of her life play out before her.

Then, she saw Mark. There had been no one like him. He was her first love. She saw herself clutching him tightly, knowing she'd never see him again, and she hadn't, until she'd laid eyes on Roman Hadley. She saw herself in college, dating a few young men whom she later jilted, choosing to go her own way and throw herself into her studies. Another scene showed her crying on the bed in her dorm room. There had been no word from Mark.

She watched herself graduate from college quite a few times. She watched the transition of age from one accomplishment to the other. Then, she saw herself as Dr. Susan Logan. The appearance of University Hospital changed through the years as did the visions. She saw her mother in a casket, and then her father. She moved boxes into her home in King's Haven.

Dean Collier appeared. He was the patient she'd failed. She couldn't stop him from committing suicide. She'd spent months with him before he'd lodged a bullet in his temple. Later, she studied parapsychology in secret, moonlighting to achieve her degree without the hospital's knowledge. There was Tracy Kimball, another person she failed. She saw it all over again—Tracy's drinking, the poltergeist activity in her house, being trapped in the basement with the team, and the car chase that ended in her death.

Why couldn't she have saved these people? Why had she failed them? The mirage showed her an explosion. She remembered it well, the one she and Agent Wiley had narrowly escaped. Roman Hadley's dying face appeared, the same face she'd last seen years before—Mark's. Her tears continued.

Then the scenes played out faster—Cedar Manor, Brett changing into a wolf, that thing in the sky at Leah's graduation, hypnotizing Dylan. The mirage showed her one last vision. She saw the fascination on her face, one she hadn't realized existed. She was gazing into the Black Mirror, and then the vision faded.

Why was she seeing scenes from her life play out before her? Was she dying? She wasn't dead. As a doctor, she could feel her heartbeat. Was there a message in what she'd just witnessed? Again, creeping hysteria threatened her sanity. She thought of her life, her work, the team, and the tears became a form of release. She had to escape, but how?

The thought of another failure struck her. Where was Angus Marlowe? Had he escaped through the gateway? Had she unleashed an evil spirit upon the world outside? She looked around her for a sign, a clue, but there was nothing, only the fog of an uncertain world.

Chapter Fourteen

~ The Ghostly Witness ~

Taryn had watched as Madison opened the door, her eyes roving around the room at nothing. She could see suspicion on her daughter's face, that narrowing of the eyes that said she was unconvinced. She watched as Madison walked over to the Black Mirror and stared into it, not with the same fascination she and Susan had possessed, but with deep distrust. She hadn't witnessed what had happened to Susan, but Maddy's third eye showed her something. The girl's innate psychic ability revealed the Black Mirror as the culprit for what she'd heard.

Now, Maddy stared into the mirror with vengeance in her eyes. Taryn thought about what would happen if that anger was unleashed. She wanted to call out to her, to reveal herself, and tell her to get away from the mirror, but she couldn't—not yet. She thought of the trauma Maddy would feel, and the incurable disbelief she herself would have to confirm. Now was not the time. She had to handle it the right way.

She watched Maddy's face and her careful steps around the room as her eyes searched for something she couldn't see. Taryn knew she'd heard her. Having heard her mother's voice, she would set out to prove it.

Taryn moved quickly around her daughter. The girl whisked around, as if she'd felt something, yet she saw nothing. Madison wasn't seeing her because her third eye was not as developed as Leah Leeds'. Maddy carefully looked around as she walked back to the door, eying the room as if monsters would jump out when she left. After lingering for a moment, Madison closed the door behind her.

Taryn's intuition told her two things. Madison would search the house, looking for Susan. She would even find her car still parked outside. The second thing was just as sure as the first. Taryn knew the portal would open. The glass would disappear once again, and Angus Marlowe would walk through the portal, back into the world again. That was his plan. He'd been imprisoned within the gateway, awaiting someone with the key to release him. Susan had the key. Angus would be free, and Taryn was not about to let him harm her daughter.

She glared vehemently into the mirror, waiting for him to return. She felt almost sure he would be able to see her, even in the ghostly form. Soon he would walk through the portal, and when it happened, she would hide from him, yet remain close enough so she could watch Madison. Her eyes didn't move from the mirror, but unlike before, it had no hold over her. She was in control. She stared into the sleek blackness, waiting.

Slowly, it began to ripple in waves. She saw the three-dimensional effect as the glass vanished, and the blackness elongated into an entryway. A figure came forward. She recognized his lanky height, his familiar stride, and his beard and mustache. It was Angus, and then another figure stepped forward from behind him. Susan, but it wasn't Susan. It was her doppelganger.

They stood within the frame, ready to walk back into the world. Still in the ghostly form, Taryn merged with the wall behind her, but thinly under the surface so she was able to see and hear. The view was sketchy, and the sound was slightly muffled, but it would do. Angus looked around the room, searching for her and her daughter, until something distracted him.

"We must leave like ghosts through the wall," he said to Susan's double. Then, he instructed the double to return to this room. Which wall would they pass through? What if they saw her? Taryn had been ready to move fast.

He showed the double how to undertake the ghostly form. Through her translucent view, Taryn watched them fade into nothing. She saw them make ghostly imprints on the southern wall. They had moved outside, to the back of the house. Taryn's instinct told her to remain hidden in the wall, and there she stayed, watching as Susan's double walked back through the wall and into the den. She watched her every move.

Madison returned to the den, distracting Taryn. She watched helplessly as her daughter spoke to the doppelganger, not completely falling for her falsifications. It was an immature masquerade, one that hadn't been perfected yet. Her little girl was far from stupid. Taryn could hear the skepticism in Maddy's voice.

"I heard a voice calling out for you," Madison told her. "I thought I heard my mother."

Taryn closed her eyes at hearing those words. Madison had heard her. Now, there would be nothing to stop the girl's incessant curiosity or her adamant suspicion. The double tried to convince her it was all in her head, that the assignment had caused the resurgence of memories which provoked her imagination. The double was cunning, a Black Mirror image of Susan Logan. If this thing was a doppelganger, a copy of the original, then maybe the real Susan was just as cunning. Maybe to the double, the cunning streak was a natural instinct, a reproduction of what the host already possessed.

"Susan" asked to see the list Maddy made, and together, they walked out of the den. Taryn followed them. She stood a safe distance away from the double, but listened to her every word. Within minutes, Charley returned from work. As the double was leaving, Taryn moved around her and watched her head follow her ghostly outline. She could see her, but just how much, Taryn couldn't be sure. She watched the double walk out the doorway and into the real world, perpetrating the ultimate subterfuge that she was a human being, but then again, Taryn was guilty of the same transgression. Charley noticed nothing. Madison told her father about Susan's strange behavior, but failed to fill in all of the details. It proved Madison was watching, waiting to investigate on her own.

Taryn knew what she had to do now. She had to tell the paranormal investigators what happened to their leader. Angus had said anyone who entered the gateway with the key would not die, but Susan would remain trapped there forever, unless the team helped her. Taryn didn't know where any of them lived. Susan's double had told Charley of a meeting tomorrow. She would make it back to room 208 for that meeting. She would reveal everything to the investigators about how Angus Marlowe had returned to this world as a doppelganger, and how an infiltrator sat quietly among them.

Chapter Fifteen

~ Deciphering the Tome ~

It was just after dinner when Paul Leeds got a call from his daughter. The tone of her voice was reluctant, skeptical.

"Dad, it's me," she said, breathing into the phone. "The team and I are on our way to see you, if that's okay. Although, I'd like to say I'm not completely on board with this, but it's your decision, Dad."

When he asked what it was about, she handed the phone to Sidney.

"Paul, how are ya, buddy? It's Sidney."

Paul was fine. The tragedy and the trauma he'd experienced in Cedar Manor were part of his past, a past that he'd come to understand from a hindsight point of view. Now, he rarely thought back to that part of his past, but when he did, it was to examine it from a studious perspective. The mental and emotional scars he'd suffered as a victim had long since healed.

"Sidney," he responded. "So, what is my daughter trying to hide from me now?"

Sidney got straight to the point. "Well, this concerns our excursion to Cedar Manor a few years ago." Paul remained silent. "Do you remember when we asked you and Leah if either of you remembered seeing a black mirror? We had discovered that it was the missing counterpart to the gold-gilded mirror."

"Yes," Paul said. "The black tome had described the gilded mirror as being a 'Porta un abyssus,' a gateway to Hell."

"That's right," Sidney confirmed. "It was unknown what happened to the Black Mirror, until now. We've found it, or at least, Susan did."

"Why didn't my daughter tell me?" Paul said, sighing as he took a seat at his kitchen table.

"Well, you know how she is."

Paul heard movement on the other end, and Sidney muttered 'ouch' under his breath.

"She worries about you."

"Let me guess, Sid. You want me to finish deciphering the black tome."

Paul remembered he'd never finished decoding the Latin words in the large black tome that had belonged to Angus Marlowe. Cedar Manor had burned to the ground that night, and he had been hospitalized. Afterward, he, Leah, and the rest of the team had put Cedar Manor behind them. They had all moved on, and Sidney never mentioned the tome again.

"If it's a problem, we'll find another interpreter." Sidney's attempt at appeasement was well-crafted, but it did nothing to conceal the hint of desperation in his voice.

Paul and Leah had never encountered a black mirror while living in Cedar Manor, only the gold-gilded mirror that obsessed, and later possessed, his wife Janet. Paul had since wanted to continue translating the tome, but he'd been well aware Leah would not have allowed him to do it. Besides, he had no intention of drudging it all up again. What his daughter failed to understand was that if something concerned her, it concerned him, especially if it involved Cedar Manor.

"Don't be ridiculous, Sidney," he said. "Tell my daughter I'll be fine. I'm a big boy now. When should I expect you all?"

"We were hoping to be there within twenty minutes."

"I'll see you then," he said, and disconnected.

Now, hours had passed as they sat around his kitchen table, watching him read and jot down notes on a small tablet. They'd filled him in on Susan's discovery, and how they'd all just come from the shop of a man who sold strange and unusual artifacts. The man had kept the mirror all these years, and then sold it to a young woman who'd gone missing. By the look of worry on Leah's face, he guessed there was much more that they weren't telling him.

Paul turned the delicate pages carefully, using his magnifying glass to make the withering page and the riddled words even larger. The last time he'd seen the book, he'd placed its origin at approximately the late eighteenth-century. Time had been civil to the book. The now fragile pages were once strong sheets of parchment. The printing had faded, but with the use of the glass, he deciphered words one at a time.

The tome described another realm within the gateway, a world beyond this one. He had deciphered that much when studying the book a few years ago, relating his theory of the 'gateway to Hell,' and citing the word '*abyssus*.' It was the Latin word for abyss, which was a reference in early times to a blackened void many believed to be Hell itself. He looked up at them and spoke whenever he arrived at a conclusion.

"It's written here that both of those mirrors are portals to an alternate realm," he said. "We talked about that years ago, remember?"

"Yes," Sidney said. "We've deduced that one of the mirrors is an entrance. The other is an exit, but we're unsure of which is which."

"One of those mirrors is gone, destroyed in the Cedar Manor fire," Leah reminded them.

"So, was the gold-gilded mirror an exit or an entrance?" Dylan interjected.

"I'm not sure that it matters," Paul said. "If they are both portals, they both lead to this alternate realm, this unearthly territory that's said to exist behind the glass."

"What about the entity that reached out from the gold mirror the night of our investigation in Cedar Manor?" Brett demanded. An awkward silence lingered between them. "We rarely talk about it, but that thing leapt out from the mirror and touched Cory Chase. It was trying to escape. Does that mean the gold-gilded mirror was just that, an exit?"

"I think you could be right on that, Brett," Paul said. "The tome is telling me the Black Mirror leads to this realm and will open with the key. The key is the handheld mirror."

"I knew it," Leah exclaimed.

"We'd suspected as much," Dylan said. "That's why Susan is going to compare the handheld mirror to the Black Mirror." Dylan looked at his watch. "In fact, she may have done that already. We're meeting tomorrow, but I may call her tonight."

Paul sat back in his chair. "I believe the mirror was primarily used in forms of witchcraft. The tome explains that when a traveler enters the gateway, something comes forward from the depths and is released into the world."

"What is released into the world?" Leah looked puzzled.

Paul continued to study the page in front of him, squinting one eye while widening the other through the magnifying glass. Two words stood out to him—*duplex spiritus*. He wrote them down on the tablet, and then held it up to the team.

"You see these two words?" He pointed to the tablet. "They mean 'double spirit.' I'm not exactly sure what that means, but it's definitely what is conjured up from this realm or abyss. I know witches were said to perform 'transmutation,' where they would take on another form and display themselves in two different places simultaneously. It's possible the double spirit is the traveler's other half, one assigned to walk wherever the traveler chooses. I notice a word recurring, and it's the same in Latin as it is in English, the word, 'walker.'"

"Double walker," Dylan pondered.

"I think there's a German word for that," Sidney said.

"Doppelganger," Brett said. They all looked at him, realizing it would be Brett who would touch so easily on such a paranormal phenomenon. "The word is 'doppelganger.'"

"So, when a person enters the Black Mirror," Sidney surmised, "their doppelganger forms within the gateway?"

Leah's voice spoke softly, contemplating what they'd just learned. "Then that doppelganger is released into the world."

Paul noticed his daughter's eyes as they met those of her cohorts simultaneously. He wasn't being told the entire story, but he would get it out of them or Susan, if necessary. His daughter was failing to mention something, something she didn't want him to know. Suddenly, he realized what it was. He turned to her.

"Really, Leah, did you think I wouldn't figure it out?" She closed her eyes. "So, this has to do with Angus Marlowe?" The other investigators diverted their eyes. Their lack of responses was all the confirmation he needed.

143

"He disappeared, along with that mirror, in 1970," Paul said.

"We can't really speculate what happened to Angus," Dylan responded. "We don't know. The mirror had been in a shop for over forty-five years, and the handheld had been in the police station since 2009."

"Until it was stolen in 2009," Brett concluded. "That leads us to wonder who could've taken the handheld mirror from the police evidence room without being noticed and why?"

"Let me get this straight," Paul began. "Do you all think Angus Marlowe entered the gateway?"

"That's a pretty big leap to make at this time," Dylan said.

"Then where the hell could he have gone all these years, unless to Hell itself? Is it a coincidence that this young woman also went missing after acquiring the mirror?"

"That's what we're investigating," Dylan replied.

Paul didn't like what he was hearing, what he was reading, and the pieces coming together in his mind. Though much of this sounded crazy, Angus Marlowe was by all accounts, an occultist. Paul pointed this out, as well as the fact he hadn't totally disbelieved all of the medieval accounts of witchery and occultism.

"Dad, he was a failed occultist," Leah said. "All he ended up doing was killing women."

Paul said nothing. He looked back at his notes, and then told them the stipulation of the key. If a person didn't have the key upon entering, their death would be assured, and the doppelganger would exist without its host. A certain foreboding feeling crept through him, but he wouldn't mention it to Leah at this moment. If she thought he was too involved, he wouldn't be able to study the situation on his own. He played it cool, while a thousand fears unwound in his head.

"I'd like to keep this overnight, if I may. I want to decipher as much of it as I can."

"Absolutely," Sidney said. "That's why we need you."

"What you've told us so far is a great deal," Dylan added.

"Dad, just don't get too overwhelmed in this." Leah pleaded with him.

"I won't sweetie. I promise." He spoke to placate her, a tactic that would end the subject.

He also promised to call them tomorrow, and now he watched them leave. Paul knew damn well the mystery surrounding Cedar Manor and Angus Marlowe hadn't died. He sat down at the table with the tome in front of him, daydreaming into the past. He recalled how enamored Janet had been of the gold-gilded mirror, and how her personality had changed. The brassy, bossy, self-absorbed woman had redirected her absorption to a clear glass set within an ornate, golden frame. She was enraptured. The sound of her grating voice had been heard less and less. Eventually, she became lost, staring into the mirror for hours on end. The look on her face portrayed a haunted soul seemingly trapped within the shell she'd become.

Had the gateway beckoned to Janet? Had someone tried to lure her into this opposite realm? Who? Angus Marlowe, or the dark force that no doubt dwelled within it? He would probably never know the answers to those questions. What happened to Janet was in the past, and he could do nothing about it now. However, there was something Paul could do if his daughter was in danger because of this Black Mirror. He would protect her at all costs.

* * * *

Sidney drove the van while Dylan rode shotgun, and Brett and Leah sat in the middle seats. They discussed everything Paul had discovered in the tome.

"I knew he would figure out what we weren't telling him," Leah said. "Of course, he began to get excited. I knew this would happen."

"Yeah, but Leah he brought up some good points," Brett said.

"Yes, he did," Dylan agreed. "Like connecting the disappearances of both Angus and Taryn Page."

"He also speculated Angus could've gone into the gateway in 1970," Sidney said. "Yet we have no proof of that. If Angus entered the gateway, he obviously didn't have the handheld mirror with him. The police discovered it in Cedar Manor in 2008. So, if he didn't have the key, he would've died within this mysterious realm, correct?"

"Maybe, but Paul said a doppelganger born without the presence of the key could exist without its host." Brett said.

"So, this man in the mirror Madison described could be Angus Marlowe's doppelganger," Leah guessed.

"We can't rule that out, Leah," Dylan agreed. "Right now, we need to touch base with Susan, find out about the meeting with Madison, and tell her about Paul's findings."

Dylan selected Susan's number from his phone and dialed her with one touch. Then, he placed the call on speakerphone. It rang four times before she answered.

"This is Susan." Her voice sounded softer than usual and somewhat calmer.

"It's Dylan," he said. "We're all in the van. We've just left Paul's house, and we're taking everyone home."

He gave her a brief rundown of their visit to Enigma's & More. Yes, the shopkeeper was a collector who admitted selling Taryn the Black Mirror. They would fill her in on the details at the meeting tomorrow.

"Paul gave us an interesting interpretation of the tome's words," Dylan said. "Apparently, there's a gateway beyond the mysterious glass of both mirrors. Much of this strange legend has to do with doppelgangers."

They all heard a silence on the other end.

"This gets more and more interesting, doesn't it?" Sidney broke the silence.

"Yes, it does," Susan said. "I can't wait to hear more."

"You sound like you have a cold," Leah observed. "I hope you're not coming down with something."

"No, I'm alright," Susan replied. "Just a little tired is all."

Now, Dylan got straight to the reason for his call. "So, did you get a chance to compare the handheld mirror with the Black Mirror?"

"I did," she said. "I'm afraid nothing happened."

Leah and Brett glanced at each other. Dylan looked to Sidney, who kept his eyes focused on the road, but his facial expression was blank, contemplating something unreadable. It was not the answer they were expecting to hear, especially now, since the tome revealed the handheld mirror was in fact, the key to the gateway.

"Maybe we should all try it when we get the opportunity," Sidney said.

"Yes, well, we'll talk about that later," Susan replied. "Are we still on for tomorrow?"

The investigators looked at each other again.

"Yes," Dylan answered. "We'll see you at three-o'clock."

"Until then," she said.

"Get some rest," Leah advised.

Dylan hung up, and then turned to Sidney. "She doesn't sound like herself."

"God," Sidney said, "I hope she's not coming down with something. You all know how bitchy she gets when she's sick."

"Here, here," Brett agreed.

"We also need to meet Madison and Charley," Leah suggested. "I want to know as much as I can about Taryn. After all, she was reading my book. Maybe I can glean something by holding her copy."

"I agree," Sidney said. "It's essential we meet Madison. She's only eleven, and those memories of when she was small are still fresh. Child psychics maintain memories for years, but the sooner we talk to her the better."

"We'll settle all of it tomorrow," Dylan said. "I have a feeling that tomorrow, we'll know a lot more than we do right now."

They drove on in silence.

* * * *

Later that evening, Paul sat behind his desktop, researching whatever he could find on doppelgangers. He hadn't discovered much, just a consistent repetition of the word's definition. Doppelgangers were said to be an exact double of a particular person, but more specifically, the spirit form of that person, often achieving physical shape. A spirit in the flesh. He scrolled through the pages of links and articles on the subject. Doppelgangers were alleged to be born within some opposite, alternate realm, much like the gateway beyond the Black Mirror.

He read through stories and legends, but none delved deep enough into the past. It was folklore and ancient tales that proffered more knowledge on subjects such as these. Medieval societies were more prone to believe in the occult and less reliant on science as the ultimate vindicator. Paul knew science could not explain many things.

Now, alone and unseen behind closed doors, he went to his attic and searched through the numerous volumes of text and reference books he'd amassed over the years. The attic itself was a small library, closed away and hidden from the world for his sole usage and refuge. His fingers ran down an assemblage of books as his eyes quickly caught the titles. He stopped on a thick, black and gold volume. He pulled the book from the shelf and read its title *Mysteries of the Dark World.*

He'd read part of the book when he was in college. Years later, he'd thought to try and research some of the things he'd experienced in Cedar Manor, but the bigger part of him chose not to indulge in what could have been detrimental to his recovery. He'd left the book alone.

Now, his finger browsed down through the table of contents, stopping at the German word he was searching for—*Doppelganger*. He read of its origins, as well as many more stories from around the world and throughout history. He discovered connections between the doppelganger and subjects like the occult and witchcraft. Many cases remained unexplained. He remembered reading some of this information years ago as a younger man in his twenties. Now, Paul sought far more urgently than he would have for academic study or paranormal fascination. He sought something specific—how to destroy a doppelganger.

Chapter Sixteen

~ Who Are You? ~

Taryn arrived at the university, minutes before three-o'clock. She was going to show up at the meeting like any other human being, tell them her story, and then tell them exactly what happened to Susan. She reached the top of the stairs in Levin Hall and walked through the hallway, her eyes searching for room 208. When she found it, the door was slightly open. She moved quickly to the other side of the door and peered inside. Only the three male investigators sat around the table. Taryn wanted to get to the investigators before Susan's double arrived. Thankfully, she hadn't yet, but Leah was not in the room either. Not only did Taryn want her to hear every word of what she had to say, but she wanted Leah to see her, this time, in the flesh.

She would wait a few minutes and give Leah time to arrive, but she worried about the double showing up before her. She would confuse the situation even more. Taryn would have to convince the investigators the woman was not really Susan, but it could be a difficult task. The double already possessed a wide range of Susan's memories. What if they didn't believe her, and the fake Susan reported back to Angus, who then sought out her daughter? If she had a mere moment alone with the investigators, she could alert them beforehand, and allow them to watch the double's performance for themselves.

She heard footsteps coming down the hallway. She moved a few feet away and hid behind the door of another room. Slowly, she poked her head around the side of the door and peered at the figure walking down the hallway. Her long, blonde hair hung down around her shoulders in wavy curls. Again, Taryn marveled at how her face seemed perfect. She was just about to come out from behind the door, stop her, and ask to join them. Leah would probably recognize her as the ghostly figure that moved through the wall, but she would explain that it was imperative she speak with them.

Then, other footsteps echoed from the direction of the stairwell. She looked past Leah. It was her, Susan's double. She traipsed, yards behind Leah, her face blank, her feet hastening as though she was late. Taryn stuck her head back behind the door. What would she do now? She would wait, but either way, she was going to expose everything. She had no choice.

* * * *

Leah heard footsteps behind her. She turned her head and looked. It was Susan. She was the last to arrive. Strange, she always arrived first. She must not be feeling well. Leah held the door open for her, and they stepped inside together.

"I'm sorry if I'm a little late," Susan said. "Today has been hectic."

"Not a problem," Dylan said. "It's exactly three-o'clock."

Dylan sat at his end of the long conference table. Leah watched as Susan hesitated before sitting at the other end, the seat that was typically hers. She thought of how Susan had lumbered down the hallway, as if she'd hurt her foot. Now, she seemed to step with a slow inhibition. In a way, she did look sick. There was something about Susan's face Leah couldn't pinpoint, like an indistinct imperfection made visible by her apparent fatigue. They all looked at Susan and waited for her to begin.

She looked back at them and paused before speaking. "So, team, as I said, no luck with the mirror. I held it up, right in front of the glass. I waited. There was nothing, no ripples, no waves, no movement of any kind."

Susan's nonchalant response sounded as if she were unaffected by the lack of results. She wasn't frustrated, yet fiercely determined, as she would be under usual circumstances. Leah remembered the same woman who'd held a press conference just recently, exposing a conspiracy that had been taking place in Green Valley for years.

"Then we need to try it again," Dylan said. "According to Paul's findings, the mirror leads to a gateway, an alternate realm, as he put it. If that's where Taryn Page is, we need to help find her."

Dylan filled Susan in on everything Paul had deciphered from the tome, including the necessity of the key. "You did bring the handheld mirror with you, didn't you?"

There was that hesitation again. Susan seemed distracted.

"Well, no, I left it at home," she said. "I didn't think we'd need it for the meeting."

"So, when can we meet Madison and Charley?" Sidney said. "We should get their consent before trying to open the gateway. The mirror is in their house."

Susan's response was quick. "I don't think that would be a good idea right now."

Instinctively, the investigators looked at each other. Susan quickly explained as she took the legal pad from her purse and showed it to them.

"This is the list Madison comprised for me. Her situation is much more complex than I'd originally assumed. The level of anger and impatience in this child is tremendous. I want to take a little more time to study her and her abilities. I also feel she remains deeply traumatized by the loss of her mother. I think she's finally realized her mother is not coming back, and that she may be dead by now. Trying to access this supposed gateway could jeopardize her situation even more. It might even set her back. As a result, I wanted to propose we suspend our investigation, at least temporarily."

"What?" The investigators uttered the same word simultaneously.

"What about finding Taryn?" Brett said, but Dylan interrupted before Susan could answer the question.

"Susan, if you think it's a problem for Madison, let me talk to Charley. I'll ask if we could remove the mirror and investigate on our own without Madison being present."

Susan fidgeted restlessly in her chair. Dylan's eyes narrowed in scrutiny. Leah watched the exchange.

"What about Angus Marlowe?" Leah said. "If there's any chance he is who Madison saw, we need to—"

"Leah, there is absolutely no shred of evidence that Angus Marlowe walked into the gateway years ago," Susan retorted. "Nor any proof he walked out of it since then. I think our investigation can wait until I help Madison first."

A vision interrupted Leah's sight. She blinked her eyes and shook her head, yet the image remained. Her third eye was projecting. She looked at the woman who sat next to her, the woman she'd known for years, the woman who helped her through a tumultuous resurgence of childhood memories and chaotic dreams that left her sleepless. Leah saw double. She saw two Susan's, one sitting, and one standing. The Susan standing was running her fingers through her hair, the look of desperation on her face. She looked once again at the sitting Susan, the one who'd stared at them, fidgeted, and now averted her eyes. Leah watched as the two Susan's merged together to make one.

Leah had seen many things in her young life, and she knew exactly what the vision meant. She leaped up from the chair and slammed her hands down on the table in front of her. She stared straight at the woman, beholding the imposter her third eye had unveiled.

"Who are you?" Leah shouted louder than she expected. "Tell me, who the hell are you?"

The imposter's eyes grew wide. The other three investigators rose quickly from their chairs and rallied behind Leah. They'd noticed something, but said nothing.

"Who are you? What have you done with Susan?" Leah persisted.

The double quickly sprang from the chair and ran. She flung the door open wide and fled room 208, leaving Susan's briefcase behind. Brett, Dylan, and Sidney ran after her. Leah followed them out into the hallway and found there was no one but the four of them. Susan's double was gone, vanished into thin air like a ghost, though they hadn't witnessed it. They turned to each other, whipping their heads around the hallway in confusion.

"Leah, what did you see?" Dylan said.

She shepherded them back inside, and then locked the door behind her. They sat back down, staring at the empty chair where the double had been seated. Leah told them about the vision of two Susan's.

"I saw her," she said, her voice quivering. "I saw the real her. She was lost, frightened. Whoever it was that sat in that chair was not Susan. I'm sure of it. The vision showed the two of them merging, becoming one."

"Doppelganger." Brett said.

Dylan interlocked his fingers together. "It looks like Susan opened the gateway and entered."

Sidney took a deep breath before speaking. "So, Susan is what, trapped?"

"Inside the Black Mirror." Leah finished the thought.

"What are we going to do?" Dylan's voice sounded the alarm.

"Get her back," Sidney said. "That's what we'll do."

Panic stricken faces stared at each other. Then, heads turned in every direction as a sudden draft swept the room.

"Look!" Leah pointed to one of the empty chairs that surrounded the table.

They hadn't needed a third eye to see what was in front of them. Within the chair, the outline of a figure grew more and more visible by the passing of seconds. Shock gripped the quartet and gasps erupted from them. Was it Susan's doppelganger taunting them?

Leah watched the figure take shape. She saw the outline of a torso, a head, and then hair that shaped an invisible face. She identified a pair of eyes as they slowly appeared. They were there, two orbs turning greener and brighter. The mass of hair turned ash-blonde, and the color of flesh filled in what was once empty space.

A young woman now sat in the chair, her green eyes pleading in the midst of their surprise. It was her, the ghost Leah had seen pass through the wall at the last meeting. Only this woman was no ghost; she was a doppelganger. She materialized into flesh and bone right before their eyes.

"It's you." Leah was breathless, her heart pounding percussion. She remembered the picture in Dylan's phone. "Who are you?"

"I'm so sorry," the woman said in a soft voice. "I didn't mean to scare you all. I'm here to help you. I'm Taryn Page."

The shock subdued them to silence.

* * * *

When the meeting in room 208 began, Taryn had merged with the surrounding wall and eavesdropped, a feat of which she was well accustomed. She'd seen Susan's double dash out the door and into the hallway, where she faded back into the ghostly form and evaded her pursuers. Taryn followed her, but Susan's double had moved fast and disappeared within the walls. She was gone.

The investigators stood in the hallway, seeing nothing, but now they knew. She followed them back into the room and sat down in a chair at the long conference table.

She had to do it this way. If she showed them what she was, rather than telling them, the story would be easier to explain. Once they had the opportunity to see it for themselves, there would be no doubts about what she was telling them. So, there in room 208, she materialized before their already bewildered eyes.

"It's you," Leah said, recognizing her. "Who are you?"

She spoke softly and apologized quickly, so as not to alarm them. "I didn't mean to scare you all. I'm here to help you. I'm Taryn Page."

Gasps of disbelief reached a crescendo of collective shock. They knew her name well; she'd expected as much.

"It was you, here in this room, at the last meeting." Leah said.

"Yes, I can explain, but there are things you need to know first."

Taryn looked at their expectant and troubled faces. They knew for certain she was not supposed to be sitting in front of them, yet she was. Brett watched her, somehow understanding. He knew what she was. She could almost feel the keenness of his senses. Obviously, they all had questions bubbling just beneath the surface of their stunned silence, yet they waited for her to speak.

"That woman that just left here was not your Susan," she began. "She's a double, a doppelganger, like me."

Her eyes met theirs, one by one, around the table. Leah's eyes widened. Sidney leaned forward, observing her with a microscopic gaze. Brett simply hung his head. Dylan stood, walked over to a desk, and retrieved a mini voice-recorder. Then, he sat back down.

"Taryn, I'm going to record, if that's okay with you."

She nodded. He pressed a red button, and Taryn watched the wheels of a small cassette turn.

"Tell us what happened to you."

"I made the mistake of bringing home the Black Mirror. Suddenly, I couldn't take my eyes off of it. It was an addiction. It lured me."

They listened with unwavering interest as she spoke. She was suddenly aware her voice was a monotone drawl, seemingly devoid of inflexion. She pictured the small cassette being played back one day, proof of a doppelganger, a live recording of a voice stuck between dimensions. She told them about leaving Madison in the living room, and going into the den to study the mirror yet again.

"I felt like it was calling me. Like it wanted me to know something that only I was lucky enough to learn. I stared into it, waiting for something that I couldn't explain. Then, I couldn't take my hands from the sides of the frame. It was as if they were glued to it. It wasn't pain I felt, but an intense pressure, as if an invisible force bore down and crushed me. Then, the glass disappeared."

She told them about the mist, the lightning, and the man who walked toward her.

"I kept trying to break away, but I couldn't remove my hands. He reached through the frame and grabbed me around my throat. He choked me. I couldn't breathe and was losing consciousness, but I could still hear a slight movement from behind me. I remember thinking and praying my daughter hadn't entered the room as she usually did. I hoped she wasn't witnessing what was happening to me. That was my last thought. He pulled me through the frame and into his world."

Taryn stared into the tabletop as if it would reveal an answer, her eyes unflinching.

"Taryn, tell us about his world," Sidney said.

She gazed upward, remembering. "I felt death when he threw me to the cold ground. I watched scenes of my life pass before me in stages. My body shut down. I felt myself die. In that instant, I knew what death was, but then something happened. I rose up from the cold ground, alive."

"You didn't have the key when you entered," Brett observed.

"So I died," she said. "The Taryn Page that once existed is dead. I am all that remains." No one dared to penetrate the lingering silence. "It's another realm that lies beyond the Black Mirror, a cold separate

Hell, a void of nothingness."

She described the rock formations, the small mountains, and the extinct birds that were doppelgangers themselves. She painted a picture of an opposite world set in the blueness of pre-dawn, a purgatory on the verge of something unknown.

"I knew he'd killed me, but I felt no need for revenge. I wanted to know what I was, and he explained it to me. He showed me how to perform that little task I just showed you all. I can be in this form, or I can take what he calls, 'the ghostly form.'"

"So, you can exist in both human and spirit form?" Dylan said.

"Yes," she answered. "It's all because of the Black Mirror. That's what it does, and it's been doing it for centuries. It recreates within the darkness, and then sends the doppelgangers into the light. Afterward, he tried to make me his servant."

Taryn told them how the man had wanted her to steal the key for him, to help him gain his escape back into the world. Leah clung to her every word.

"So, you were the one who stole the handheld mirror from the police station," she said.

Taryn nodded and noticed it was all beginning to make sense to the investigators. "Yes, but I didn't bring it to him. I left it on my husband's desk. I knew that he would know what to do. When Charley brought it to Susan, I had no idea who she was. I made no connection between you and her. I left the mirror behind, so the man would never escape into this world. I stayed here, and I've lingered for years, though I know nothing of time anymore."

"Taryn, I know you've read my book. Tell us, who was the man who killed you?"

"You already know, Leah," she said. "The man is Angus Marlowe." She watched Leah's eyes close upon hearing the dreaded words. "But your Susan isn't dead. She's very much alive and trapped in the realm. The woman you saw emerged from the gateway with Angus. He is free, and now he seeks vengeance."

She looked into Leah's eyes. "My psychic intuition has remained a part of me. I'm afraid he's after you. I can feel it. He somehow continued to see this world through the passing years. Throughout that time, he's been watching. He's also threatened my daughter, Madison."

She told them about the mirages, the visions, and the clear glass portal she had walked through.

"The gold-gilded mirror," Leah said.

"Yes, it was a gateway," Taryn confirmed. "He couldn't escape through it without the key. He explained I could leave, because I had not entered willingly."

Leah closed her eyes again, envisioning something. She nodded her head, putting it all together.

"I'm seeing that night over again in my mind. I see the flames destroying Cedar Manor, flames for which I am to blame. That's the reason for his vengeance." Leah opened her eyes.

Taryn continued. "I must apologize for something else. I watched Susan as she gazed into the mirror. I saw in her exactly what had possessed me. Her obsession was the same. I transitioned into my human form and tried to warn her, but I wasn't fast enough. I yelled for her just as she hurried through the open frame. She heard me and ran back, but the glass had solidified, closing on her."

Taryn told them how Madison had heard her yell, and how she'd hid. Then, Madison had opened the door, finding nothing.

"She sees things, but not like you can," Taryn said to Leah. "She still hasn't seen me in that form or in this one. I can't let her see me, not now, not yet."

"Taryn, none of this is your fault," Dylan said. "You are yet another victim murdered by the hands of Angus Marlowe."

"Right," she agreed. "Only, I've been lucky enough to linger here for possibly an eternity, though I wouldn't recognize the duration either way."

Then, she told them about how Angus and "Susan" had entered her den, and how she remained hidden within the walls, watching as they quickly departed. Susan's double had returned, assigned to the task of deceiving Madison.

"She tried to convince Maddy she'd imagined my voice in her head, and that it was triggered by the memories Susan had asked her to list. I listened to her spew that psycho babble as she tried to sound like Susan. Susan's memories will become the double's memories more and more as time passes."

"So, she hasn't had enough time to remember everything," Sidney observed.

"That would explain the awkwardness she displayed," Brett said.

"And why she wanted to suspend the investigation." Leah added. "She's doing it for him. She's now his servant. Where could he be right now?"

"Anywhere," Taryn said. "Doubles have no need for rest, lodging, food, or water. We exist in light, and in darkness, like ghosts. Time is all one entity. It is infinite."

"So, the man is Angus Marlowe's doppelganger," Dylan said.

"He has Angus' soul," Taryn said. "His soul and the doppelganger became one in death. Susan is not dead, so she and the double will coexist, at least until Susan is rescued."

Sidney grabbed the legal pad left behind by Susan's double and held it up in his hand. "Taryn, tell us more about Madison. I've studied and worked with child psychics extensively. I know I can help her. We'd been planning on meeting with her and Charley, but now, it's imperative."

Taryn told them how she and Charley had noticed Madison's clairvoyance early. "She was only five. That's another reason I took an interest in your story, Leah. According to your book, you were the same age when you realized your ability.

"Maddy knew too many things before they happened. Charley and I knew all of it was too much to be coincidental. Then, when she became impatient or angry she would break things, but not with her hands, with her mind." Taryn revealed all the instances when she'd witnessed Maddy's telekinesis.

She gave an upward nod with her chin. "Right there is a list of the extent of Maddy's ability. There are things there that even I didn't know about. Now, I've been watching her grow older. I'm a silent witness unable to speak, or hold her. Charley has forbidden her to use her ability, but she has tried to break the mirror."

"We need to meet Charley and Madison tonight," Leah said. "We have no time to waste. We have to find Susan and bring her back."

"That's going to be difficult," Taryn insisted. "Angus has the key.

He's taken it from Susan."

"Then we're going to need you to help us find him," Dylan said.

"That's right." Leah's fear for Susan combined with her anger. "Angus wants to avenge Cedar Manor by coming after me, but it's not going to work that way. I'm going to coax him from his hiding place."

"We're going to coax him," Brett corrected her.

"We will get Susan back," Leah vowed. "If I myself have to walk through Hell to do it, then so be it."

The overhead fluorescent lights buzzed through an uncontested silence. Leah's words were affirmed. They were now in charge, and they would get their leader back, even if Hell awaited them.

Chapter Seventeen

~ A Cry from Beyond ~

No day or night existed in this realm. Susan couldn't tell how much time had passed, but if she had to guess, she would estimate about a day. She relied on how her body felt. She'd been awake most of the time, giving way to occasional dozing for what felt like minutes. Then, she would wake, jumping up like a jack-in-the-box, only to rediscover the nightmare was real. She'd also counted how many times she'd squatted and pissed in 'No Man's Land,' holding her bowels that had weakened from fright.

The background of this eerie place never changed. It remained the deepest indigo blue, never fading or darkening. It knew not daylight or nightfall. A dim, shadowy world without time or end surrounded her. Lightning flickered above, casting brief flashes of light that quickly died away.

She'd seen the strange birds that flew above her before, but only in books. One of them had flown at her, it claws snatching at strands of her hair. She flailed her arms against it like a windmill. In that moment, she recognized it—a pterodactyl. The extinct ancient bird thrived in this alternate realm unknown to the real world.

She ran from the bird and cowered behind one of the many rock formations. She sank to the cold, hard ground and stayed there, afraid to move for what could have been hours.

She touched the hardened rock, but it wasn't earthly rock. It was harder, glassier, like onyx. She thought of the mirror and wondered if there was a connection.

Something crawled through the white mist toward her feet. She focused her gaze on it, and then jumped to a standing position. The largest spider she'd ever seen, maybe two feet in diameter with its eight legs reaching out far and wide, approached her. She gasped and rose quickly from the ground. It came closer, but she refused to retreat. Anger boiled inside her, and then erupted.

"ARRRRR!" She yelled and jumped into the air.

She landed hard on the spider's back. A crunching sound, almost like the breaking of bones followed. Then, a pop like the bursting of a balloon occurred as the spider's legs shot outward and curled up around its body. The oversized arachnid sagged inward, deflating in death. Susan watched it, awed by its freakish size.

Something was happening to the dead spider. It was changing. The more she looked, the more it appeared as though there were two spiders, but there weren't. Something crawled out of the dead spider, an exact ghostly image. It wasn't as visible as its dead host, but it was a perfect reproduction of the spider she had just killed. She watched as the new spider grew in visibility becoming blacker and fuller, an exact replica of its dead host. Then, the new spider crawled away, leaving the dead carcass behind.

It made her think of the reason she'd dashed rashly through the mirror's frame. She'd glimpsed an image of herself. What or whoever it was had spoken to her and lured her through the gateway. At that moment, all logical thought had abandoned her. She'd been obsessed with the mirror, just like Taryn.

She had to discover who the mysterious being was that bore her face, her body, her voice. Was it a ghost? She thought of the omens foretelling the fate upon seeing one's self. When a person saw his or her ghostly image, it was said to be a portent of doom, a harbinger of danger, tragedy, or worse. She'd studied the subject years ago, and now she recalled the name for a person's double. It was a German word— Doppelganger.

Had her doppelganger lured her through the gateway? If so, where had her double gone? She hadn't seen Angus after she'd woke on the cold ground. It started to make sense now. She'd felt Angus' grip on her shoulders. He was no ghost. He was real. He was somehow alive in the physical sense. Was he a doppelganger?

She couldn't think of any other possibility, especially after seeing that ghastly spider, and how its exact double had crawled away only moments later. She thought of the pterodactyl, a bird extinct for many eons. So, the gateway was a realm that gave birth to doppelgangers.

She thought of the team. Surely, they would be searching for her by now. Madison would have realized she'd gone into the mirror and would tell her father. Suddenly, her mind flooded with thoughts of her doppelganger taking her place in the real world. Fear gripped her, making her convulse. The sweat ran down her face. She breathed deeply as paranoia thrived. She wanted to scream, but this world would not respond.

Then, it came from somewhere in the distance. A deep mournful cry bellowed out in agony. She jumped and turned, searching her surroundings. It sounded of torturous confusion, displacement, and eternal damnation.

"AAHAHHAHH..."

Fear speeded her breathing. She exhaled harshly with a shushing sound. Then, she thought of something, or someone. There was no one to hear her in this hidden world, this darkened realm that the Earth would not acknowledge. Yet there was someone in the real world who might hear her—Sidney.

Sidney primarily heard the dead, but she'd studied him since he was a little boy. She knew the extent of his capabilities. He'd once heard Ryan Quinn calling out to him. It was worth a try. It was probably the only hope she had.

Susan tried to muster her voice, but the soft sobbing of defeat snuck in between breaths. She surveyed the surrounding indigo that encompassed everything. The mists rose around her. She closed her eyes and concentrated, picturing him in her mind, seeing his face, his glasses, and his round form. She called out as loudly as she could, projecting her voice into the vastness that surrounded her, ignoring the echo that answered back.

"Sidney. Sidney, help me!"

She called out again, listened to the return of her voice, and prayed.

Black Mirror

* * * *

Sidney was about to the leave the house to pick up the other investigators. They had arranged to meet Charley and Madison at their home at seven o'clock. He walked toward the door, his keys dangling in his hand, when deafness overcame him. The sounds around him ceased—the jangling of his keys, his footfalls upon the floor, even the soft ticking of the hallway clock.

Then, a scream erupted in his mind. "Sidney. Sidney, help me!"

The sound of it startled him. He placed his hands on the wall and leaned against it for support. He focused on the voice. He knew the voice well. It was Susan. Then, he heard her again.

"Sidney. Please, help me. Please!"

His hearing returned, and so did the sounds around him. It was as if a giant cork had been unplugged, and water had been allowed to surge back through. Susan was calling out to him. She was alive, trapped in the gateway beyond the Black Mirror, just as they'd suspected at the meeting. Leah's vision had been accurate as always. He whisked the door open, closed it behind him, and ran to the van. He would tell them all before reaching the Page's house. Then, they would figure out how to rescue Susan.

Chapter Eighteen

~ Revelations ~

"I know it was her voice," Sidney said. "I heard it just as I would if she were sitting next to me. It was Susan. She's alive, and she called out to me."

Sidney drove the van and retold the story over again as he picked up Leah, the last of the passengers. They were now on their way to the Page's house.

"What you heard backs up my vision," Leah said.

"It's the dead who I normally hear," Sidney continued. "That's what scared me at first, but I could tell by the sound of her voice that she's alive. I know it. I could hear it."

"Look, there's no doubt that we're all in agreement," Dylan said. "We have to enter that gateway somehow and rescue Susan. We'll be risking our lives, but we have to save her."

"It's not the first time we've risked our lives," Brett said.

"Right, but we need to figure out how we're going to get into the gateway. It will be impossible without the handheld mirror," Dylan reminded them. "Taryn told us Angus had the key, and that he'd taken it from Susan."

"That's why I'm hoping to lure him out," Leah said.

"That's our initial plan of action." As chief investigator, Dylan had taken the lead in Susan's absence. "But what would happen if Madison could shatter the Black Mirror? Could Susan make it out?"

"Madison has tried to break the glass many times," Leah remarked. "She's failed. That doesn't surprise me. It's too powerful an entity, too strong a portal to be broken down by a little girl."

"From what I've read on that list, I wouldn't underestimate that little girl's ability," Sidney said. "I hate to see what she's capable of at an adult age."

"We'll speak to Charley first, alone," Dylan said. "We have to tell him about Taryn. It will help us explain what happened to Susan. Taryn said she'd be helping us. Let's see if she shows herself to Charley, or Madison."

"It's also crucial for us to study the extent of Madison's ability," Sidney said. "He needs to understand that, and allow her to show us what she can do."

Leah voiced her usual "with or without you" stance. It was what got them into Cedar Manor so quickly a few years ago. It was also what got them trapped in a snowstorm.

"If Madison can shatter the glass, I'm going in."

"One thing at a time, Leah," Dylan said. "First, it's time for us to meet this girl."

* * * *

Charley watched from the door as a white van pulled up in front of the house. Madison was kneeling on the couch, watching from the living room window. Three young men and an equally young woman stepped out of the van. He recognized the woman by her long blonde hair. She was the girl whose memoir Taryn had read.

His nerves jittered, wondering what they were going to tell him, and contemplating what he did and didn't want Madison to hear. Dylan Rasche had phoned him a little over an hour ago with a brief rundown of why they would be visiting. Now, he watched as they walked down the sidewalk. He opened the front door and let them inside. They exchanged greetings, shaking hands in introductions.

"I'm Charley Page," he said. "I'm sure Susan has filled you in on my visit to her. I've been looking forward to meeting you all." He shook Dylan's hand, and then pointed at him. "Dylan, I apologize for my pushiness awhile back. This time, the questions are all yours." He smiled and joked, hoping to lighten the mood before a dark discussion.

"Not a problem," Dylan said, grinning. "You're right, we have much to discuss."

"Nice to meet you, Leah," Charley said, shaking her hand. "My wife read your book and couldn't put it down. I hear you and my daughter have some things in common."

"I'm flattered," she said. "That's what we're here to find out."

He led them into the living room, where his daughter now sat turned away from the window, waiting.

"This is Madison," Charley said, his hand outstretched. "Maddy, these are the paranormal investigators from the university. They've come to meet us and get to know you."

Leah walked over to the couch and sat down next to Madison. Charley noticed his daughter's eyes widen on seeing her.

"Hello, there," she said. "I'm Leah. These are my friends, Sidney, Brett, and Dylan. Susan has told us a lot about you. It's so nice to meet you."

Madison looked at them placidly. "Are you here to find out what happened to my Mom?" Leah looked over to the others.

"Well, Madison," Dylan responded, "Leah and Sidney would like to talk to you and study your ability, if that's okay with your father. Today, Brett and I are going to talk to your Dad about your Mom, if that's okay with you."

Charley said nothing. Dylan looked over at him, searching for any sign of his consent to allow his daughter to demonstrate her own natural, yet unnatural ability. It scared him to know she was using it, but he also knew the investigators came with highly regarded reputations, even if they were a little secretive. They would be honestly studying Madison, and they were the only people who could help her understand this ability that she possessed.

Madison was nodding, a response Charley repeated. He was well aware the investigators wanted Madison to show them the Black Mirror, and then describe to them what happened the day her mother disappeared. He agreed to allow it only under their close supervision, and also because of something Dylan had said to him on the phone about Taryn.

"Maddy, why don't you take Leah and Sidney into your mother's den?" Charley suggested. "Give them a show and tell, so to speak."

Madison appeared surprised. Charley simply nodded to her, letting her know that it was okay. Madison scooted off of the couch and motioned with her hand for Leah and Sidney to follow her. They walked down the stairs, and Charley, Dylan, and Brett watched as they disappeared behind the door. The three of them sat in the living room.

"So," Charley began, "you said that there was much I needed to know, specifically about Taryn?"

"It's hard to know where to begin," Dylan answered. "Since you write about paranormal subjects, I'm assuming you believe in all of this, otherwise you wouldn't write about it. Am I correct?" Charley nodded, prompting him to continue. "Then, you need to understand what the Black Mirror really is. It's the reason your wife disappeared years ago, and it's also the reason Susan is in danger right now."

"What?" Charley exclaimed. "I saw Susan when she left here yesterday—"

"We'll explain," Brett interjected. "First, you need to listen."

Dylan began by telling him how the Black Mirror had once belonged to the Marlowes. He told him about the tome that Paul and Sidney had been deciphering for years. It was the tome that revealed the Black Mirror's purpose.

Now, Charley began to fully understand the connection between the investigators, Cedar Manor, and the Black Mirror.

"It's a gateway to another realm," Dylan said. "Some opposite, alternate world exists beyond its black glass, and we now know Angus Marlowe disappeared into this realm back in 1970. He'd broken through to the other side and became trapped there." He then related the story behind the handheld mirror and that it was the key to the unknown alternate realm. "Angus' mistake was not having it with him when he crossed over."

"It's what happens inside this realm that you need to prepare yourself for," Brett said. "I've read your stories, so I take it you've researched a wide range of paranormal subjects. Have you ever heard of doppelgangers?"

Charley looked at them both, not even sure if he'd heard correctly. "Doppelgangers? Seriously? Yes, I've read a little about them. They're said to be a person's exact replica, a ghostly double capable of appearing in the flesh."

"That's right," Brett said. "A person's doppelganger is said to be born within that realm. Without the key, the person who enters the realm dies, and the doppelganger continues. If the person holds the key when entering, then both the person and their double will coexist."

Charley listened carefully, putting the pieces of the puzzle together, one piece at a time. "So, you're saying Marlowe's doppelganger has been trapped all these years."

Dylan nodded. "It was he who pulled Taryn through the mirror and into the gateway. Charley, every word your daughter has told you about her mother's disappearance is true, all of it."

Charley felt himself surrounded by a sudden heat wave. His ears burned from the stun of Dylan's words, revelations he had not expected to hear. He'd assumed they would agree with him that there was some other explanation for Taryn's disappearance, and then help Madison to understand her psychic abilities. Now they were supporting Maddy's story, saying that it was all true. He had been a parent who failed to listen.

"How do you know all this?" he demanded. The two investigators looked at each other before answering.

"Taryn told us," Brett said.

Again, Charley questioned what he heard. The words were there, but he failed to grasp them as they triggered quick and automatic denial.

"Taryn told you?" The sound of it was incredulous. Only one thought came to him. "So, she's alive?"

"Sort of..." Brett left a lingering pause, failing to finish what he wanted to say.

Dylan took over. "As I've explained, Angus Marlowe pulled Taryn into the gateway." Now, Dylan paused and looked him directly in the eyes. "Taryn did not have the key with her."

Charley understood what Dylan was trying to say, but it was hard for him to form the words. "So, you're saying Taryn's dead?"

"But, alive," Brett said.

Charley stared at them both. Why didn't they just spill it?

"Are you saying Taryn died, and now she's a doppelganger?"

"She showed up at our meeting today," Dylan said. "She's been dwelling in this house. She's been watching you and Madison for years."

Past incidents flashed quickly in his mind: the cool drafts that suddenly swept by him, the soft peck on the cheek he once felt, instantaneous thoughts of her that overwhelmed him out of nowhere. All of it made sense now; it had been Taryn. Then, a bigger piece of the puzzle suddenly fell into place.

"The handheld mirror," he said. "She's the one who left it on my desk."

Dylan nodded. They told him how Angus forced Taryn to leave because he couldn't. Her assignment was to steal the handheld mirror and bring it back to him, so he could gain his freedom.

"She was the one who stole it from the police station?" Charley was flabbergasted, but beneath it all, something began to bug him.

"She didn't bring it back to him. She brought it to you, and you brought it to Susan," Dylan said. "She's remained free all of this time—"

"Yet, she never bothered to show herself to me, or to her daughter. Why?"

"Charley," Brett interjected. "Suffice to say this whole thing is somewhere along my line of expertise. The last thing in the world Taryn wanted was for you or Madison to know what she was, to see what she'd become. It wasn't something she'd ever been ready to face."

"Given Madison's clairvoyance," Dylan added, "Taryn ran the risk of her figuring out her mother was dead, but alive. She feared what it might do to you or to Madison."

"Sometimes a psychic ability or a supernatural thread that is sown within a person can be a curse to them and their family." Brett sounded as if he spoke from experience, and Charley wondered what he was personally leaving out of the story. "In Taryn's case, who she became was forced upon her. She didn't want to expose her family to it."

Christopher Carrolli

"We still haven't told you the reason Taryn showed up at our meeting," Dylan said. "Yesterday, when Susan was here, she left Madison in the dining room and went into the den. Her task was to compare the handheld mirror to the Black Mirror. In doing so, Susan opened the gateway, and according to Taryn, she'd gone through. Taryn tried to warn her, but the glass solidified, trapping Susan inside."

"Taryn claims that doubles of both Susan, and Angus Marlowe, reentered through the mirror. They were right here in this house. She watched them inside her den."

Brett's words raised the hair on the back of Charley's neck. His daughter had been only feet away. "She says Angus left this house, and Susan's double stayed behind."

"That's why Madison thought Susan was acting strangely," Charley said. "She said Susan had been less talkative after coming out of the room. She said she'd seemed 'different.' So, the woman I sat here and talked to yesterday was not Susan, but her doppelganger?"

"That's right," Dylan said. "Now, you know the main reason we've come here. We have to save Susan, but how we're going to do that is our next dilemma."

Brett leaned in closer to Charley, conveying the seriousness of the situation. "The only way we can get into this gateway is to find Angus Marlowe's double and steal the handheld mirror away from him. That's going to be easier said than done. We may need Madison to try and shatter the glass."

"That may not be necessary."

A woman's voice startled them. They shifted in their seats and looked at her. It was the first time Charley had seen her in over six years. She stood only feet away, right under the arch that separated the living room from the dining room. His heart pounded and skipped beats in between. He tried to catch his breath. It was her, his wife. It was Taryn.

* * * *

Taryn had promised the team she would help them in any way she could. She'd been in the house the whole time, watching as Dylan and Brett told Charley the story of what happened to her. She'd watched

170

every twitch of Charley's face, every blink of his eyes, and the intermittent rise and fall of his chest at things still too painful to hear.

She remained hidden as she materialized around the side of the arch that separated the living room and the dining room. The men sat facing each other around the sectional sofa. They mentioned the possibility of Madison shattering the Black Mirror, but Taryn had a better plan. Now, Charley was aware of what had happened to her. She was expecting this. Telling him was crucial to finding Susan, so seeing her now was inevitable. It was time to reveal herself, at least to her husband. She stepped around the corner and took advantage of their break in conversation.

"That may not be necessary."

They shot quick glances toward the sound of her voice. She stood only feet away from them. Charley's face sagged upon seeing her, as if all of his facial muscles had suddenly weakened. His reaction displayed the pain he felt inside, the years of living with unending grief. Charley rose from the couch in slow motion, lingering for seconds in a bent position before straightening himself. They gazed into each other's eyes without blinking.

"Taryn?" Charley's voice faded into a dumbfounded whisper.

"It's me, Charley."

He stepped slowly toward her, careful and skeptical at what stood in front of him. She could see his heartbreak, and something like it lingered somewhere deep within her. They stood inches apart. His lower lip quivered as his eyes squinted, fighting back tears. He touched her left cheek with his right hand. She felt his fingers touch her flesh, and then he pulled her towards him in a tightened grip. He sobbed heavily, yet tried to muffle the sounds so Madison would not overhear. His hot tears ran down her neck.

"Don't cry, Charley, this is my fault, all of it. I'm here now, and I'm always with you, no matter what happens."

She held him until he pulled away from her, clasped both sides of her head in his hands, and kissed her on the lips. It awakened something within her. Memories flashed in her mind like a slideshow: the two of them kissing on the Ferris wheel, meeting him at the end of a long aisle in her beautiful white gown, and then him in green scrubs, clasping her hand as she pushed and screamed and breathed.

Dylan broke the spell of their reunion. "Taryn, you said our plan with Madison may not be necessary."

Charley stepped to the side, but still held on to her. She looked at both Dylan and Brett.

"That's right," she said. "I have an intuition as to where Angus and the handheld mirror can be found. I'm sure he and the double are inhabiting Susan's home. The handheld mirror is there. I feel it. If I stole the mirror once, I can do it again. I'll wait until he's not there."

"No, I don't want you anywhere near—" Charley began to protest.

"Charley, there's nothing more he can do to me. I am what I am now. The important thing is that you'll all be here with Madison. We have to get Susan back, and soon, or she will die. I'll go to Susan's house, find the key, and then you all can begin this rescue mission."

"They're in there with Madison, now," Charley said. "What if she breaks that mirror?"

"She won't," Taryn replied. "I don't know that I want her to see me yet. Surely, Charley, you understand. I have to do this." She broke away from his grasp and stepped backward. "Watch, Charley, see what I've become."

She faded into the ghostly form, slipping away little by little before his eyes. She saw his lips part and his mouth drop as her flesh became paler, and her figure turned ghostly, lessening until it was non-existent. His head darted in all directions. His eyes searched for her. Dylan and Brett simply hung their heads.

She floated through the room and merged with the wall, until she was outside. She would find the handheld mirror in Susan's Logan's house. Her intuition told her so.

* * * *

Madison showed Leah and Sidney the artifacts her mother had collected over the years. She showed them the strange statues of twisting, serpent-like humans, the African death masks, the exotic violet that inexplicably lived and breathed in its glass container, the dragons, and in the corner, the stone gargoyle. Leah and Sidney shared the excitement with the girl, and then casually turned their heads to the opposite corner across from the gargoyle. There it stood, a sheet of shimmering blackness almost taunting them, as if it expected them. They stared at it, and then back at each other as Madison rambled on about the gargoyle, apparently her favorite.

Madison turned and pointed in the opposite corner. "That's the Black Mirror," she said. "I hate it. It's evil."

Leah knelt down and wrapped her arms around her. "I know you do, sweetie. I hate it too."

Madison reminded Leah of herself, and how when she was younger, she'd thought back many times to the gold-gilded mirror that obsessed her mother, the mirror she blamed time and again for her mother's death. Like Madison, she had hated that mirror. Two young girls from two different times both recognized and came to hate the evil represented by two mirrors, which were opposite ends of another realm. How strange.

Suddenly, Leah's third eye revealed something. An iridescent glow hovered and shimmered in the center of Madison's forehead, like someone manipulating a magnifying glass over her small face. Leah recognized Madison's chakra, a third eye much like her own.

She pulled Madison in closer, hugged her, and then glanced at Sidney. He always knew when she saw something. She nodded to him discreetly.

Sidney addressed the young girl. "Madison, Susan told me how you can move or break things with your mind. I've read the list you made. Susan also told me you tried to break this mirror, much like you did with the glass and the window in the garage."

"That was an accident," Madison said.

"Of course it was, sweetie," he said. Leah shot him brisk glance with her narrowed eyes.

"Madison, I want you to turn around and look back at the mirror. I want you to tell us exactly what happened the day your mother disappeared, while keeping your eyes on the mirror."

Madison slowly wriggled out from Leah's embrace. Leah stood close beside her as the girl stared into the Black Mirror. The deep anger in Madison displayed itself in the form of a glare that glossed over her eyes.

"I want you to keep your focus on the mirror while you remember," Sidney continued. "I want you to tell me everything from the beginning."

Leah knew what Sidney was trying to accomplish. She prepared herself. Madison reiterated how Taryn obsessed over the mirror more and more.

"I knew it was evil when I first saw it," she said. "In my mind, I saw it opening. I don't know if my mother believed me. I was watching TV when she came down here. I waited, and then I followed her."

Leah and Sidney watched as Madison's small chest rose up and down, and she began to breathe more heavily.

"When I opened the door, she sounded like she was in pain. Her hands were gripping the sides. Then, I saw the glass disappear, just like in my vision. It was a doorway, like I'd seen in my mind."

Madison's face twisted into a snarl. Her heaving breaths became more rapid, her anger more intense. "I saw what looked like mist. There were flashes of light, but I couldn't see that well, so I stepped a little closer..." Madison closed her eyes, a childish attempt to quell her anger, but Sidney provoked it further.

"Madison, what did you see next, or should I say who did you see next?"

"A man, it was man with evil eyes. He came closer and closer from the other side. He reached out and grabbed my mother by the neck. He choked her."

Madison's breathing turned to a rapid panting as if she was running a race. Leah noticed the girl's face flush to a fiery red. A slick stream of sweat dampened her hair. Leah suddenly felt unsure.

Madison opened her eyes. They focused right at the Black Mirror.

"I screamed." They heard the rage in her tone, the anger that stowed away deep inside, blatant and unresolved. "He pulled her through! I was too small to do anything. I couldn't help her." She breathed faster and faster. "He took my mother!"

Leah and Sidney were startled by the sound of movement, clinking glass and clunking wood, a sudden shaking within the room. The Black Mirror rocked slowly from side to side, affected by an invisible force. Madison's anger had been unleashed and now rampaged throughout the room. Leah looked around her. Artifacts danced on the tables. The overhead lights flickered on and off. Suddenly, they heard the popping sound of breaking glass.

The shaking stopped. Madison's heaving breath now broke down into sobbing. The mirror was unaffected. Once again, Leah pulled Madison into a tight hug, and she and Sidney looked at each other.

What had broken, if not the mirror? Sidney looked around, and then picked something up from the floor. It was the glass case that housed the exotic, seemingly immortal violet, one of Taryn's prized possessions. Sidney held the broken container in his hand as Madison turned around and saw it.

"Oh, no, Mom's violet."

The captured wild flower was now exposed to the air. They watched as it suddenly wilted, withered, and faded. Madison cried out. Leah knew well that the flower reminded her of her mother. She comforted the girl and looked at the Black Mirror. Its dark glass remained untouched by Madison's fury.

* * * *

Madison had tried to shatter the Black Mirror many times since she was a little girl. This time, something was different. She adored Leah from the moment she walked into the living room. She liked Sidney too. He was funny. The both of them understood her. They made it okay to remember what happened and to be angry about it. They were both well aware of what she could do. She told them every detail of what happened to her mother that day. They were details she would never forget; images she would carry with her forever.

As she retold the story, the anger she'd stored inside grew larger and larger like a balloon about to burst. Her heart beat faster, and her breath ran away from her. It happened whenever she became too angry. She felt feverish, enveloped in a wave of heat that made sweat dampen the hair above her face. She stared into the black glass, almost challenging it. She saw beyond its blackness. It had no effect on her.

She trembled. Soon, her inner shaking reached beyond her body. The objects around the room moved, teetering from the quaking within her. She felt something she hadn't before. It was as if her anger breached some invisible barrier that normally protected the Black Mirror. This time, she imagined beyond the glass and projected her anger into the mirror. She sensed the thickness of an unseen energy around her. She mustered that energy and sent it in the direction of the mirror. Suddenly, the legs of its stand rocked back and forth against the floor in unison to the clink and clank of moving objects.

Sweat poured down her face. Her skin burned. Madison pictured shattered glass as she watched the mirror move. She unleashed one final surge of the mysterious energy from her, pushing it out with all of her emotion and directing it toward the Black Mirror. She heard glass break, the popping, shattering sound with which she was so familiar.

The shaking stopped. She broke down into sobs when she looked closely. The mirror was unaffected. She hadn't broken it. Instead, she'd broken something else. She turned and saw Sidney pick something up from the floor. She recognized the deep purple flower amid the broken glass case—her mother's violet. The strange flower that had lived for some time in the special glass case now wilted and dried up in front of her. Madison burst into tears. It was like losing her mother all over again.

She fell into Leah's arms. She never stopped mourning her mother, but she did momentarily find some solace in Leah's tightened grip. Sidney kneeled down beside her and spoke to her at eye level.

"Madison, I'm so sorry this happened. I didn't know this experiment would backfire on us, and I'm sorry about the flower."

She shook her head, the tears tapering off. "It's not your fault. I thought for sure I could break it, and this time I almost did. I felt something I hadn't before, like a force. This..." She gazed around at the objects now strewn out of place. "This never happened before."

"Madison, are you telling us this was the first time the mirror physically moved the way that it did?" Sidney said.

She nodded and looked up at Leah.

"I could feel myself moving it. I was sure it would break."

"Don't worry about that now, sweetie," Leah said. "We'll figure something out."

Then, Sidney's phone rang.

* * * *

Black Mirror

Paul had finally finished with *Mysteries of the Dark World,* and a few other books he'd pulled from a shelf in his attic. Then, he went back to the tome. He wanted to examine a few final pages, and he did that now under a bright desk lamp. In those remaining pages he'd deciphered yet another answer, a blatant explanation for the mysterious Black Mirror. The remaining pages described the realm beyond the gateway as a "birthing canal." The realm was the womb, and the key was the male counterpart. Once these two things were brought together, a successful "birth" was accomplished.

Paul stumbled on something else in the tome's remaining pages—one of the primary reasons for his search. The Latin words warned of the events that would follow the Black Mirror's destruction. After translating the words, he read the undeniable warning they conveyed. The meaning was clear. Once the Black Mirror was destroyed, all it had brought forth unsuccessfully would also be destroyed. All it had brought forth unsuccessfully...

On the Black Mirror's destruction, any doppelganger born unsuccessfully would die along with it. Much to Leah's dismay, Paul had deduced that Angus Marlowe had entered the gateway. Yet if he entered the gateway, did he have the key with him? Paul didn't know. He'd been fed only bits and pieces of information by his daughter and the investigators. They needed to know what he'd just discovered. If Angus Marlowe had become what the tome described as a "double walker," then there was a way to destroy him.

He grabbed his phone and called Sidney. On the third ring, he answered.

"Sidney, this is Paul. I've finished deciphering the tome, and I've discovered something that may be vital." He heard a pause on the other end.

"I'm here," Sidney said.

Paul got straight to the point. "The gist of what I've discovered is plain and simple. You destroy the mirror, and the doppelganger dies. How's that for simple?"

Sidney scoffed under his breath. "Easier said than done."

"So, then I was right," Paul said. "Angus entered the gateway back in 1970." Sidney didn't answer him. "I take it my daughter is there with you?"

"You got it."

"Then, listen to me. This is important. Just answer yes or no. Did Marlowe have the handheld mirror with him when he entered?"

"No."

"Good, then if he didn't have the key, he dies with the mirror. Got it?" Sidney agreed.

Paul knew they would keep him posted. After he ended the call, he had a feeling there was more to Sidney's reticence than Leah's presence in the same room. Something was happening, something more sinister than he'd imagined.

Chapter Nineteen

~ Doppelgangers ~

Angus wandered about through the world aimlessly, taking in as much of it as he could. The sky, the birds, the trees, human beings, the sudden appearance of it all once again revived him. He saw subtle hints of the passing of years in things like cars, clothing, and buildings. Time was something he hadn't experienced since entering the gateway, but the sights of what had been unseen for so long provoked a tinge of yearning. He saw the world once again, but he'd postponed revisiting one particular destination—home. Now, the delay ended, and flesh and bone materialized within the stone ruins of Cedar Manor that were not yet completely removed.

The foundation of the great house had not been excavated, and portions of stone walls still stood erect, broken and withered, with jagged edges jutting out like jigsaw pieces. What were once walls looked like the aftermath of bombed out, war-torn shelters. War was precisely what had occurred here.

He knew he was largely responsible for the surrounding devastation, the end result of demonic rage conjured up by his rituals. Yet, if the girl with the third eye had stayed away from here, he would be safely ensconced in his home again, dwelling within the magnificent rooms and marveling at a different day and age from behind its immense structure. Now, only the destruction of what once was met his eyes.

Angus remembered his childhood. His mother and father had been so happy. He recalled the Christmases, the huge tree in the grand

179

hallway, the myriad lights that adorned the house, and people who would stop to admire the spectacular holiday display.

As a youngster, he'd been transferred from school to school, labeled as "different" simply because of his desire to be alone. His introspection was often misinterpreted, which led to his being sent somewhere else, until finally, his schooling was left to tutors.

All of his life, he'd heard whispers about how he was an unexpected child born to middle-aged parents, which led to the rumors of his being different, and even special. None of those descriptions had contained a speck of truth.

He was an only child. He had no one except Mother and Father, and both of them were caught up in the whirlwind of trying to balance a quiet, private life with the renown that came from success and prestige. As a child, he'd been practically hidden away, a reality that became voluntary at some point. He began to lead his life in his own world and in his own time.

The early sixties became the late sixties. He watched as a society changed before him. Soon, he began to seek out his own crowd. He found them hanging around in communes, groups, and gatherings. Young people searched for answers about the state of the world around them. Drinking, drugs, sex, preaching, and philosophizing filled their days. He told them about a world far beyond, a place of release, and distant realms that existed here on Earth, ones the human eye failed to see. He mesmerized them with his talk of other dimensions.

He began to immerse himself more and more in the occult, dabbling in rituals, séances, and ceremonies, all in search of an alternate path than the one prescribed for him. A better path existed. He spoke of a way out for those who chose not to conform to the world's expectations.

He studied the tome backwards and forwards and decided one day, he would seek that alternate path through the Black Mirror. Then, he'd finally been led astray. First came death, and murder followed.

Victor Roth had been his cohort, his follower, an underling protégé with an interest in the occult that equaled his own. Long ago, he and Roth indulged in a night with two young ladies. The basement in Cedar Manor provided the privacy for their intimate party. The two females expressed an interest in the occult and worlds beyond. Angus and Victor satisfied their curiosity.

The slightly older and more flamboyant of the two girls had stared fixedly into the Black Mirror. Then, she volunteered herself for the ritual Angus would perform. During this undertaking, something had gone wrong.

Angus needed blood for the ceremony, the ultimate human sacrifice offered to the dark gods. The older girl became obsessed in her pursuit, impatient to show her readiness with a daredevil flare. In a fit of wild fervency, she cut herself. The slash to her open wrist formed a bloody bracelet around her hand. Angus filled the golden chalice as she bled, but the blood began to seep and gush. The cut she had made was too strong, too deep. She'd sliced through an artery.

She realized the extent of her injury. Blood was everywhere. She began to scream, but her voice grew weaker and fainter. The other girl cried out to save her friend, but it was too late. Her eyes closed. The gushing of blood was unstoppable. Angus ripped an old sheet and wrapped it around her wrist as a tourniquet, but her skin grew cold and clammy. Her complexion paled to grayness. The younger girl's screams were stifled into muffled protests as Roth clamped his hand around her mouth.

It wasn't his fault. She'd caused her own death through a childish attempt to show how unafraid she was and through her senseless but fearless commitment to what dwelled beyond. Her attempt to impress, to show bravery failed her. She died in the dankness beneath Cedar Manor.

Roth lost control of the other wriggling girl he tried to subdue. She fled through the basement, her screams echoing and bouncing from the limestone walls. Angus had to stop her. He had no other choice.

They chased her though the vast basement. She'd fled in the wrong direction, but Angus couldn't risk her becoming lost, and then somehow finding her way out through one of the secret tunnels. He had already been accused of rape, a deed Father had made go away. However, this time he would pay. The girl died on his makeshift altar from a self-inflicted wound. No one would believe the truth.

The other girl ran screaming through the archways, losing herself in a never ending maze that provoked her swelling panic. Angus followed the sound of her screams, desperate cries that echoed around him. Soon, her screaming stopped, and her crying tapered to a soft whimpering.

He and Roth began searching in different directions. He'd tiptoed through one room, feeling her presence, but unsure of where she'd hidden. She could've been anywhere within this vast labyrinth, but he was sure she was here in this room. He crept back out of the room and waited.

Soon, she bolted from her hiding place in a flash and dashed past him. He gave chase. Roth followed quickly behind him. He couldn't let her get away. He would lose his life, and for what, a young girl's stupidity? He was not going to let anyone make this his fault.

He caught her around the waist, and she wriggled wildly in his grip, kicking her legs against his in a futile effort to escape. What came next was quick. He reached his hand around her neck and squeezed. She coughed, choked, and gasped until she fell limp in his arms. He hadn't wanted this. He held her until she grew cold. Then, he let her body fall to floor. The solid thud was the sound of his worst deed. It amplified in his ears. He and Roth would figure out what to do with the bodies later. Now, he had to clean the mess left behind.

Roth looked at him with eyes wild with fear. Angus remembered how pathetic Roth had appeared in that moment, knowing he was just as responsible for what had occurred.

"What are you going to do now?" Roth whined.

"You mean, what are we going to do?" Angus answered him. "You're going to help me get rid of this mess, and remember, neither of us knows a thing about what happened to those girls. You'll follow my lead, or we're both going down for this."

That marked the beginning of it all. One murder led to another. The thrill of it never left him. It became an addiction for him and Roth, a sick, obsessive satisfaction that bordered upon ecstasy.

There had been a few others over the years, girls whose fanatical interests went far, and then faltered in the final moments. It was a pattern he began to enjoy, watching their false courage turn quickly to fear, and then failure in death. He felt as if he wielded the power of life and death.

Roth grew complacent. His young mind turned rabid, an effect from multiple doses of LSD. Angus remembered how his once vibrant eyes suddenly narrowed into a maniacal, almost demonic stare. He and Roth tore apart the basement walls and stashed the remains of their dirty work. Roth later shot himself in the head in 1969. Now, from the look of the ruins that surrounded him, their deeds had been discovered.

He remembered how he'd contemplated the possibility just before walking through the mirror and into the gateway. He'd been right about eventual discovery. He hadn't been here to accept his just reward because he escaped. Now, the modern world appeared before him with its fast-paced assault against humanity, its bright lights, its vast web that spun around the world, and its handheld gadgets. The world he'd always known lay crumbled around him, a grand domain laid waste by a young woman and her connection to darkness.

He would find her. He would wrap his hands around her throat as he had done to the others. He knew his current existence depended upon the safety of the Black Mirror. In life, he had been an unexpected child, and even his rebirth had been a failure, an unsuccessful birth brought forth by the gateway. He had to find the girl, but more importantly, he needed to move the Black Mirror from its present location. His new existence depended upon it.

* * * *

Taryn lingered outside of Susan Logan's house, taking a moment to marvel at how the light rain failed to touch her in the ghostly form. Her intuition remained strong in this moment of careful contemplation. Angus was not here. Susan's double was somewhere inside and so was the key.

She glided through the outer wall of Susan's house, merging with the sturdy brick and moving through the dark-red matter, as if it were nothing more than a curtain. She stepped into the house, an invisible intruder sent to save its owner. No one was in the lofty living room or anywhere in the lower level of the house. Taryn turned her head upward. She felt a presence stirring upstairs—the covetous, copycat imposter who had taken Susan's place.

Taryn closed her eyes and felt the vibes inside of her. It was like searching with her soul. In an instant she knew. The handheld mirror was in Susan's office, the first door in the hallway just beyond the living room. She was only feet away. She floated fast and slipped through the closed door. The black, handheld mirror that could save Susan's life lay on the desk. She grabbed the mirror from the desk, and then penetrated the door once again.

Taryn made straight for the wall by which she'd entered. Her ghostly presence covered the distance in seconds until the sound of a voice stopped her.

"I know you're here," the voice said. "I see you."

Susan's double stood on the staircase, her hand clutching the railing. Her eyes saw right through her, one doppelganger spotting another. Taryn materialized and stood visible, exposed as the intruder she was, but if it was confrontation the double wanted, she was ready.

"So what?" Taryn said. She stepped forward and faced her from across the room. "What can you do to me? We're both in exactly the same position."

"Not exactly," the double said.

"Why continue to be his servant? You're free, or at least you will be when I return this." Taryn held up the mirror. "You may not be able to remain in this house, but you'll be free, and you and I both know why."

Susan's doppelganger simply stared, stunned into silence by the sting of Taryn's words. The double's mouth twisted in a strange half-grin, one that displayed her acceptance at being defeated.

"I know he's not here. Why do you think I risked coming here? I'm leaving now, and I suggest that you take my advice and do the same."

Taryn walked toward the wall she'd entered through, keeping her eyes fixed on Susan's double the entire time. They stared at each other from the across the room. No words passed between them. The silence signified acceptance of the unspoken agreement.

Susan's double stood frozen on the stairs, her hand still clutching the railing, and then she turned her head away. Taryn got the message. She faded into the ghostly form and trudged through the wall once again, until she emerged safely in the rain. She had retrieved the key. Now, it was time to rescue Susan.

Chapter Twenty

~ Plans into Action ~

Sidney hesitated to tell Leah it had been her father on the phone, but he would have to reveal Paul's discovery to her and the team. Madison was still in the room, still shaken over the violet and its glass casing. Someone knocked rapidly on the door and then swung it open. It was Charley.

"Is everything alright in here? Maddy, are you okay?"

"We were studying Madison's telekinesis," Leah said. "There was an incident with the glass case. We apologize for the damage—"

"Don't worry about it," he said.

Charley pulled his weeping daughter toward him and hugged her. Madison's sobbing soon quieted, and she wiped her eyes with her hands as Charley carefully picked up the broken glass case. Sidney noticed his reaction when he saw the violet, wilted and dead after mysteriously thriving for so long. Charley's eyes winced in worry, as though the dead violet was some sort of an omen. Either way, Sidney took advantage of the moment.

"Charley, I need a quick moment to speak with Leah and the team in the other room, if that's okay with you?"

"Yeah, sure." Charley spoke without looking at him. His eyes remained fixed on the violet, his mind deep in distraction.

Sidney looked at Leah and nodded toward the door. She followed him into the living room, where Dylan and Brett waited. Sidney glanced back toward the den before he spoke.

"I have some news," he said.

"Who was that on the phone?" Leah demanded.

"It was your father. He's discovered something in the tome." Sidney spoke in a low voice, and Dylan and Brett moved in closer to hear. "The tome revealed that if the Black Mirror is destroyed, anything brought forth from it unsuccessfully will die. Paul said that if Angus entered without the key, his double would be destroyed along with the mirror."

"So, he knows?" Leah's frustration was evident.

"Yes, Leah, he knows," Sidney said. "However, he knows nothing about Susan."

"So, if we destroy the mirror, we also destroy Marlowe's double?" Dylan said.

"Precisely," Sidney confirmed.

"You'll also destroy me." Once again, Taryn's voice was sudden and out of nowhere. They turned around quickly and saw her standing in the room along with them, holding the handheld mirror in her hand.

"That's alright," she added, handing Leah the mirror. "I just ask that my daughter doesn't see me, that she doesn't go through losing me yet again."

"We won't let that happen," Brett said. Leah agreed.

"Besides, there's no need. We have the key now. I'm going in there after Susan."

Taryn looked at each of them, carefully choosing her words before she spoke. "I was thinking maybe it would be best if I went in after Susan. After all, I know the way in. I've been there before."

"No," Leah said. "We can't risk that. You escaped that realm. We're unsure of what will happen to you if you return. If you become trapped there, Susan will be also." Taryn lowered her eyes. "No, I'm going in. The guys are trying to stop me, but they know how stubborn I am."

"Maybe you're right," Taryn said. She looked away, tracing some inner revelation that stirred deep within her.

"Taryn, what is it?" Sidney said.

"I have a feeling Angus will be here." She looked at them with those same pleading eyes. "I think he's coming for me." Then, she turned her gaze toward Leah. "I think he's coming for the both of us."

"Then Leah, if you're going to do this, we need to move now,"

Dylan said.

Sidney looked at Dylan. His lips were moving, but to Sidney, all sound had suddenly died away. Susan's voice exploded in Sidney's mind.

"Sidney! Help me!"

His body shook. His head felt the slightest rush. Then, sound returned. He heard one or two of Dylan's last words.

"Sid, are you feeling okay?" Dylan caught sight of his sudden spell.

"Yeah," he said, eying him with a serious glance. "You're right. We better move, now."

* * * *

Angus entered Susan's house and walked through the living room, curiously eyeing the surroundings. He detected no sign of his underling, the masquerader who now lived here. He stepped through the door and into the office. It was the sight of the desk that made him materialize.

The key. It wasn't on top of the desk where he'd left it. His hands yanked the drawers open in a fit of rage. Fury, the one human emotion that remained, consumed him. The key was gone. Someone had stolen it.

He flung the office door open, and then galloped up the stairs in freakish strides, his legs spanning far apart in leaps and bounds up the staircase. She was not in the bedroom, or anywhere else that he could see. He opened all the doors on the upper level until it became clear that he was alone in the house. His servant was gone.

"Susan? Susan!" His scream suddenly turned into a psychotic, playful coaxing. "Su-san? Suuuu-san?" She was gone. His tone turned back into raging fury. "I will find you, Susan. I'll find you!"

He began throwing objects, vases, knickknacks, furniture. Anything he laid his hands upon he hurled through the air. Glass crashed throughout the house. She had deserted him just like Taryn. He ran down the stairs and continued his assault. He overturned tables, threw chairs, and ironically, broke a mirror.

He stared into its cracked glass. He hadn't known he was still capable of such emotion. He thought it had died away with his body. He stared at his reflection in the cracked glass. The cast of his maniacal eyes was an image he hadn't seen in ages. His chest heaved up and down, a human reaction in a human form. In the reflection, the crack in the glass ran across his face.

* * * *

Brett and Sidney ventured outside to the van to retrieve the video and audio equipment. What was about to take place would be documented for the society's archives.

"I really think Madison should witness this," Leah told Taryn. "Madison not only needs to understand her ability, but she needs to be able to put an end to this mystery in her own life, as well. Yes, she's still a child, but she also needs closure from this. It's going to be impossible to shield her any longer from the truth that there are mysterious things in this world, and that she, and her ability, are among the unexplainable."

"Charley will be there," Dylan said. "I don't know how you intend to handle the truth about yourself to your daughter, but if you were hoping for her to accept that you're gone, this may be your chance. If that's what you want."

Taryn closed her eyes, and then shook her head. "I don't know how this will end," she said. "He's on his way here. I can feel it. I'm going to wait for him. I will not let him harm my daughter."

"None of us will let that happen," Dylan promised.

The front door opened, and Brett and Sidney stepped back inside. The video camera was slung from a strap over Brett's shoulder, and Sidney carried a high-tech audio recorder like a briefcase. Taryn began to fade into a ghostly form before their eyes.

"I'll be watching," she said. The sound of her voice grew fainter.

They stared at the spot where she'd stood, as if taking time to pay their respects. For a brief moment, they let their minds record what they'd seen, realizing they would never grow accustomed to what their eyes had shown them. For them, bewilderment would never cease. Everything was all part of the strange world they'd immersed themselves in long ago.

"Let's go," Leah said.

Brett and Sidney followed her and Dylan into the den, where Charley and Madison cleaned up broken glass. Dylan motioned Charley aside for a moment. He and Leah needed to speak with him, privately.

"I'm going inside the mirror," Leah said. "We want you and Madison as witnesses. Charley, trust me, Madison can handle this." She reiterated the need for closure, as she'd already pointed out to Taryn. "In her own way, she's already aware something has happened to Susan. Madison and I shared the same vision, and I can explain it to her." She raised the handheld mirror up to his face. "Taryn brought this to us. She's here, and she's watching. We need to rescue Susan, but Charley, whatever you decide about Madison is up to you. I'm convinced that witnessing this will help her."

Charley took a deep breath and exhaled. "I understand, Leah. Please, do whatever you have to do to get Susan back. I trust you with my daughter. When it's over, I don't ever want to see that damn mirror again."

"You got it," Dylan said.

Sidney helped collect the last of the shattered glass, and then everyone assembled in the middle of the room. The girl watched in wonder as Brett tinkered with the video camera, and Sidney set up the recorder on the small coffee table. Leah asked Madison to sit down beside her on the sofa. She had something to tell her.

"Do you remember when you had the vision of two Susan's?" Leah said. Madison nodded. "Well, I had that vision too."

Leah looked at the rest of them, including Charley. No one expressed any visible objections to what she was about to reveal to the eleven-year-old.

"Madison, you were right when you said Susan was acting strangely after seeing the mirror. When she was in here, and you were in the dining room writing your list, something happened to Susan." Leah paused. "She went into the mirror, just like your mother."

Madison stared back at them, her crystal blue eyes wide with fear and hopelessness.

"But I saw her."

"You saw someone, Madison," Sidney said. "That someone was pretending to be Susan."

"You see, the vision you and I had about the two Susan's was accurate," Leah continued. "Our Susan went into the mirror, but another Susan walked out."

Madison shocked them with her next words. "Somehow, I knew. She didn't walk like Susan. She walked and talked slower, and she was quieter, like she wasn't as smart."

The investigators glanced at each other. They had all noticed the slightly different demeanor when the double tried to fool them. That day, "Susan" had seemed detached, at a loss for words. Leah remembered noticing the slightly different walk, the slower, clumsy plodding. Even an eleven-year-old, who hardly knew Susan, had been able to discern the differences the double couldn't hide. Leah realized Madison was smarter and much more intuitive than any of them had realized.

"You're a smart girl, Madison," Leah said. "You were right when you said that the mirror opened and that it led somewhere."

"So, where does it go?" Madison said.

"That's what I'm going to find out. I'm going to find Susan, the Susan that picked you up from school yesterday. I'm going to bring her back to us. That means I have to walk through the mirror and discover where it leads."

"No, don't!" Madison's protest was quick and adamant. "You can't go in there or you'll never come back!"

"I will, sweetie, I promise. Out of all of us, I'm the one who's best fit to go in because I see things like you do. It's my third eye. I'll be able to find Susan much faster than anyone else, right guys?"

She turned her head to them as they stood behind her. The guys grunted inaudible verbal agreements, unwilling to debate the issue in front of Madison.

Madison's next question stumped Leah into speechlessness. "So, if Susan is inside the mirror, then is my mother there too? After the man grabbed her and pulled her in, I never saw her walk out, but I heard her. I know I did. I heard her calling Susan's name."

Leah looked into her eyes, not knowing what to say. Secretly, she hoped Taryn would jump out of her hiding place and put an end to this charade once and for all, but she understood why that was easier said than done.

Sidney spoke, placing himself in Susan's role and issuing a half-truth. "Madison, we won't be able to answer that question until after Leah comes back."

"I'm sure all things will be revealed." It was the best answer Leah could give.

Her heart fluttered inside, knowing this venture would be risky, but her third eye kept showing her shattered glass, much like the dream she had years ago before reentering Cedar Manor. She knew she would return. She saw beyond today.

"Whatever happens, I want you to stay here with your father and the team. I want you to tell the guys if you see anything. Don't be afraid. We study things like this all the time. We know what we're doing. This is our lives. This is who we are as people. We're the ones who help in times like these. So, I want you to stay focused. After all this is over, I want you to move on with your life, whatever the outcome is, okay?"

Madison lowered her eyes and nodded.

None of them had any other choice. Leah rose from the sofa and looked to the team.

"Alright, guys, let's do this."

Dylan instructed Brett and Sidney to start recording whenever they were ready. Sidney pressed a button, and two reels of tape spun slowly for the purpose of picking up all sounds both heard and unheard by the human ear. Brett walked over to Leah and began pinning something to her collar. It was a mini camcorder.

"Leah, I want you to wear this. It will be recording everything you see. I can't promise that it will be of superior quality, but it may give us a glimpse of what's beyond." Brett hoisted the main video camera up on his shoulder, and a flashing red light signaled the start of the recording.

Leah stepped slowly toward the Black Mirror, the handheld key gripped firmly in her hand. The team stood in a circle behind her. Charley stood off to the side, his arms embracing his daughter in a protective hold.

She held out the handheld mirror, searching with her eyes for the reflection of black glass upon black glass. Quick images flashed fast in her mind—mountainous rock, everlasting azure, birds swarming in a strange sky above. Her human eyes focused on the black glass, while her third eye showed her an unearthly blue realm. The images flashed quickly, vying intermittingly with the black glass before her. Then, the images vanished.

She continued to gaze into the mirror, wondering about the dark fascination that had captivated Susan, and the similar obsession that engrossed her stepmother long ago. Leah wasn't experiencing that obsession. Her third eye would not allow it. Suddenly, the black glass shifted within its frame. The movement was quick, but she caught it, and so had the others.

"Did everyone else see that?" she said.

"I saw it," Brett replied.

The others agreed. Leah took a few more steps forward.

"Leah, be careful," Dylan warned.

"I'm not afraid of you." Leah whispered to the mirror.

The black glass shimmered and then quickly jiggled. They watched as the glass rippled in waves, and what looked like black water moved within the frame in a rolling motion. Gasps erupted in the room. The distorted glass vanished, revealing an entrance. The mirror had been merely a door, and now the door opened. What lay beyond was now laid bare. Leah remained calm. In front of her was their one chance to rescue Susan.

She saw a mist, a foggy whiteness veiling the black, like smoke in the dark. She stepped closer and peered deeper into the frame. Her eyes winced at a flash of light from within—lightning. It flickered brightly, illuminating the dark beyond for only an instant.

"Leah, I'm going with you," Sidney said.

"No. We can't risk it. The more of us inside the gateway, the greater the danger. Don't be afraid. I'll get her."

Her hand reached up and touched the front of her chest. The ruby cross Hollywood had given her just before they'd gone into Cedar Manor lay secure. It had been with her then, and it would be with her now.

"I'm going in now. You all know what to do if I don't come back."

She strode quickly as she spoke, stepping through the frame before any of them could stop her. Still, she heard their protests behind her.

"Leah, wait," Dylan yelled.

"Leah," Brett echoed.

As she entered the gateway, the voices went mute behind her. She turned around to look at them, but the portal had closed. The entry she had walked through was now solid black glass growing fainter in the foggy mist. Her heart pounded. She may have trapped herself, but this wasn't the time to think about it now. She had to find Susan.

Chapter Twenty-One

~ Beyond the Black Mirror ~

Angus found his way back to the house that had once been Taryn's—too late by the looks of it. He'd merged with the southern wall of the house until he lingered just beneath the wall's surface, yet enough to allow him a view into the room housing the mirror. A small group of people surrounded it. A girl stood in front of the mirror. It was her, the girl with the third eye. Worse, the portal had opened for her. She quickly stepped through it and into the gateway. He'd arrived too late to intervene.

He'd seen it all from his hiding place in the wall, an unseen ghost well within their midst. The girl had the key. The stolen handheld mirror was gripped firmly in her hand, and she'd held it to the glass. The Black Mirror opened its entranceway to her.

He had no doubt she was trying to rescue Susan. When it was over, if she was successful, she would destroy the mirror, just as she had done to his home. He was not going to let that happen. She took the handheld mirror when she entered. She might find her way out or she might not. Either way, he would destroy her first.

Angus heard her friends scream after her. So, her name was Leah. Her friends moved fast, surrounding the mirror and pounding on the glass with their fists. They continued to shout her name, but she wouldn't hear beyond the glass. How easily she had done it, as if the glass had welcomed her. She'd offered no incantation, only presented the key. Amid the mayhem, Angus spotted another small person—Madison. So, they'd allowed the girl to witness the whole event. A man held the girl tightly—her father.

He had to act fast. If Leah failed to return, they would destroy the mirror to get her back. They would kill him to save both Leah and Susan, but not if he kidnapped the girl. He glimpsed a glass object on a small table inside the room, a statue of some kind. He'd seen it before among the bizarre collection in the room. The time to act was now.

He slipped into the room and conjured his flesh and bone with a speed he'd grown well accustomed to long ago. He shot through the room, too fast for their eyes to catch, and snatched the small statue from its place. Angus ran to the girl and her father, brandishing the glass statue high above his head. He brought it down hard on top of the father's head, shattering the figurine into pieces. The father fell to the floor, knocked unconscious by the blow.

"Daddy!" the girl screamed.

Angus moved fast to grab her. Once he had her as collateral, they wouldn't touch the mirror. He would take her away from this house, and they would only get her back for an exchange—Madison for the mirror. He ran towards her, barely noticing the fiery flare in her deep blue eyes. She recognized him. He knew it. He moved faster toward her.

"You!" The scathing sound of her small voice stopped him cold.

The weight of his earthly form rose in the air, as if pushed by some invisible force. His feet lifted up from the ground as his arms flailed backwards. His back smashed into the wall behind him. The heavy phantom force pinned him to the wall and bounced him repeatedly against it. He tried to slip into the ghostly form to evade it, but he couldn't. His head pounded the wall.

The force was coming from Madison. Her deep blue eyes narrowed in a devilish glare at him. Angus knew Taryn's daughter possessed some psychic ability, yet he'd never known the extent of the child's capabilities. Witch? Surely she was a witch of some kind. Her breath heaved as her chest rose up and down. Deadly anger boiled just beneath her skin. She unleashed that rage on him.

"You!" she shouted. "You took my mother."

For an instant, he felt release. He made a bold dash toward her, but the unseen energy violently threw him backwards yet again. Once more, his back smashed against the wall. His human form felt the pain, and he couldn't escape it. He couldn't escape her. Then, the strange force threw him face down to the floor. He lay, unable to move, as an invisible crushing weight pressed him into paralysis.

* * * *

Taryn lingered in the ghostly form, remaining hidden behind a shelf in the den to ensure Madison wouldn't see her. Charley and the investigators knew of her decision not to reveal herself to her daughter just yet. They also knew she'd be watching from somewhere in the room, safely hidden from human eyes. She'd seen it all unfold within the midst of what she'd once lovingly called her "gallery."

Angus had entered the room, swiftly snatching one of her most favored collectables from its place. It was the white statue of a vestal virgin, a replication of innocence either blessed or cursed with multiple eyes that kissed the glass icon from head to toe. When Angus raised the statue and struck Charley over the head, Taryn began to materialize. She would stop him one way or another.

She had been ready to reveal herself as Angus went for Madison, but then something happened. Madison spun around and faced him with a glare in her eyes Taryn had never seen before. She watched as her daughter's telekinesis exploded into a full scale assault against the man who had taken her mother, and now attacked her father. The strange and powerful energy coming from Maddy threw Angus against the wall with an unseen rage, pounding his head off the wall and then throwing him to the floor, writhing and squirming, pinned down by the telekinetic force Maddy projected.

Sidney and Dylan attended to Charley, who lay unconscious. Taryn wanted to defend and protect her family, especially her daughter, but there was no need. Madison's unthinkable ability shielded her, or had she protected herself? Taryn didn't take the time to ponder the question because now, Madison turned her explosive attention toward the mirror.

* * * *

Beyond the Black Mirror, the misty darkness gave way to a vast landscape, an undiscovered world set against a deep blue backdrop. Leah gazed around her and realized she'd just proven the existence of opposite realms. Here was proof that the tome had revealed the truth about dark worlds hidden within the real world.

Here, rock formations and odd looking mountain ranges rose in the distance. A swarm of strange birds cawed and flew above her. The collective flapping of their wings sounded closer than it was as the gaggle flew hastily across an ominous sky. It was just as her third eye had shown her only moments ago.

She stepped carefully on the rough, coarse ground beneath her feet. How foreign and unearthly it felt when she bent down and touched her fingers to its rigid, rocky texture. She rose and continued to walk into nowhere, feeling the chill of this strange atmosphere surrounding her. It had a bleak coldness, like death, and she moved through it seeing no one.

A loud bellowing startled her. She jumped at the sound of it. The clamor of desperation and anger surrounded her. She closed her eyes and tried to focus her third eye, but saw nothing.

"Susan!" She yelled as loud as her voice allowed.

Her voice echoed around her, but it was a different kind of echo, one that reverberated, and then returned like a boomerang.

"Susan-an-an!" Only the ghostly echo responded.

Leah touched the cross around her neck. "Please don't let her be dead," she prayed. She called out her name again; this time, louder. "SUSAN."

Nothing but the echo responded. She continued to walk through the mist until she arrived at some sort of empty space, a clearing of some kind. Something shimmered in the not too far distance. It was an image, slowly becoming clearer and more visible. She closed her eyes again and reopened them. It wasn't her third eye showing her the vision of Susan; it was the clearing itself, as if some unseen storyteller dwelled here. It was like watching a film: Susan laughing, her lips moving. It was a familiar image of the last time she'd seen her. Then, another image formed alongside it. Susan standing on the staircase in her home, her hand grasping the railing, but it wasn't really Susan. The double. She'd made herself right at home.

Leah knew Susan was here somewhere. That's what the images confirmed, both Susan's coexisting. She turned from the clearing and walked back, this time, taking a detour in another direction. She passed more mountainous formations with craggy, rigid rock so unlike anything she'd ever seen before.

She heard something. It was a soft, helpless weeping, not the loud, desperate moaning she'd heard earlier. This was human, not phantom-like. She walked faster, following the sound of it as it grew louder and louder.

She arrived at the end of the long, mountainous range, turned, and walked along its opposite side. Her heart jumped when she saw Susan. She was on top of a large rock that was low to the ground, but one she'd obviously had to hoist herself up to sit atop. She lay curled into a fetal position, emitting the helpless sobbing Leah had followed.

"Susan," Leah cried out.

The echo startled Susan into a sitting position. She pushed the stray hair from her eyes. Leah saw the disbelief on Susan's face followed by careful contemplation in case she turned out to be nothing more than a vision.

"Leah, is that you?" Susan's voice shook, reflecting fatigue and confusion.

"Yes, Susan. It's me."

Leah ran up to her and grabbed her by the shoulders. She shook her lightly to wake her, to stir her into action, and to let her feel her touch. Susan responded to the feel of Leah's hands grasping her. The look in her eyes changed from disbelief to realization.

"Leah."

She jumped from the rock and ran into her arms. The joy of answered prayers reverberated around them.

"There's no time, Susan." Leah's voice echoed eerily through the vastness. "We have to get out of here. The others are waiting."

Susan clutched Leah's arm and squeezed tightly. "This isn't just another dream, is it?"

Leah ached at the desperation in her voice. "No, Susan. It's not a dream. I have the key." She showed her the handheld mirror. "The gateway closed behind me. This may be our only hope."

Leah wrapped her arm around her and ushered her quickly in the direction she'd marked in her mind. Susan was obviously fatigued from this nightmare. Her legs wobbled, yet they treaded steadily through the misty fog with Leah's help.

"This place," Susan said, "I think it's Hell." Her voice quivered slightly.

"I'm not sure that it's Hell," Leah replied. "It's surely somewhere not far from it."

Suddenly, a sound came from behind them. Leah, still escorting Susan, stopped walking.

"Shh. Listen," she said.

They stopped walking and remained silent. Footsteps plodded heavily behind them. They turned around slowly. A figure was following them through the mist and quickly gaining ground. Leah knew it was not a vision. The figure was real. She moved with not quite the same gait, but her long blonde hair hung in luxuriant waves. The figure's eyes were deep blue and set in a dead stare that gazed directly at her, watching her as it walked toward them. The eyes were hers. The face was hers, but an inanimate, expressionless copy of the original. The figure was her doppelganger.

Leah dug her nails into Susan's shoulders. "Come on," she yelled. "We have to get out of here."

Susan's legs moved more freely, and soon, they were running through the mist that surrounded them in thick wisps and clouds. Again, Leah looked behind and noticed the double coming closer and closer. A large bird screeched and flew fast above their heads. They ducked to avert its path, and as they did, Leah felt something slip from her loosened grip. The sound of crashing glass echoed devastation in her ears.

"No!"

The handheld mirror lay on the cold hard ground, shattered into sharpened slivers still stuck inside the frame. She bent down and picked it up, their only hope now lay smashed into pieces. They'd stopped for just a second, but now Leah's double loomed only feet away from them. They ran faster, until a vision interrupted Leah's sight. In her mind, she saw a black door. It was slightly to the right of where they were running.

"This way." She pulled Susan by the hand, and they ran faster.

The door flashed in her mind again just as the deep indigo died away, and the gateway's dark entrance loomed before her. Now, she stood right where the vision had appeared. Leah held out her hands, palms flat, and moved them around in front of her. She searched for a hard surface in the darkness, knowing they were close to the entrance. She envisioned the black door once again as lightning flickered briefly above them.

Susan followed Leah's example and searched with her hands. Leah's hands felt nothing, only the empty atmosphere. She turned her head. The doppelganger was close enough that Leah could see the exact details she saw every day in the mirror.

She flung her hands wildly, until her palms smacked something hard. She felt around. It was the entrance, the portal.

"I found it!"

She held up the broken handheld mirror in front of the hard surface, maneuvering it slightly. Nothing happened.

"Come on," she yelled.

The surface remained hard. She grabbed Susan around the waist, just as a hand touched her shoulder.

* * * *

The Black Mirror somehow returned Madison's gaze, silently taunting her. As far as the man on the floor was concerned, she wanted to crush every bone in his body, but something about him made it an impossible feat. She collected the thick energy that was part of her, pulling it around her as weapon. She closed her eyes and felt her rage, her pain, and her strength of mind. She exerted it all toward the mirror and watched as the dark Victorian masterpiece rocked back and forth on its legs. It shook, shuddering from the force overpowering it. Her breath came harder and faster. Sweat drenched her face.

Suddenly, she heard her mother's voice loud and clear. "Break it, Maddy. Smash it into a million pieces."

She heard, but she kept her attention focused on the mirror. Not even the sound of her mother's voice would distract her now. That voice urged her onward. Mommy had finally given her permission. She directed the energy one more time with an invisible push toward the quaking mirror.

She quickly pulled her hands away as if she'd felt it happen. The Black Mirror shattered, showering endless slivers of black glass down around them. Leah and Susan tumbled outward to the floor and lay among the broken pieces.

Madison caught her breath, and then breathed again.

Chapter Twenty-Two

~ Aftermath ~

Leah had shaken the phantom hand from her shoulder. She and Susan hit the hard surface with their bodies in attempts to break it with their weight. Suddenly, it shattered into shards, and a million slivered pieces sprayed through the air. It was just like the recurring dream a few years ago. Now, it all made sense. She and Susan landed on the floor amid the broken glass. A voice called out to them.

"Leah, Susan!" Dylan ran over and swept Leah off the floor.

Sidney did the same to Susan. They patted them down, searching for any signs of cuts. Luckily, neither of them was hurt. Leah had a small cut on her arm, but it drew little blood. She clamped her hand to it.

"God," Susan cried out in relief. "I'm okay, Sidney. I'm okay."

"Look!" Leah pointed beyond the silvered frame. The glass was gone, but they saw into the gateway. They glimpsed the blackness and flashes of lightning that flickered from within. Leah told them about her double, and how her hand had touched her shoulder. "She was right behind me, and now she's gone."

Madison stood watching the inside of the gateway. Leah looked at Sidney, who motioned his head toward Madison. It was she who had broken the glass. Charley was sitting up on the floor, holding the back of his head. A crash of thunder suddenly burst from inside the gateway as the lightning grew more frequent. Then, a brilliant flash exploded throughout the room, bathing it in a bright, blue light. They threw themselves to the floor and took cover.

The lightening vanished as if nothing had happened. There was no fire, no smoke, and no blue light. Leah watched as Madison rose from the floor and stared at what was once the Black Mirror. It was nothing now but a silver frame. Black glass splattered the floor in pieces. The frame now showed the wall behind it. There was no gateway.

Leah noticed a man wriggling and twisting on the floor, cursing amid his exertion and anger, but it was no ordinary man. It was Angus Marlowe. Taryn had been right. He had come for her. Now, she saw the man of her childhood visions with her naked eyes.

He stood upright, free from the invisible bond that had gripped him, but Madison simply watched. Leah understood why. The sight they beheld was one for their archives, and Brett was recording it all on the video camera. Angus began fading like a ghost, dissipating and dissolving into nothing more than a silhouette. He screamed a last angry shriek that faded in volume as did his presence. He disappeared, destroyed along with the mirror.

Then, an unexpected voice broke the silence. "Well done, Maddy."

* * * *

Madison had finally broken the mirror. Her ability had reached its peak. Taryn had known the day would come. It was inevitable. Now, she would perish along with Angus, but she had helped take him out of this world. It was her contribution to the world, her gift to her daughter. She knew what she had to do. She'd told Maddy to break the mirror, and her daughter had heard her. Now, she stepped forward from behind the shelf and revealed herself.

"Well done, Maddy," Taryn said. She was fading fast. Her message would be quick. Madison spun around and saw her.

"Mommy!" Maddy ran towards her, but Taryn was a mere ghost of her human form.

"I'm proud of you, sweetie. I'll be watching over you, always."

"Mommy, wait!"

Taryn had no time. She sensed herself lessening, fading out of this world and into the next one. She had helped her daughter. Now, her daughter would move on, and put this all behind her.

"I love you, always." Her voice faded to a whisper.

A warm heat from a bright light enfolded her.

Chapter Twenty-Three

~ Home ~

At Susan's insistence, they'd taken her back to her house rather than the ER for a quick checkup. They discovered the house in shambles when they opened the door. Furniture was overturned, glass was shattered, and chairs had been flung about the house. Susan walked through the mess, making a steeple with her hands in front of her face.

"Oh, no," she groaned.

In the van, they'd told her what had happened while she was gone. Angus and her very own double had set up shop here in her home, but she never expected this. She closed her eyes and fought back tears.

"Marlowe must have flipped when he discovered the key missing," Dylan observed.

"Susan, why don't you go upstairs, and get a bath," Leah suggested. "Let us clean this up. When you come back down, you won't have to see this."

She thanked them, wiped her wet eyes, and collected herself. She took their advice, but first, she attended to the cut on Leah's arm. As she disappeared up the stairs, the investigators righted chairs, cleaned up glass, and placed broken items in a box Susan could rummage through later.

When she rejoined them, they sat in her living room, surrounding her and pampering her.

"Susan, I still think you should go to the hospital and get checked out." Dylan urged.

"Just what should I tell them, Dylan?" she countered. "I'm not going. I'm fine."

"They say doctors make the worst patients," Sidney pointed out.

"Then it must be true," she said with the slightest hint of sarcasm.

They had a lot to discuss. Susan began by telling them everything that happened after she'd picked up Madison from school.

"I still have no idea what came over me. I couldn't get that mirror out of my mind. As I stared into it, I began to realize I was overcome by it. The glass began to change. Then, the gateway opened. That's when I saw her, my double. She was beckoning me. I followed her into the darkness."

"Yes," Sidney said. "The secret of the gateway was that it produced doppelgangers, and then sent them back out into the world through the other mirror, a sort of birth canal, if you will. The Black Mirror was said to be a tool used in witchcraft and sorcery. We discovered all this from Paul's work with the tome."

"We even encountered your double," Brett said. "She sat in on the meeting we planned."

"Until we busted her," Sidney bragged.

"Until I busted her," Leah corrected.

"It was through Taryn that we found out what happened to you," Dylan said.

Susan closed her eyes and shook her head. "That poor young woman gave away her second chance at life to save mine. Someone called out to me after I entered the gateway. I recognized her from the picture Charley had sent us. I ran back towards her, but it was too late; the gateway had closed. Poor Madison, I'm sure this has been like losing her mother all over again."

"Not necessarily," Leah said. "I think Madison will receive some sort of closure from all this in the long run. We never told Madison her mother was a doppelganger. I don't think Charley will either, until she's older. In Madison's mind, she saw Taryn's ghost, which is not far from the truth. I think she understands it's over now. I predict that she'll move on with her life."

Susan stared aimlessly at nothing. "Even the birds were doppelgangers," she said. "The pterodactyls, they were doubles, all of them were, even the insects. They were extinct creatures cloned and living within an alternate realm. Like everything else that walked out of the realm, the realm itself tried to recreate in an almost exact image, but failed. It tried to be our world, but like the human doppelgangers, there were imperfections."

Brett had been transferring the feed from Leah's camcorder to his laptop. "Do you want to see what the camcorder picked up?"

"Sure, but I don't think Susan and I will ever forget." Leah said.

Brett turned the laptop around to face them. They watched as the shaky video focused in and out. They could see the mirror frame, the open gateway, and Leah moving closer to it. Leah's voice was faintly heard.

Then, blackness overwhelmed the video as it showed Leah dashing through the portal. The camera caught the flickering lightning, though it looked more like disruption to the video. The rumbles of thunder were so slight Brett adjusted the volume. They could see someone walking through the darkness, and then there was nothing but gray static. The crashing interference absorbed the remainder of the video feed.

"That's it?" Leah looked dismayed.

"I'm afraid so," Brett responded. "I haven't yet transferred the main video showing everything that happened in the den after you walked through, but as you can see, this video cuts off where the static begins."

"That must have been the moment when I entered the realm."

"The blue realm, I call it," Susan offered. "It's interesting that it wasn't visible in the recording."

"Well, we both know what we saw." Leah said.

"I wouldn't be discouraged, team." Susan's voice sounded weak, even to her.

She'd been through an agonizing ordeal, but she mustered her strength and took the lead again, though it didn't stop the team from worrying about her. "We've proven to ourselves the existence of other worlds within our own. Don't let it scare you. Remember, our world is the dominant one. Our world will always prevail over that which remains dark and hidden.

"I'll continue to see Madison, and so will Leah and Sidney. I think it's important for us to help her get through this and to study her.

Through us, she will realize the extent of her ability, if she hasn't already. She will also learn who she is as a psychically enabled individual. We can show her how to control her ability and how to live with it.

"I think you're right, Leah," Susan continued. "Madison will be alright. She still has her father, who luckily has only a concussion by my diagnosis. She's with her father right now in the ER, and when they get back, they'll start life anew. They will rebuild. Madison will always feel her mother around her. She will always be there, one way or another."

They changed the subject from Madison, and Susan revealed more about her nightmare. Then, Leah spoke of her experience.

"I can't get the sight of my own double out of my mind. She was identical, but expressionless, a copy of me that drew closer and closer as we tried to return. The gateway wouldn't open. I'd broken the handheld mirror. She touched my shoulder just before the glass shattered. After we made it through, and all of us looked into the gateway, she was gone."

"Her birth was unsuccessful," Sidney said. "It was a miscarriage, so to speak. She didn't make it out of the gateway before it was destroyed."

"So, she was destroyed along with it?"

Sidney nodded before he spoke. "Angus and Taryn perished because they didn't have the key when entering the gateway. According to what Paul told me on the phone tonight, any doppelganger born without the presence of the key would die if the mirror was destroyed."

There was a pause, and then Susan posed a question. "What of those born successfully with the key?"

Another pause ensued as Sidney looked around in thought. "I don't know," he said.

Susan sat forward. "You don't know? My double was born successfully. I had the key. She entered this world. She was here in my house, yet she isn't now. What does that mean? Where is she?"

Now, the pause grew into a deep silence. No one had an answer.

Sidney hesitated before drawing the most logical conclusion. "I think it means she's still out there."

They cast quick glances at one another. Fearful eyes met in confusion. The thick, lingering silence was one they knew all too well.

Epilogue

Susan's double had taken Taryn's advice. "You may not be able to remain in this house, but you'll be free, and you and I both know why."

Now, free she was.

After Taryn entered the house and absconded with the handheld mirror, it made the perfect excuse for her to flee, to free herself of Angus's dominance. She knew he would be destroyed, and the investigators would reclaim their beloved Susan. Now, her predictions had come true.

She was aware of everything that had occurred as Susan's thoughts and memories had become her own. When Susan was free, she was free. She experienced the same glorious feeling of freedom and release, the same sadness and joy.

Angus had taught her much in their time together. She understood what Taryn had meant by being free, and they both knew why. She, unlike Taryn, had been a successful birth within the gateway. Susan had carried the key with her upon entering. She and Susan would coexist, indefinitely. A devious streak somewhere inside her found this hard to ignore.

A world she'd never seen before had become familiar through Susan's eyes and memories. It wasn't a perfect world, but it was a better one than she'd known. It was a world she didn't want to leave, a world she wanted to remain in as long as her host survived. She wouldn't give it up. Soon after Taryn had left Susan's house, so had she.

She left King's Haven and moved through the world effortlessly and without limit, marveling at her speed of travel. Now, she sat in a dimly lit café, about twelve miles west of Green Valley. She sipped an espresso, though she had no need, no appreciation for it. Her intent was to conduct herself as a normal human being and pass as an everyday person. Quietly, she sat making plans.

She would need to acquire the essentials— a phony birth certificate for one. She already knew Susan's Social Security number. All she needed was a replacement card. She had taken her driver's license, not that she would need it. She'd also taken a few of Susan's credit cards, the pin numbers of which came to her automatically. She would establish herself as Susan Logan, and she would be gone before anyone figured it out, except for maybe Susan.

She meant no harm toward Susan or the team. She loved Susan. She was Susan in more ways than either of them would ever understand. She had no hesitation about keeping her distance from Susan and the team. She would stay far away. Breaking that promise to herself would infringe upon her newfound freedom. It was life she wanted, and there was a big beautiful world out there. She finished her espresso, paid with one of several twenties she'd lifted from Susan's purse, and walked out the door.

The autumn chill invigorated her, giving her the feeling of being alive. The sunshine cast a dim orange glow on this brisk morning. She walked freely, absorbing it all, until a familiar face approached her.

"Dr. Logan, how in the world are you?" A young woman, approximately in her mid-thirties addressed her. Her long black hair was pulled back into a ponytail. "Imagine running into you here. How have you been?"

She knew the girl's name, but she couldn't recall Susan's memories fast enough.

"I've been fine. How are you...?"

She tapped the side of her skull to show forgetfulness.

"Angie," the girl said. "Angie Roberts. I've always wanted to thank you, Dr. Logan, for everything you did for me."

She grasped the young girl's hands in hers. "You're more than welcome, Angie. It's what I do."

Angie wrapped her arms around her and hugged her. "You take care, Dr. Logan."

"I will, and the same to you, Angie."

She watched Angie walk away down the sidewalk. Then, Susan's double turned and continued onward. Her transition into the role of Susan Logan was complete.

THE END

Legal Disclosures

"Telekinesis." *Random House Webster's College Dictionary.* Random House. New York. !991. p. 1372.

Photographer: Tara Manon

About the Author

Christopher Carrolli is a full-time writer, who lives in Western Pennsylvania. He is a graduate of University of Pittsburgh at Greensburg and holds a BA in English Writing, and an AA in English. He has also won the Ida B. Wells Prize in Journalism.

www.facebook.com/ccarrolli
ccarrolli@facebook.com (Facebook email)
www.christophercarrolli.blogspot.com
carrollic@aol.com
www.goodreads.com/carrollic

Other Works by the Author at Melange

Pipeline, The Paranormal Investigator, Book 1
The Listener, The Paranormal Investigator, Book 2
The Third Eye of Leah Leeds, The Paranormal Investigator, Book 3
The Skinwalker's Tale, The Paranormal Investigator, Book 4
Phantom in the Sky, The Paranormal Investigator, Book 5